AN EMPTY EMBRACE

Cyril Mezden

GRENDEL PRESS

An Empty Embrace

CYRIL MEZDEN

ISBN: 978-1-960534-07-1 (paperback)
ASIN: B0CTFTM4B9 (ebook)

Cover art by danycomicarts.com
Edited and typeset by Susan Russell
Proofread by Astra Bijoux, Rachael Swanson, and Kasey Kubica

Published by Grendel Press LLC
www.grendelpress.com

Dedication

To my friend,
my Queen,
thank you for believing in me.

To my queer and trans peers,
I know you and see you.
Our rights are human rights.

Chapter One

Deep within the Elvyn Wilds, three adventurers run full force through the winding trees and foliage. Crunching underfoot are thousands of golden-red leaves spirited off their trees by the pull of autumn. The setting sun, relaxing into a lower angle in the sky, hints at nightfall. Usually around this time, the three would be diligent in setting up camp and collecting enough wood to last through the cold night, but their attention is captured now by something more demanding than the threat of icy fingertips.

A dry, guttural wail booms through the forest, sending winged creatures scattering above the canopy of trees. The sound is followed by the heavy thuds of wood meeting wood, and the less-grounded trees succumb to gravity. One of which falls forward, its whistling branches warning of collision.

"Sable!"

Hearing the urgent call of her name by her warrior companion, the smallest of the three adventurers, a halfling witch with petite, dark features and tightly curled hair, momentarily spins around on her heel and holds up a sure hand to the advancing hazard. With a burst of purple energy emanating from her gloved palm, the falling tree seems to hit an invisible barrier that ripples with a pearly shimmer upon impact. They continue on with quickened breaths as another deep wail echoes through the woods.

Up ahead, burnt orange sun slices between the tree trunks. It looks to be a clearing and, with any luck, an escape from the impending bludgeoning. Running through the light, our adventurers find themselves perilously placed at the lipped edge of a cliff. The healer of the group, a spindly young elvyn man with long, white hair wrapped into a bun, inspects the terrain below and asks in a shaky stutter, "Viktor, where do we go from here?" Over a hundred feet down, a crystalline river refracts the blooming ruby of the setting sun, and the three are presented with a choice.

The warrior turns to face the quivering woods. A pit in his stomach sinks deeper now, well below the navel. "Good question," he replies between heavy breaths. Will they stand and face the threat, or jump and risk a fatal fall?

Thrashing out of the forest's edge comes a massive wooden club smoothed to a shine by years of labored use. Holding the weapon is a twenty-foot-tall forest giant with a hefty, muscular build. Gnarled, moss-gray hair covers its mostly naked body in patches. In a language unspoken by our three, the giant taunts its prey and lifts the club overhead with both monstrous arms. Viktor, the largest in the party, a half-orc with desert-brown skin, makes the call in his mind. Hastily, he grabs the other two into a tight, sweaty hug and falls backward off the cliff, narrowly missing the clubbed strike save for the tip of his beaded braids.

Down they fall together, screaming as loud as their voices will allow. They plummet into and are consumed by the frigid waters of the river. A mixture of adrenaline and impact, broken slightly by the half-orc's inhuman build, leaves the adventurers conscious for only a few moments to feel the cold touch of the water seep through their clothes, their skin, and deeper still. Soon enough, awareness leaves their bodies, a hush settles in their minds, and they float away into a quiet black expanse.

Along the stony riverbank, three wet bodies lie unconscious. The crisp evening air is accompanied by a whisper of muted sunlight, so close to setting yet still bleeding through the muddled foam clouds. Celest is the first to wake. Glistening threads of white hair, now unbound by the rolling currents, veil his face haphazardly like a wavering bride. A groan of confusion is followed by a gasp of realization as he looks to the left and sees his friends sprawled across the waterfront. "Viktor—Sable—be living, oh Goddess!" he pleads while stumbling to meet them. Checking their breath, he finds them alive and hot tears of relief well up in the corners of his narrow, yellow eyes before sliding down the flat bridge of his nose. "Thy mercy knows no bounds, my divinity," says Celest. "Thank you, a thousand times over. Thank you." His palms press into the ghostly gray stones of the bank as prayers of protection slip through beholden lips. Faint white light gathers at his words and heals a small portion of the damage taken by the party.

The soft sound of Celest's murmurings slowly rouses the other two. Sable's round, starry eyes open in panic. She jolts up with a yelp that sends Viktor scrambling to his feet, clenched fists ready to swing. A pause, as the two take in their surroundings, is broken by a frustrated whine from Sable. "What were you thinking?" she asks. "You could have gotten us killed—or worse!"

Viktor's upper lip twitches with irritation.

She shuffles through the pockets of her dress, taking inventory. "I think I lost my powdered mandrake root. Shit. There go my suggestion spells," she says under her breath, but loudly enough for him to hear.

"Yes, thank you so much, Viktor, for saving our lives. If it weren't for you, we'd be giant's stew right now. How valiant—how noble you are!" says Viktor sardonically. "Maybe you could show a little gratitude to your hero instead of moaning over some dried potatoes!"

"Mandrake root," Sable snaps. "That was the last bottle I had. You know what we had to go through so that I could get my hands on that stuff."

Viktor shakes his head like a wet dog sending droplets of water flying in all directions. "Was that the time in the jungle with those vines that nearly ripped Celest's arm off, or the time when you were charmed into believing that horse was your grandmother?" he asks with a wry grin.

"The former. And we agreed not to talk about the horse thing. Please, just forget that ever happened. Honestly, it's cruel that you keep bringing it up."

"Hmm. Never," he says, then turns his attention to Celest. "Alright, Sunshine. Enough chatting to your mommy in the sky. She's probably sick of you by now."

Celest moves to sit on his feet and looks up at the warrior with still-dewy eyes. "She is a *goddess*," says Celest, clearly offended by his teammate's choice of words.

"Ah, yeah," says Viktor as he helps Celest stand upright. "Sorry."

"We could have stayed and fought, you know," says Sable. "I had plenty of spells prepared." She takes out a thin piece of sandalwood bark and snaps it between her fingers with a spin. A gust of hot wind dries her clothes and radiates outward to catch the rest of the party.

Viktor scoffs and crosses his brawny arms. "I don't think magic would have done us much good. You didn't even have enough mana for that spell to hide us, remember?"

"My illusion spell takes a lot of energy," she replies, "and that's hilarious coming from you, o' valiant hero who swings an axe first and asks questions later."

"As if that's actually—" He pauses mid-sentence as the color in his face fades to a greenish-gray. "My axe." Viktor swings sharply to the right and sprints into the water. A few minutes pass as the others wait, but with each surface and subsequent dive, Sable grows more and more impatient. After the seventh try, a deflated and empty-handed Viktor drags himself back on shore. "Let's find a taphouse," he says, "I need a fucking drink."

"Oh yes, I'm sure we'll find a cozy inn brimming with sweets and ale in the middle of the forest!" says Sable as Viktor stomps off downstream, and she moves to follow.

The once-foamy clouds condense to silver wool and allow a light fall of rain to escape their form as the three head south. Dense wintergreen trees crowd the forest's edge, reaching out wantingly toward the sparkling waters of the river. "How far did we float? These trees look nothing like the ones in the Elvyn Wilds," Sable asks.

Celest stops to ponder the question but is unable to explain the change of scenery. Viktor continues ahead, stride unbroken, determined to find anything that could turn their situation around.

After a half hour's travel down the bank, they catch sight of a dock jutting out into the calmer waters. Bits of rotted plank have fallen away, and a frayed old rope tied to the piling suggests it was once used to anchor a small boat. "There's a welcomed sign of civilization," Celest says with a slight smile.

"A dead one, maybe," adds Viktor as he scouts the surrounding area. Directly across from the dock, a scanty trail, overgrown with moss and fern, snakes into the woods. "But this looks promising." They follow the path for a time with some trouble. The sun is gone, and not only is Celest's light orb enchantment dim, but he also can't quite find sure-footing on the moss. After stopping twice for the cleric to heal his own scraped knee, Viktor hoists Celest onto his back and continues forward.

"I'm so sorry, Viktor. I'm such a burden to both of you. After everything you've done for me thus far, the least I could do is walk on my o—"

"For the last time, Sunshine. It's fine. You're fine. I'm fine."

The minutes creep by like thick sap sagging down a towering deepwood trunk, but eventually, the forest thins and opens. The three adventurers find themselves facing a fortified city of dark, milky stone. The mammoth gates of which are rusted and ajar.

Celest taps his teammate on the shoulder to be let down.

"Certainly didn't expect to find a city out here," says a bemused Sable as they slip through the gates. "No map I've studied of the Wilds ever mentioned one."

The structures of this city languish with neglect. Broken roof tiles litter the pavement, most of the street lanterns have been shattered, and a musky smell of rotting cloth and soot tickles the back of the throat. Still, on the main road, a larger building holds a warm, orange light that leaks through the windows and onto the wet pavement. A sign hanging from the door reads "The Red River Tavern" in red lettering.

"Sweet medicine after a piece of shit day," says Viktor as he heads to the entrance. "Why is it always me who has to pick up the slack?"

"Don't pretend you have any other skills besides making bad guys bleed. You're not allowed to complain. You're the one that got us into this mess after all," Sable quips. "We're in some busted city in the middle of nowhere and completely off mission. We probably won't even make it back to the Wilds in time to collect the eclipse bow from the temple of the moon."

Viktor gives her an exceptionally stale look and then swings open the door with a thud.

The halfling lets out a joyless chuckle. "I need some time to myself, Celest. Why don't you make sure our guard dog doesn't bother the locals." Since entering the city, a drumming headache has been creeping up behind her eyes. After the elf nods in compliance, she meanders down the street with a thumb to her brow and disappears into a thick blanket of fog.

Inside, the hearth is smoldering warm. It drives back chilled fog that laps at the leaded-glass windows. Viktor sits at a timeworn table that is dwarfed in comparison to his imposing build, and Celest opts for the seat next to him. One leg of which clicks on the floor with any shift of weight. "Shit day. Shit service." Viktor eyes the bar maiden, who is preoccupied with another patron.

"Would you like me to calm you?" Celest holds out a welcoming hand.

"Nope." Viktor leans away and pushes himself to a standing position. "All I need is some damn ale." He goes to slump over the bar counter and asks the barkeep for a drink. The man pours a chalky rose wine from the bottle and slides it to the half-orc. It appears this wine and some stale bread are the only things they're selling. He downs the bitter liquid and pounds his fist down twice for another.

"Ow," says a figure whose forehead and arms are pressed like a wax seal into the bar top. "You must be strong." They look to be human, short with sandy blonde hair. Sitting up, Viktor can see that their round face and smoky, jade eyes are pointed in his direction but not focused on anything in particular. "My name's Nyx. You ever been anyone's bodyguard?"

"I'd say. Why? You need someone to protect you?" Viktor downs the second drink as if it were spring water.

"Not me. It's... my sister who needs protecting." Nyx takes out a coin and taps it on the wood, getting the attention of the barkeep. When the man walks over, Nyx says, "A glass for me and another for the big one."

"What's wrong with your sister?" Viktor asks as he sucks down the third brew. "And if she's in danger, why are you here and not with her?"

Nyx chews on their lower lip. "I needed a drink, same as you. There's only... so much I can handle," they say in a hushed voice. "It's a demon. That, I'm sure of. It comes in the night, but gods know what it actually does. Memories are fuzzy when I try to focus, but I know its voice. It's poison." Their thumbnail digs into the tabletop. "Last time it came, it bit her. Her neck was bleeding, and she was just standing there in the drawing room. I don't know where I was before my other sister and I found her, either. I think, in some way, we've all been under the beast's illusions. So, what I'm wondering is... if the coin is right." Nyx bows their head and sighs before asking, "will you help us? Otherwise, I just—I don't know what to do."

Meanwhile, drifting along on the somber flagstone alleyways a block away from the tavern, Sable talks out loud to herself while the aching pressure in her skull thumps for attention. "If I were taller, he'd take me more seriously. Maybe I should lose the dress and go for something more... utility based?" She shakes her head and continues. "No. Definitely not. This dress has so many pockets." Sable sighs, rubbing her temples in an attempt to ease the pain, and wonders how much time away from her teammates would fix this knotted headache. Leaving the two of them alone for too long, however, could prove to be even more stressful in the long run. Her reflections are interrupted by the low howl of sobbing.

With a hardened demeanor, she responsively follows the sound to a middle-aged human man curled around a pastel blue child-sized blanket. "Hello, sir?" says Sable. "Are you in need of any assistance?"

The man looks up, snot and tears sticking to an unkempt, brown beard. A look of hope and confusion lasts only a moment before his face is overtaken with grief.

"What's the problem here?"

"Briar," he spouts. "My daughter is missing. Sweet child—she won't survive out here!"

"Out where exactly?" asks Sable, quickly taking a small notepad and enchanted quill from her dress. "Could you give me a description of what your daughter looks like?"

"Here! Markovia! Outside!" he screams. "She's never been out on her own before. She-she's a petite thing. Black curled hair. Just passed her nineteenth year. Eyes like blue crystal. She's been gone since yesterday." The sobbing starts again, and he smothers his face in the tattered blanket to cover an agonized expression.

"Briar: black hair, blue eyes, nineteen," says Sable as she steps closer to the man. "I'll try my best to find out what's happened. This is your home?"

He follows her pointed finger to the nearest building and nods weakly in agreement.

She considers, for a moment, inquiring about the city itself but decides against probing for answers from a clearly broken man. More than likely, she thinks, he would not be the most reliable of sources in this state. His grief, though, is heavy and certain. It pulls on her own.

He looks her in the eyes, now stricken with confusion, and asks, "You would help me? Why? I don't have any coin—I couldn't pay you if that's what you're after."

"I know what it's like to be on the receiving end of misfortune, sir," she says while putting the paper and quill away and carefully removing one of her gloves. Old burns have disfigured her obsidian skin. The scars start at the fingertips and disappear under the bell of her sleeve. "I help because I've needed help. My village was attacked by a horde of goblins in my youth. They came in the night and burned our farms to the ground, stole our food and animals, and slaughtered dozens of my people. It all went to ash. Halflings aren't much equipped for violence, you know, and there was no one there for me then. We were sitting ducks." She slips back into her glove and rests a hand on his shivering shoulder. "Sorry if you didn't care to know, but I'd like you to trust my intentions. I will try to help you. No coin required."

The man squeezes tightly to the blanket, nods while avoiding her sympathetic gaze, and quietly stands to return home.

The witch takes her leave after waving goodbye, but soon after starting to walk, the drumming in her skull ignites into a sharp buzz. Her forehead crinkles together as she winces. Stumbling to the side, she braces herself against the wooden planks of a cracked barrel that has been abandoned on the street. Her vision momentarily fades to black before she finds herself somewhere entirely new.

A terrible rain permeates the cold dead of night atop a black marble balcony. Along its railing leans a woman with hands clutched so tightly to the stone that it looks like her fingers could snap. The wind rips wildly through her chin-length brown hair and the pastel yellow fabric of her nightgown as she looks in horror behind her.

"You are mine. There is no escaping this," a man's growled voice chases through the rain.

The woman frantically shakes her head in denial as the man corners her escape. A hooded black robe conceals his form.

"You will not deny me any longer." His open palm swings toward her, but she catches it before it hits her face. A struggle ensues as he attacks, attempting to grab and hold her still, and she defends until the hand gripped over her mouth is bitten. He yells, pulling away before retaliating with a shove to her chest. The wet stone causes her foot to slip as it tries to stabilize her, and she stumbles over the railing, falling down into oblivion. "No!" The man's voice cracks like lightning.

Sable gasps, the shock bringing her back into reality.

"What?" she huffs between strained breaths. "What was that?" She dusts off her gloves in an effort to self-soothe and collect herself, then takes off toward The Red River Tavern.

Chapter Two

B ack at the tavern, an energized Sable bursts through the entrance. She's successfully shaken the strange vision from her mind and is now fully focused on the new task at hand. Spotting Viktor's hulking frame at the bar, she shouts from across the room.

"New objective," she says as the warrior and various other patrons turn to recognize her. "Let's put a wrap on it here, and I'll bring you up to speed."

He turns on the barstool to face her. "Oh yeah? Just so happens I've found us a new mission, myself. It's a family in need of our services."

"Are you drunk?" she says. "You expect me to believe that as if you haven't been mucking about in the booze this whole time?"

He leans to the side so that Nyx is visible. "This nice person just hired me in the protection of their sister. Say hello, Nyx."

"Hello, Nyx," they say with a joyless smile.

"H-hi," says Sable. "Uh, I'm sorry. What's the situation?"

"Nyx has invited us to stay the night. Beds. Supper. Very hospitable, right?" says Viktor boastfully. "But I guess we could just decline and run off to whatever you've got lined up."

"No, that's quite alright," says Sable, shifting on her heels. "It's getting late. I'm sure we could help her and her sister. Nyx, is it?"

"They, not she or he. Particular about that, this one," corrects the warrior.

"Oh? Pardon my mistake, then. It's a pleasure to make your acquaintance," she continues. "Um, unrelated, but very important, would you happen to know the whereabouts of a young woman named Briar?"

Viktor finishes another drink and then collects Celest from the corner table while Sable asks around the bar if anyone knows a girl fitting the missing person's description, but unfortunately, no one has.

Nyx unfolds a worn, metal walking stick and proceeds to lead the party out of the tavern and down suffocated cobbled streets to a manor nestled in the middle of a forgotten garden. Fresh chive blossoms bob to the rhythm of the raindrops as they approach the front steps. "Here we are," they say. "Home sweet home."

A dilapidated signpost reads "The Lasaunt House of Unattended Youth" in copper lettering that has bloomed green with age.

"This is an orphanage?" asks Sable as she runs her fingers along the sign's splintered wood.

"Used to be," they reply. The door opens with a painful creek. "I'm home… Brought some guests."

A tall, gangly woman with fluffy brown hair peeks out from around a corner. "Guests?" she asks worriedly. "Who are they?" Her dusk-honey eyes scan the party with the attention of a cornered rabbit.

"They're adventurers," says Nyx. "Big one's Viktor, the small one's Sable, and the quiet one's named Celest. I asked them to help us—help Adinine." Humble greetings are extended from the party, all feeling a bit awkward for intruding.

"Oh, I see," she says. "I'm sorry. It's not often that we have foreigners come through these parts. My name's Cassianna. We were just about to have some roasted onion soup. Would you folks care to join? There's enough for everyone."

Viktor agrees without hesitation, and they follow Cassianna to the kitchen.

A large oak table is set for three, and savory sweetness emanates from a large cast-iron pot. Sitting at the table, a striking young woman with long, copper hair and sharp, old-world features wrings a napkin between slender palms. She introduces herself, with a voice like summer doves, as Adinine—youngest sister of the Lasaunt home.

They situate themselves around the table as Cassianna collects more bowls, spoons, and rags from a high cabinet. She pours the golden-brown liquid into each with a ladle and serves the guests first, followed by her siblings and then herself. Bits of charred black onion and pepper float on the top layer of the soup. A warm, earthy flavor invites the thought that one could ward off the coming winter with this meal alone.

"So, your sibling brought us here for a reason," says Viktor in an uncharacteristically cordial tone. "Could you, Adinine, in your own words, describe what has been happening?"

Silence falls in the room as Adinine's face contorts with worry, and her shoulders reflexively tense up to guard the skin around her neck. Her voice is barely a whisper. "It started last week on the day of my nineteenth year. I was alone, sleeping in bed, when I heard tapping at the window. From there, everything is a blur, but—" She pauses to swallow the mass of stress welling up behind her tongue. "I remember his eyes. Like blood-filled pools. Hungry. More than that. Insatiable. I thought... It was a nightmare." She looks down into the soup bowl, trying desperately to keep her composure.

"She told us the next morning, but we didn't take it too seriously. The second time was a few nights ago. There was no way to dismiss it after that. We had all fallen asleep in the common room," says Nyx, sparing their sister the pain of recounting her trauma. "When Cassianna and I woke up, Adinine was gone. The demon slipped past us somehow. We found her later in the drawing room. She was in some kind of strange trance, standing in the corner as stiff as a board. Her wrists were dripping with blood. And, we heard it. It... has the voice of a man. I remember hearing an awful laugh just before we found her."

Another empty silence hangs in the air as the horrific image manifests itself in the adventurers' minds. In the most passive voice she can muster, Sable asks, "This creature, it drinks of your blood?"

Adinine nods, eyes still fixed on the bowl.

"Perhaps it's a vampire, then." Sable takes a deep breath in and continues to eat. Between casual spoonfuls, she says, "We've dealt with undead beings before, and I've read a few texts regarding different types of undeath. Plus, Celest is a cleric of The Order of the Sun. Dealing with the undead is practically a specialty of theirs."

Adinine's eyes flutter as fear shifts toward an unexpected hope before asking, "A vampire? You're aware of a monster like this?"

The witch dabs her mouth with a rag, nodding. "Mm, yes. The libraries in Hightower are filled with all sorts of things. From what I understand, vampires are a very rare sort, and the only few documented accounts are from overseas. Nothing I've read about them spoke of mental enchantments, but you can rest assured that you'll be protected under our watch. We are nothing if not professionals."

With that, the acute tension subsides, and the meal continues.

After its completion, bellies are full, and eyes hang heavy from the long day. Cassianna offers to show the party to their rooms. "Luckily enough, there's a bed for each of you," she says. "The three of us have taken to sleeping in the old master room—*if* we fall asleep tonight, that is. It feels safe when we're all together."

Viktor and Sable stand to follow, but Celest's attention lies on Adinine, whose delicate fingers are clenched into solid fists.

Celest stands and moves around the table to her side. "May I?" he asks, extending a tender hand. With a puzzled expression, she relaxes as best she can and meets his palm with her own. A frigid jolt of fear pings through Celest's nerves, finding a home in the center of his torso, directly under the rib cage. He takes a deep, careful breath in—pushing on the feeling with the bottom of his lungs until it's swaddled in a film of warm, white light. Slowly, he exhales, letting the fear float up through his throat and dissipate with a glimmering iridescence past his lips.

Adinine gasps with relief, and a single tear slides down the ridge of her high cheekbone. "Thank you, Celest. I feel—" She pauses to wipe away the salty droplet. "a bit better." He offers her a friendly smile and goes to meet his friends in the doorway.

Cassianna guides them through the home, dropping each off at an empty room. "Here we are, Celest. This last one belongs to Adinine. Sorry about the mess. It's been—"

Celest cuts her off with a hand on her forearm. "There's no need for apologies. Thank you for letting us stay. And for the meal. It was delicious."

"I'm the grateful one, really." A warm, toothy smile bounces from ear to ear. "You and your friends have given us hope. That's more than anyone else in this city has even tried to do. The people around here are reserved and usually keep to themselves. I can't tell you how nice it feels to have some fresh faces nearby." She steps off down the hallway and gives a final farewell before sliding around the corner.

Celest has no trouble falling asleep. Beneath the linens, the chill of night finds no purchase on his golden skin. The plush, wool-stuffed pillow cradles his head like an attendant mother and smells of whispered lavender, matching the scent of Adinine's hair. As a member of the elvyn race, Celest has no dire need for sleep, but the act of drifting into the subconscious and allowing himself a moment of quiet vulnerability, especially after such a demanding day, is practically irresistible.

A few hours pass, accompanied only by the music of falling raindrops on the roof tiles, until a new sound rouses the cleric from his dreams. Three polite taps at the window are followed by an absolute silence as if everything outside the bedroom suddenly ceased to exist. A dazed Celest slowly opens his eyes, turning to face the noise. Outside, heavy black fog licks at the windowpane, and in an instant, his focus is captured by an arresting crimson gaze floating amongst the smoke. A smooth, sensuous voice shakes the stillness as the deep-red eyes transform into shimmering gold. "The night is cold. Invite me inside."

Without a thought, involuntary words escape Celest's lips. "Yes, of course. Please come in." He mindlessly gets out of bed and unfastens the lock at the window. Fog spills through the opening and collects on the wooden floorboards, shaping itself into the form of a man. The figure is taller than Celest, almost Viktor's height. A flowing black robe lazily holds his pale frame and is cinched at the waist by a silky, scarlet sash. Void-colored hair cascades down his back. Under sharp brows, his golden eyes fade back to red as Celest's mental daze returns to clarity.

The reality of the situation quickly sinks in, and Celest takes a sharp inhale to scream, but the man lunges forward with the grace of a sea serpent, and the elf is met with a death-cold palm over his mouth. "Yelling would be terribly unwise," says the man. "How about instead, you tell me your name." His hand lingers for a moment, then falls as he takes a step backward.

Through tight, trembling lips, the cleric manages to respond. "Celest."

With a flourish of his robe, the man holds out an arm to the side and takes a deeply dramatic bow. "It's my pleasure to make your acquaintance, Celest. My name is Julian," he says in a silken voice. "I do appreciate your composure. Truly, there's no need to be afraid." He turns and walks to the bed, touching the pillow delicately with the back of his hand. "Now, tell me. Where is the young lady, Adinine?"

"No," says Celest reflexively, a bit louder than intended. "You can't have her."

Julian meets his eyes for a moment, sending needled tingles down his spine, then looks away and relaxes into a lounging position on the bed. "It's rare that more than one outsider finds their way into this place at a time. Always a very interesting event—doubly so when they're questers by trade." Worry flashes across the elf's face. How did he know about the others? Had they been followed? Celest wracks his mind for an answer. "Don't give me too much credit. It's a bit obvious to tell your profession. Your type all have that wistful gem caught in their eyes. So, where is the rest of your party, priest?" asks Julian as he meticulously absorbs every detail of the elf's form. Celest stares back at the man, silent as a mouse.

The quiet gap between them stiffens the air. "Well, since you seem determined not to share anything of yours, maybe I should lead by example and be more giving." The man pauses a moment as if deliberating the consequences of a choice he's already decided to make.

"Let me tell you a story, Celest. But be warned. It is a tragedy. You may not have the heart to bear it." After a lengthy sigh, he closes his eyes and continues. "Once, long ago, lived a prince. His life was filled with successes of every kind. In the face of opposition, he always stood victorious. The prince conquered this land by twenty, and built a castle for his mother and brother. He was content with the days watching as his city grew around it. They prospered under the system he had built." The vampire's hand drops to the scented pillow. "Until he met a beautiful woman full of will and spirit. Her name was Katya. She was a devotee at the church, not a noble by any standard, but one of regal grace. He would win her heart... However, it was stolen from him all too soon. She died. Abruptly. As quickly as he'd fallen in love, she was gone."

Julian's eyes open, and he stares idly at the ceiling. "He became obsessed. Her death twisted his mind. It beguiled his thoughts until he no longer recognized who he had become. In an act of desperation, the prince sought the aid of forbidden magic and, in doing so, cursed himself and the land he had once called home. Even still, he wanders his forsaken kingdom, forced to witness the disaster of his mistakes."

Celest's stiff body softens a bit, and as if noticing, Julian effortlessly rises from the bed and slowly walks toward the cleric. "Besides the guilt, however, there is hope," he whispers, now inches from Celest's face, "to lift the curse and save the people of Markovia from their unending isolation and despair." Julian's lustrous, sanguine eyes smolder like the dying embers of an abandoned fire pit. The elf loses himself in their depth as a compulsory hand reaches up to touch the vampire's chest and unburden his mind.

Darkness clouds Celest's vision. It clots in his lungs as if he were gasping in tar and strangles him like a bladed noose. An endless expanse envelops the cleric, void of light, color, and warmth. An echoing silence, the sound of an unvoiced scream, chokes tighter as he tries to escape, tearing at the ceaseless nothing with a weakness only found in one's dreams. He reaches outward, writhing in the violence. Somewhere in the void, however, another is present. A ghost of a person, chained down and unable to move, shares its space with the elf. It's almost imperceptible through the full-bodied pain, but, in the darkness, the ghost stares at its guest and feels something different for the first time in centuries.

A beat breaks the aching silence. Celest is still alive. Despite the agony, his heart keeps warm. Its rhythm is steady. The thought washes over him, followed by a sense of self to cling to. He focuses inward, feeling the cadence at which his spirit pulses through delicate veins and buzzes on the tips of his fingers. It reminds him of her, of the goddess abiding within him. The shadows sink away from a soft light now emanating from his core. Her mercy is boundless and divine, and this borrowed body was proof of her favor. He holds firmly to the gift of his life and bursts, becoming the radiance inside of himself. Taking in a bottomless breath, Celest lets everything else melt away with an exhale.

He finds himself back in Adinine's bedroom, hand still resting on the vampire's chest. He looks up to see that Julian's face is stricken with quiet tears of reprieve. "What did you do?" asks the vampire breathlessly. "How did you do that?" Before summoning an answer, Julian draws the cleric into a tight embrace. One hand drags through the alabaster strands of Celest's hair, and the other securely fastens to his slender hip. Celest lets out a surprised yelp that is muffled substantially by the black robes enveloping his mouth. Otherwise, he makes no move to stop it, choosing instead to become a passive observer.

Julian's clothing gives off a strangely pleasant scent, sweet like myrrh and honey, but his frame is solid and still as a marble statue. The hug lasts longer than expected. With each passing moment, an unfamiliar swollen heat expands in the center of the cleric's breast. Its fever grows hotter and ever more distracting until, finally, the vampire loosens his grip. He takes a slight step back but keeps his hands firmly planted. Julian stares down at the elf with a captivated look. "Dearest Celest," he whispers. "You alone may be the salvation I'm searching for."

Struggling to find his voice, Celest stammers, "I—"

Julian's eyes melt to gold. "You are feeling very tired now. Get to bed and rest. You'll need it."

Celest yawns, eyes glazing over with sleep. Julian guides him to the bedside and gently lays him down. "I'll be seeing more of you. Sweet dreams, sweetest Celest."

The last thing the young elvyn man sees before returning to the pull of sleep is Julian's animated black robe flicking the latch of the closing window to land perfectly in the lock as it clicks shut.

Chapter Three

Meanwhile, a few doors down, Sable is dreaming.

She carries an oil lantern between the prodigious isles of a library while running her fingers across the tomes' spines. She is comfortable wading in the sea of literature. It's a comfort that feels like home. Aside from their educational purposes, which she considers their most important aspect, books promise an escape from the ever presence of reality. In adolescence, around her fourteenth year, she would spend hours reading and rereading a book she had stolen from a trading shop artificer who had stopped at her village to rest for the night. The title of which was *The Seven Doors Within: A Soul's Life-Study and Thesis of Transmutation and Its Underlying Properties* written by an ancient elvyn alchemist with a name too long to bother pronouncing. The books in this library all momentarily shake loose from their individual bindings and transform into the text in her memory. All but one, who continues to curiously shiver. It stands out like the bright white beacon of a lighthouse amidst the sea of navy blue leather bounds.

"What frightens you so, little book?" she asks as she floats up to its shelf. Upon inspection, it appears the book has no title or author. Its only identifier is a golden sun imprinted on the cover of the bleached white paper. "Show me what you will. You aren't the only book in need of my attention." The tome shakes again, violently, as the golden sun melts to a garnet red. The once-white pages turn to black and burst open, flipping through themselves like a colony of bats breaking free from the mouth of a cavern.

It lands on a page toward the end of the book as words begin manifesting on the paper in an elegant yet hurried manner. "*He seeks to punish me,*" says the script. "*Out of spite, he will strike in the place most dear—my faith. I know if I protect the Angel, it will leave me vulnerable, but if I don't and the shrine is destroyed, my abilities will be weakened regardless.*" The invisible pen pauses for a moment on the period of the last sentence. Ink wells up underneath, bleeding onto the page below before continuing. "*I wish it hadn't come to this. Once, I thought the chance to make him laugh was all I ever wanted. But, I confess, his proclivities have always been disturbing. Only mother's grace was capable of bringing him to his senses. If she were still here, maybe things would be different. In a way, it does feel like we're children again in the playgrounds. If he saw me with a toy, he'd take it for himself. Selfish child! It didn't matter then, of course. I'd give anything to see him content, but we are not playing games anymore.*

"*To treat a life with the flippancy of an object? To deny one an agency of their own? How could it come to this? I won't stand for it. I may not have been able to save her, but I must protect the shrine. In truth, I don't know if it will be enough to keep the Angel safe from him, but the shrine must remain. I must keep faith alive. It's the least I can do in the wake of this disaster. The brother I knew is gone. The regret is simply impossible. The pain is wholly unbearable. But, I must keep my faith.*"

The book flies from Sable's hand and slams itself back into the open slot on the shelf. A seeping of white, gold, black, and red emanates from its spine like an oil spill. Each book the colors touch adds to the profound display, which now covers the entirety of the towering bookcase. For a moment, Sable is bewitched by the battle of wills before her eyes. The colors seem to stake their claim, fighting for territory and their existence within it; until suddenly, all turn gray. Sable cautiously descends back to the floor, eyes fixed on the bookshelf, but just as she is about to land, an image projects across the spines, connecting the individual book bindings into one cohesive message. The witch lets loose a startled gasp and accidentally drops the lantern, sending globs of oil and flame into the shelves. "Oh, shit—shit!" she says as she tries to stifle the flame, but it's already spread too wild to contain.

Sable steps back and watches as fire engulfs the paint-like strokes of the image. She tries to take in as much detail as she can before the fire chars it all to dust. It depicts a clearing of yellow flowers. A single tree stands to the side, one of its thick branches supporting a small swing with a wooden seat held in place by rope. Two children with dark hair and light skin play. The taller child pushes the smaller one into the air on the swing as the sun blooms overhead, saturating the clearing with its warm, orange rays. In the bottom right corner, almost undetectable among the bladed grass, two letters sign the image: DM. The fire intensifies, leaving Sable with an all-too-familiar feeling of dread. Flames reflect like cut rubies in her round, raven eyes, and beads of sweat pool on her chest and palms. Head throbbing, she curls into a squat, hugging her arms to her knees, and wills herself to wake.

Soon enough, she feels her body between the sweat-damp sheets and the pulsing of a throbbing headache. With a groan, she rolls to the side and peers behind the duvet out the leaded-glass window. It's raining, but the sky's hue suggests that behind the clouds, the sun is shining. Sable allows herself one final sigh before stretching out of bed and readying herself for the day.

Already in the dining room, the Lasaunt siblings and Viktor sit around the table drinking a strong black tea spiced with mint. The morning keeps still as they slowly prepare themselves for hours to come. Sable peeks behind a doorframe into the kitchen and is spotted by Cassianna, who offers up a hearty smile. "Good morning, Sable. I hope you slept well. Was my bed comfortable enough?" she asks politely. "Oh, would you like me to fix you some tea?"

Sable hops up to sit at the table, feet dangling from the chair. "No, thank you. I'm partial to my own morning brew," she says, pulling a twisted bottle from her dress pocket. A swig of the potion causes her eyes to glow with the potency of an astronomical event. "Woo! The bed was lovely, Cassianna," she says with an elevated perk to her voice. "My dreams, however, were less so."

"You had nightmares, too?" asks Viktor. A deep furrow buried between his brow appears to age him up by a few years. He holds this intensity as he stares down at the oak table, running his thumb absentmindedly along the rim of an empty teacup. "In my dream, there was this woman, but not really a woman. It was more like a bird with tits."

"Gods, Viktor, could you please keep your absurd sexual fantasies to yourself?" says Sable, rolling her eyes.

"It wasn't like that!" Viktor slams his fist on the tabletop while keeping Sable's gaze. Unblinking, she hoists up an incredulous eyebrow in response to his tone. "She cried at me to save her while clawing at my stomach with her talons. When I looked down, I could see the flesh at my feet and the front bones of my spine." A flash of unease paints his expression before he breaks the stare. "My dreams are never like that. It's always the same. Fight the monster, rescue the babe, and get the treasure. For fuck's sake, I couldn't even move."

"I'm so sorry," says Adinine timidly. "I do understand, though. Up until last night, my dreams have been riddled with all manner of horror. Celest's magic truly helped. Could he not do the same for you?"

Viktor's face softens to its regular demeanor as he pushes a few ocher-brown braids behind his ear. "Maybe. I mean, it might if I let him, but his spells make me feel kind of—"

Just then, Viktor is interrupted by a flurry of footsteps down the staircase, followed by an airy gasp and two loud thuds. "Ow," says a voice from the common room.

"You alright, Sunshine?" Viktor shouts from the kitchen. He turns to the siblings. "Don't mind Celest. That boy's always tripping over something. Poor fellow can't find his own feet."

The elf slides through the doorway with a glowing white hand placed on his swollen cheekbone. A glossy teardrop hangs from the sharp outer corner of his eye, not yet ready to fall. "I had a bad dream," mumbles the cleric.

Viktor stands, giving his seat to Celest, then leans over the chair and pats the top of the elf's head twice before heading to the kitchen for an apple.

Cassianna pours the cleric a cup of tea and pushes it his way.

Accepting the offering, Celest takes a deep breath and holds the warm liquid to his lips, letting the malty flavor trickle through and drag across his tongue. Immediately, it comforts him, allowing him to relax in his seat and begin the new day.

"You did?" asks Adinine. "I was just telling Viktor how well you helped with my own sleep last night. What frightened you?" She places a soft hand on her jaw and listens intently.

"Well." Celest fidgets with one of the tassels of his cream-colored robe. "I dreamt that in the dead of night, I was visited by... a man." He looks around the room to see the differently pigmented faces surrounding him, each fading to an ashier hue. Most noticeably, Adinine's deep bronze complexion dims to a satin brass as she unwittingly bites down on her lip. "In my dream, he was so lonely and enthralling... like a black hole." The elf takes a few more sips, inhaling the steam as it rises from the cup. He continues. "He told me the story of a prince who built a castle here for his family and who lost a woman he loved. Does the name Julian Markov sound familiar to you?"

Adinine abruptly stands to her feet, knocking the chair she was using backward, to the floor, with a loud clack. "Castle Markovia," she chokes out the words. Nyx rises from the seat, feeling their way across the table to drape a supportive arm around her shoulders.

"There is a castle?" inquires Sable. "I haven't seen one since we've been here."

"The weather," says Nyx definitively. "You probably wouldn't have seen it through the fog and rain. It's west of here on a hill overlooking the city. Obviously, I haven't seen it myself, but apparently, it's a monstrous thing. The locals here have stories that it's haunted. Most are too fearful to test the theory."

"I once heard music from there," sputters Adinine through shaky lips. "When I was young. Some friends and I were playing on the outskirts of the city. They challenged me to make it through the courtyard and knock at the door. I was a proud child. I thought I was fearless." Hesitant tears carve across her cheekbones. "I made it through the gates and hedges, but when I got to the doorstep... this haunting music froze me in place."

"What kind of music?" Sable asks, readying her paper and quill.

"I remember it played like a piano but sounded like a giant flute," she answers. "I've never heard anything like it before nor since."

Sable swiftly scribbles the details. "What happened next?"

"I did it. I found some courage and knocked at the door," says Adinine, shaken to the bone. "The music stopped. That's the last thing I remember. When I made it back to the other children, they were scared and about to leave. They said I'd been gone for an hour. They'd thought I'd been eaten by a monster. Maybe they weren't wrong. Maybe that day was the start of my curse."

"And the name Julian Markov?" presses the witch. "That name is significant?"

"Uh, yes," Nyx replies for their sister. "He's the prince in our storybooks. The stories say he discovered the land here and built his kingdom on top of it. Once upon a time, they say streets were full and lively, but I guess something bad happened. No one wrote any books about that... It's been a long time since then, longer than anyone living now can remember."

The witch's lips roll over her teeth like a metronome as she thinks. "Could this be a sort of spell en masse? This city is quite dreary for its size. The few people I've met here all seem to be defensive," she considers aloud.

Cassianna nods. "You aren't wrong. The culture here is that of privacy. If I had not read so many stories of places unlike our own, I would think it natural to be cold or withdrawn. I guess being detached from other settlements for as long as this place has, is a recipe for despair. What kind of spell could—"

"Ah, yes," the halfling cuts in. "Where are we actually? The three of us were in the Elvyn Wilds, searching for an artifact before being sidetracked by a club-happy giant. We then washed up on the riverbank to the south."

A shared look of disbelief is scrawled on the sibling's faces. "The city's name is Markovia, surrounded almost entirely by forest aside from the Achered River," answers Cassianna.

Nyx sighs, fidgeting with their nails. "I've overhead hunters at the tavern tell tales of getting lost in the woods only to end back up at the city gates, nicknamed it the 'Turnaround Forest.' Fishers have trouble, too. Fog and whitewater make boating impossible at a certain point. I swear this place is a cage. I guess, by some miracle, you all must have floated from upstream. But, uhm, you said *giant*?"

"Oh, yeah," huffs the half-orc. "The big ones are thirty feet high with feet the size of buffalo and jaws that crush a man in half with a single bite. But, that's beside the point. Sable, shouldn't that river we fell into have led to the mirror springs, or am I mixing my geography?"

An uncomfortable hush hangs in the room for a moment until a spark of recollection happens across Sable's face. "Wait—" She pops off the chair and grabs Celest's arm for inspection. "If we are assuming that you weren't, in fact, asleep, you said the creature was inside the room? Are you hurt? Were you bitten?" She gets in closer, searching for a wound on the cleric's neck.

"No—stop, that tickles," whispers Celest. He's blushing a bit at the attention. "I'm fine."

Sable takes his face between her gloves and looks into his yellow eyes with the scrutiny of an owl. "Are you feeling faint at all? Dizzy? Why would a vampire just leave without feeding? Maybe he bit down somewhere covered by your clothes." With assured precision, the witch begins to unfasten the tasseled ribbon around his waist.

Celest's slender hands clap over hers. "Sable, please. I checked. I'm not bitten, I'm not faint, and I'd like to keep my robes on, please. I also entertained the idea, but it wasn't the case. I... only assumed it was a dream because I'm completely unharmed." She backs off a bit, giving the elf some space.

"I can't do this," says Adinine, who is leaning into Nyx. "We can't stay here. There's a lively inn on the far east corner of the city. We'll disappear in the crowd. Anonymity. Maybe if we're surrounded by people, the demon will leave us alone."

"A location change isn't a bad idea. I still need information on the missing Briar, but all of this may be connected," says Sable. "I'll escort you three. What's the name of where we're headed? Oh, I should mention, too, that I'm afraid we don't quite have the funds to pay for our stay. We might need to camp out close by or maybe squat in an available building."

"Nonsense. We'll pay your way," Cassianna replies. "Our mother left us enough in this estate to get by when she passed. Harvest Tavern Inn. It's the only building on New Arbat Street with round windows—couldn't miss it," she continues as she picks up the teacups from the table and dries them in the kitchen with a well-worn cloth.

"Perfect. Your city... it doesn't happen to have a portalsmith?" asks Sable. The sister shakes her head no, looking at the witch as though she is speaking a different language. "It's a mage who can summon a portal for you? Never mind, I assumed not. No dwarves," she says, then turns to Viktor, adding, "I'm letting you and Celest handle a side quest of sorts today, okay? I need you to check out where the people of this city go to worship. Ask whoever's in charge if they know of a shrine in the area. It would be an old one. And, the undead are active at night, so you shouldn't run into any trouble."

"Who died and made you guildmaster, eh?" Viktor crosses his arms and shoves his chin to the ceiling. A tattoo on his neck, in the style of his orcish heritage, peers down condescendingly at the halfling.

Sable silently stifles the impulse to polymorph the warrior into a goat. It isn't worth the effort, of course, but the look on his face makes it almost impossible to resist. Instead, she clenches the irritation in her fist and says, "I believe there's a shrine somewhere in the woods that is significant to this situation somehow. I had a dream that seemed... prophetic. We're already off mission. Clearly, we've all decided guild business can wait. If you have a better idea of how we should proceed, I'd be happy to hear it. Otherwise, let's get on. Meet us at the inn when you've finished. New Arbat Street. Round windows."

Viktor huffs an exhale through his nose. "Sure, but if shit goes south, you'll wish I was with you all instead of babysitting Celest."

"I can go by myself," says Celest. "It's just visiting a temple, right? I don't need to be watched."

"Not a chance, Sunshine," replies Viktor. "The last time we left you alone on a mission, you were moments away from being sacrificed." He turns to the Lausants and continues, "We ended up having to beg goblins to help save him from The Rat King. All the gold in our pockets, Sable's flying broom, and most importantly, the Shield of the Fallen. They didn't even know how to *use* the damned thing. Those bastards probably have it boiling gruel over a fire."

"I'm sorry," mutters Celest. "I remember." His eyes slightly glaze over and fall to the floor as he apologizes.

Viktor puts an encouraging hand on the cleric's shoulder before going to grab his gear from the bedroom. After taking a golden ribbon from his pocket, Celest flips his head upside down to fasten his free hair into a high, tight bun. After getting directions to the temple from Cassianna, they head off out the front door and down the alleyway, safe from the pelting rain under the warrior's arched shield.

Chapter Four

L ater in the morning, one would expect a city of this size to be busy with activity. Markovia, however, is as animate as an elder in their twilight days. The two adventurers, strolling through the rain-soaked streets, find themselves off-put at the quiet of it all. Aside from the street lamps, enchanted with perpetual fire, only half of the buildings they pass are lit from within. "This place is depressing, ay?" asks Viktor after passing two small children on the street that were poking soundlessly at a worm in the gutter.

"Maybe it's the weather keeping everyone inside?" Celest offers in lieu of an agreement.

The half-orc slides him a side-eyed glance and remarks, "I don't think this place gets much sun."

Not wishing to gossip, Celest turns his attention to a tailor's shop coming up on their right. Its sign hangs by its last hinge over a rotting doorframe. In the window, dust-cloaked dresses are displayed on wooden mannequins, and beyond them, an old woman and young man sit despondently at the counter. He appears to be stitching a quilt while she supervises his progress. It's brown with a pretty sky-blue trim but is gone from the elf's sight as quickly as it came.

The two continue down the road.

"Think we'll find a blacksmith around here?" wonders the warrior. "I feel naked without a weapon. We don't have the coin to buy anything worthwhile, but I don't know, maybe I could pawn you off or set you up on the street corner for some extra earnings." A hearty laugh follows his own joke.

Celest stomps off ahead, offended, but slows again to be shielded from the rain. Glaring, he replies, "The vulgarity is unnecessary."

"You know I'm kidding," chuckles Viktor. "But if you change your mind, I'm sure we'd make some quick coin. You're pretty enough."

The cleric scoffs but ignores it, knowing that his teammate will keep poking fun at him if given the opportunity. The rest of their walk is spent in silence.

In the center point of Markovia, a spired edifice extends to the sky. Celest's eyes take a few moments to run themselves over the entirety of its face. Blue and silver tin enclose the roof. The metal, dented and bent by unnatural means, hangs for dear life from the eaves. Hosts of birds and insects have made their homes among the broken walls that form tiny waterfalls at the end of each deep crack in the stone. What once was a painted mural of a giant woman is now an unsightly illustration, vandalized by all manner of vulgar additions and violent defacements. Looking into the woman's face, Celest feels an uncomfortable twitch in his chest. Her eyes are hollow and elongated from old black paint pulled downward by the near-constant rain. "How awful," he says, turning his gaze to the ground. "I couldn't imagine what would possess a community to let this happen to their place of worship."

Viktor scoffs mockingly before heading up the steps and pushing the double doors open with an agonizing creek. "You don't know too many normal people, though, with the whole growing up in your citadel thing. When folks have had enough, they've had enough."

Inside, darkness hovers over pools of murky water that collect themselves on the marbled floor. "Hey, you can see in here, right?" he asks.

"I can see," replies Celest. "Can't you?"

"Not that well in the dark. I'll manage, though," says Viktor, venturing further inward.

Large sections of the roof have fallen on crushed wooden pews, and the altar has been split in two. The splintered edges of which hold a pile of paper-colored bones. They appear to have been picked clean by the scavengers calling this building home.

The cleric swipes a hand over his mouth with a gasp, followed by a quick prayer of peace sent to the remains.

Viktor crouches down to inspect the body. "Looks like a human to me. Don't think we'll find any answers from a dead man. Cassianna mentioned to me that they weren't religious, but you would think that they'd at least know the priest was dead. Why is everyone in this city so fucking weird? I knew this was gonna be pointless."

Just then, an echo of hooting bounces around the walls.

Celest tracks the noise to the open rafters above the altar. An old, gray owl stares down at them with colorless eyes.

"You got somethin' to say?" yells Viktor in irritated jest. The bird swoops down to land on the skull of the remains. It offers an elongated hoot, as if in reply to his question. "Oh shit. Maybe you do know something after all." The owl turns its head with the precision of a machine to face the elf.

"Uh—hello," says Celest nervously. "I used to help with the aviary at my citadel. We would use a spell to speak with the messenger birds and ask how we could make the process more efficient or attend to their specific requests. Some are quite intelligent." He turns to Viktor and adds in a whisper, "I never did enjoy their company. All living creatures are lovely, of course, but the birds were always so rude."

Viktor laughs. "Could you cast a spell on me? Never got to chat up an animal before."

Hesitantly, Celest nods. His eyes close, and he traces a circular symbol on his forehead with the tip of his finger. The symbol illuminates soft yellow light and then sinks under the skin. The cleric's eyes reopen, shining with the same yellow light.

"A bit creepy," says Viktor as Celest steps toward him. The elf stretches up to the warrior's ear on his tiptoes and gently blows as the light fades. The feeling of fresh water washing through Viktor's mind sends a tingle trailing down his back. "Did it work?" asks Viktor. "Hey, owl, you know somethin' I don't?"

"A great many things, I would bet," says the owl. "Why have you come to this ruin, half-man?"

"Half-man? Ha! I'm all man, bird," he grunts back, puffing his chest.

"Your looks betray you, teeth jutting out from the lip. Blood of the beast runs through you, half-man."

"Is it... insulting you?" asks Celest, tilting his head to the left.

"Pfft—it's just complimenting my strong jaw," jokes Viktor before turning back to the owl. "What happened here? This place is a shithole."

"Human cruelty, a common theme. Years ago, they came with torches and blades. The lady of the temple was murdered by throwing stones. Scornful. Contemptuous," says the owl as it scratches at the skull with its talons. "They blame the church for their sin. They blame the gods that they go to sleep hungry and frightened. They blame the lady for failing to protect them from themselves, foolish humans. They know not that the demon is to blame."

"Yes, exactly! A demon. Do you know him? Some fuck named Julius or something. That's why we're here," spouts Viktor. "We're also looking for a shrine? Old. In the woods, maybe? Hoping the lady could have told us where it was."

"Useless in death as she would have been in life. The place that you seek was abandoned or forgotten by the people, perhaps centuries ago. Maybe you are less senseless than you appear, half-man."

"Thanks. So, you know where it is?"

"I do."

"So, where is it?"

"Where is my return? Something wanted is never free."

"Uh—" Viktor shuffles through his utility belt, looking for something of value, and finds a metal coin at the bottom of one of the pouches. "Do you take copper?"

The owl lets out another loud hoot. "Brainless. Stupid. Moron," it chides, unfurling its speckled wings to reveal a fluffy down tucked close to its breast. With a whoosh, it flies over to the half-orc, snatches the coin, and perches back up on the rafters. "I accept your waste. You and the spineless one will find the shrine in the woods northwest of the city. Two hours of travel on foot. So primitive. I suspect that the trail has long since grown over. Luckily for you, I am feeling unusually generous, so I'll answer your second query. I know not of the demon, only that he stalks the night and confounds the minds of mortals."

"Could you be more specific?" The warrior sighs. "I'm working with breadcrumbs here."

"Breadcrumbs would have made a better offering, but I've lent you more of my time than you deserve, half-man. Now, leave me be. I wish not to be in your company any longer."

"Tch—fine," says Viktor, turning to leave the church. "Come on, Sunshine. We've got what we came for."

After respectfully bowing toward the owl, the cleric follows close behind.

Outside, the rain picks up. It begins to fall in sheets and turns the cobbled streets into a city-sized black mirror. After a few minutes of getting pelted by it, the warrior leads them down a mossy stone pathway to the ruin of a once-stately home. The front door is ajar, and the two let themselves inside in hopes that the weather will lessen in severity. It appears they weren't the first to do so. Signs of squatting tenants are obvious. Old ashes lay burned in the hearth, a few soiled rags are strewn haphazardly around the living room, and miscellaneous scrawl is etched onto the walls and flooring. Whoever once was here, however, seems to have left a long time ago. It isn't a wonder as to why. In places, the roof has collapsed, leaving bits of rafters littering the floor. At the back of the home, a door leading out to the garden yard is missing its entire lower portion. A hole in the floor, more than likely caused by water damage, opens up to the crawl space underneath, and growing wildly from the soil, a vine-dense tomato plant bursts with wine-red fruits.

Celest kneels to pluck a small one and holds it for a moment outside of a broken window to let the rain rinse off any dirt. With his thumbnail, he pokes through the skin, peels it in half, and upon adequate inspection, pops the portions into his mouth. His face brightens as the tang hits his tongue, and he hums. "These tomatoes are perfectly ripe. What luck! We should take these back to Sable for her to try. If I remember correctly, tomatoes are one of her favorites. But I may be mistaken. Maybe it's pickles that she likes?"

The half-orc plucks one and bites down. "Mmm, yeah. These are good. Strange that they're growing here, though. Maybe there will be a chef at the inn who can make us a free meal out of these." He glances up from the fruit. "I'm gonna look around some more. Rich people always hide their good shit. If we're lucky, the owners may have left some of it behind, that is, if this place hasn't been picked through already." With Celest following him close behind, Viktor steps into what once was the master bedroom. Knocking on the floor with his boot yields no inclination of reward, so he pivots to the peeling, papered walls. To the left of the bed, on the side furthest from the door, a hollow sound echoes back. "Ah see, what'd I tell 'ya?" he gleefully sings. "Let's hope this isn't just a rat's nest." Rearing back his fist, the warrior punches through the wall and tears away its planks, revealing a rusted metal safe on the other side. He whistles, picking up the item. The safe is so rusted that all it takes is a twist of the lock for it to break open. Inside lies a bundle of jewelry, a few loose gemstones, and the deed to the home. Ecstatic, Viktor nearly crushes Celest in a celebratory hug that lifts the elf off his feet.

After shoving the treasure into his waist pouch, they both return to the tomato vine and pluck as many as they can. Celest turns his outer robe into a makeshift basket as the rain outside calms to a manageable drizzle. Thrilled to have acquired their unexpected treasures and excited to share the bounty of fruit, the two set out for the inn on New Arbat Street with a new pep in their spirits.

Chapter Five

Sable's head weighs heavy in her hands at a table in the Harvest Tavern Inn. At some point after leaving the Lasaunt house, her optimism was squashed. For the past few hours, she has been stopping every person they come across to ask about the missing Briar. Not only has no one seen the young woman, but no one knows who she is, either. It's like searching for a ghost. "I knew the father said that she didn't go outside, but I assumed he meant regularly or without him. Certainly, I didn't think he meant it in general. How are we supposed to find someone who wasn't even here to begin with?" she asks Cassianna, who occupies the seat directly opposite the witch.

"Some folks around here are quite strange. Most of them aren't so friendly. They've been dealt a poor hand being born in this city, I'd say. But don't let your spirits fall, Sable," encourages Cassianna in a pleasant hum. Deep brown curls frame her face and bounce on themselves as she speaks. "I admire what you are trying to do for the girl. It's not your responsibility, yet you are determined to help. The same can be said about what you are doing for the three of us." She gestures to her siblings sitting cross-legged on a bearskin rug by the hearth. They are playing a dice rolling game, and the smug look curling on the corner of Nyx's lip suggests Adinine is losing.

"She could just cheat. It's not like Nyx can see which side the die lands on," says Sable bitterly.

"The dice are carved. Nyx can count the notches with their fingers. But even if that weren't the case, they can always tell when Adinine is lying. She isn't very good at it." Cassianna covers her mouth, masking a warm giggle.

"You all seem to get along so well. I wish I had the same understanding with my companions," says Sable, "I can tell Viktor thinks I'm not strong enough to be the leader, and Celest is so passive. He usually follows Viktor because he's the most bull-headed. Ugh, it's such a bother. I am technically in charge, you know. When the guild placed us in a party, they made *me* the lead. We haven't been together long, only a few months, so I haven't had many opportunities to prove myself, but they should respect that at least."

Cassianna leans over the table and cups one of Sable's gloved hands in her own. "You are super strong, Sable. I know it. You have this energy. I feel I can almost see the way it shimmers from your person. You're radiant."

A buzzing sensation emanates from their touch, like the flapping wings of a thousand butterflies. It moves up Sable's arm, through her sternum, and up to her brain. The buzzing sits there for a moment until something clicks. "Cassianna, have you ever explored the possibility of casting magic yourself?"

"Me? No, I'm just a normal human," she insists. "Well, almost normal." She sinks back into her chair like an empty sack.

"Didn't you feel something just now? When we touched? A buzzing? Something?"

Hot, red patches flare up on her wide cheeks. She crosses her legs and interlaces her fingers on her lap. "Maybe. A bit like waves." She looks down at her feet. "It was probably just my imagination."

Sable can't help but crack a smile as she extinguishes the candle on the table with her finger and thumb. "Light this candle."

"How?"

"With your intention. It's good practice for a novice witch," says Sable. "That's how I learned, anyway. Just focus on what you want to happen and relax. Saying a few words might help, or chanting in your mind. Whatever feels right to you."

Cassianna hesitantly places her hands palm-down on the table and closes her eyes. After a few beats, she peeks at the candle. "How will I know if it's working?"

"You'll know," whispers Sable. "For me, it feels like a vibration. Resonance. And when I find the right frequency, everything falls into place." She offers an understanding smile and winks. "Try to manifest the waves you were talking about. Waves of flame catching the wick. Use the word *Ignius*."

Cassianna complies, mimicking the pronunciation. She takes in a deep breath and concentrates on the rising and falling of her shoulders, but focusing on that is uncomfortable. She shifts gears and instead focuses on the image in her mind. The blazing hearth. An oven. The strength of an imagined tropical sun. She repeats the word again. An ebbing and flowing heat moves outward from her fingertips until, suddenly, a sharp jolt sparks through her palms.

"Ah, look!" exclaims Sable. Cassianna timidly opens her eyes and sees a small flame flicker on the hemp. "You've done it! Guess I'm not the only mage in the tavern."

"Are you sure you didn't help? I couldn't have possibly..."

"Did it feel like I helped? Or did you feel the magic in yourself?" asks Sable with a wicked smile.

"I did feel... something. I don't know if it was magic." She stares at the flame. Orange light reflects on the rich soil color of her irises. They express a childlike wonder as her gaze moves from the candle, then burns into Sable. "Will you teach me? If I could learn to protect Adinine and Nyx, I'd finally be able to pull my weight."

"Pull your weight? You're holding your family together. You don't know that? I don't need to be a witch to see it." Sable snaps her fingers, creating an illusory firework show that's accompanied by celebratory musical tones. "Of course, I'll teach you. I couldn't imagine one more deserving to be my very first student of the arcane arts." The white of Sable's toothy smile is dazzling on the backdrop of her onyx skin.

The blush on Cassianna's cheeks returns as they share a laugh that brightens the entire room.

Outside and around the corner, Celest and Viktor catch a glimpse of amber light leaking from the round windows that they were told of earlier in the day. The two dash the building, eager for the warmth of a fire, and find themselves amid a bustling scene. The contrast between the somber city and the evening crowd at the tavern inn is startling, for Celest, at least. A group of locals loudly argue over a game of cards, drunkards laugh at each other's stories at the bar table, and exotically dressed dancers in translucent silks have skirts with metal charms woven into them that clack together when they move their hips.

"This day's getting better and better," says Viktor, whose eyes are fixed on one dancer in particular. The two head to the barkeep, the elf relieves himself of the tomatoes weighing down his robe, and the half-orc calls out, "Do what you will with these. Just make sure we get a taste, right?" Viktor gives the chef a wink when she comes to collect the fruits in a large wooden bowl. Celest then sits by the hearth to dry his rain-dampened robes. Flames flick light into his yellow eyes as he stares at the blackened logs, but when the brightness overwhelms him, he turns his body to scan the room more thoroughly.

Celest spots Sable and the Lasaunt siblings at a round table. The witch is speaking fast as an auctioneer while Cassianna listens intently, scribbling on parchment. The other siblings talk between themselves, both holding large goblets of red wine.

"Magic is just as much something you think as it is something you feel," explains Sable to her class of one. "Intention starts in the mind. A simple matter of focusing on what you'd like to do. Some forget that truly feeling magical, though, takes practice and patience. Write that down."

Cassianna fervently complies.

"Use of ingredients or tools can aid in reaching the proper mindset, of course, but the most powerful witches of all needn't even lift a finger to cast their will."

"That's amazing," Cassianna says, beaming. After a moment of consideration, she adds, "and properly terrifying."

"You're correct on both fronts." She sighs. "And it's also quite random as to who is predisposed to use magic, a quirk of birth. Thus is the nature of harnessed chaos, I suppose." Sable's gaze trails from Cassianna's smile to her eyes.

For a moment, as Celest watches from a distance, he picks up on a glint of intrigue on Sable's part. Her body leans forward over the table. Her mouth is parted slightly with a generous grin, eager to engage.

As if being alerted to something unseen, she blinks and turns her head to find the cleric staring. "Celest! You've made it," she yells from across the room. "Get over here and tell me what you found."

The cleric gets up after one more moment by the flame, but halfway to the table, one of the dancers, a short human woman with spiked blonde hair, stops him. She reaches up to twirl a delicate finger around a strand of hair not long enough to be held by his high bun. "I like your ears," she purrs through curled lips. "Elves are a rarity here. I've only ever heard stories. Tell me, elf, is there anywhere else..." She trails the finger down his chest and halts just above the waist. "Endowed with length?"

Celest freezes as hot blood floats to his cheeks. He tries to speak, but all that escapes is a high-pitched squeak.

The dancer takes one of his arms and presses it around her hips. "You are a man, aren't you? I don't care either way." The chimes on her skirt jingle as she twirls around to press her ass into his pelvis. The cleric hadn't noticed he had been holding his breath. A sharp exhale from Celest is followed by a catty laugh from the dancer as she sways deeper into him. "You definitely have one. Take us to a room, and let me see. You're too pretty to charge. Consider it a welcome to the city, yeah?" The friction of her charmed skirt against his lap causes a deep, involuntary heat to swell to the area. Still, he is frozen in place.

Sable pops up from the table, scurries over, and swiftly takes the cleric's free hand. "Come along, darling, much to discuss," she interrupts.

Disappointment paints the dancer's face. "No room for a third? An elf and a halfling would make a huge dent in my wish list. I already told your friend here, no charge."

"Sorry, love. This one would probably cry before any fun could be had," chimes the witch in a singsong voice.

"Just a halfling then?" she shouts over the crowd.

"I'm rather busy," says Sable before they arrive at the table. "Alright. I do hope your day was more fruitful than mine. The temple. The shrine. What have you got?"

Celest stumbles onto a seat, tightly crossing his legs. The warmth from between them causes him to stutter for a moment before responding. "Oh, uh, there was an owl in the temple, nothing much else there. It's been out of use by the people for years. It told us that there is a shrine in the northwestern woods." Celest waves off a barmaid trying to take his drink order, unable to look her in the eyes.

"Vague." Sable sighs. "But it's better than nothing. I don't know why, but I feel like Briar could be there. Hiding. We just have to find it—find her. Or, maybe... Ugh. I don't know. We'll just have to head out first thing tomorrow morning. The sooner we figure this out, the sooner we can address the... vampire issue." The witch looks around the tavern with disdain. "I had barely noticed how fast this place had become crowded. Cassianna, would you wish to continue your lesson somewhere quieter? One of the rooms here, perhaps?"

A flash of surprise turns to giddy excitement. "Yes, whatever helps the process, I'm ready for," she replies.

"Perfect. Let's get something to eat and take it to a room. There are some easy taste-enhancing spells that we could have a lot of fun with." The master and apprentice scuttle away and Celest is left with the remaining two siblings.

Adinine seems deep in the bottle, describing other patrons to Nyx while trying to hold in her laughter.

"What's happening over there?" asks Nyx. "I hear whistling. How can a whistle be off-key?" They both laugh. "It's awful. Who is that?"

Celest follows Nyx's pointer finger to the open dance floor.

Viktor has found himself straddling a stool in the center of the chaos. A deliciously thick-thighed woman with pitch dark-hair seals herself onto the back of his shoulders. Arms wrap around his chest, then tug at the belts on his armor. She whispers something through supple lips into his ear, and again, he lets out a loud whistle.

"It's our bodyguard!" yells Adinine, and the two almost choke on their laughter.

Celest, too, stifles a giggling smile. Despite not participating much in conversation, the two make him feel welcomed. By the average citizen of Hightower, the elvyn cleric was treated with a detached respect, and barely engaged, as if he were encased in a precious glass. But the siblings treat him like they treat each other, casually, like they have known him for years. Spending time at the table quickly becomes effortless.

The evening continues with this jubilant tone well into the night. The kitchen makes a few batches of roasted tomato pie, four servings of which Celest and Viktor share free of charge. The elf's eyes twinkle a bit as he takes the first bite, and the chef looks proud to see the improvised dish received so well. Comparatively, it's nothing close to the decadent meals served at the High Elvyn Citadel, but probably the tastiest thing he's eaten in weeks. The roasted fruit inside is seasoned only with garlic, onion, and salt, but the flavors are rich and robust—too good for an inn in the middle of nowhere. Celest reflects on the ever-present dissonance of this place. It echoes through the city's streets that are too wide and the homes that wilt with vacancy. Aside from congregations like this, with food and drink, local folk are few and far between. Sometime between its heyday and now, the spirit of Markovia had been siphoned. That much, at least, is painfully clear.

After licking the plate clean, Viktor and the pitch-haired dancer he was talking to before move to a more private corner of the bar room. She is a large woman but virtually invisible behind his frame, except for a droplet-shaped calf and single-heeled shoe that wraps behind Viktor's knee.

The siblings pay for their stay while Nyx keeps Adinine upright. They try their best to guide them into room number one, visible from the hallway on the first floor, and eventually, the two stumble in and lock the door.

Despite the lively tavern, Celest is content to watch the people enjoy their time while he sits by the fire. Refreshed from the good company, and toasty from the hearth, he hums hymns under his breath and relaxes.

"Hey, Sunshine," yells Viktor, half carrying his dancer companion as he approaches. A delicate silver chain, one of the few treasures found in the manor, adorns her neck. She wears it well. "I got a room for me and my friend and a separate one for you." He tosses the key, and it bounces off the hand that Celest had intended to catch it with but is clumsily secured by the other.

"Caught it! Thank you, Viktor." He wasn't expecting to. This night is full of little joys. Turning to face the woman, he adds a sweet, "Hello." She waves, and mouths back the word with a smile. "Are... the two of you heading to sleep now?"

The warrior's eyes glide to meet his companion's. Through a sultry grin, he replies, "Something like that, I'd expect."

She chuckles, pulling him in the direction of the upstairs bedrooms. The two disappear above the staircase.

Chapter Six

Viktor and his companion barely make it one step into room number twelve before seizing each other in an impassioned kiss. The scent of his leather hangs between them as he backs her up against the wall. Pulling away from the kiss to admire the look in her eyes, his tawny, brown armor softly creaks with his movement. Beads of sweat glisten from her forehead as she stares up at him, entirely engaged. On either side of her face, Viktor's hands thud against the wall behind her, and an airy sound leaves her lips as she tilts her chin to keep his gaze. Their breaths pick up together as he shifts his weight to his elbows with another loud thud. His tightly braided hair dangles over the cleavage close to spilling out from her clothing. She smiles wickedly, bringing a red, painted fingernail to the lowest brass rivet on his breastplate.

"What's your name, pretty lady? I should have asked downstairs when you were dancing for me. Pardon."

"Mashateil," she replies, biting slightly at her lower lip. "But my friends call me Marsha."

The warrior bends lower to whisper in her pierced ear, "I'm Viktor. Do you think that I could be your friend?"

Marsha's head turns to the side to meet his gaze. Her breath is hot on his face. "Why else would I have brought you up here, Viktor? To be my enemy?" she asks in return. "Though I might be craving a bit more than friendship tonight."

"Whatever gets you off, Miss Marsha," he teases before planting another kiss and lifting her off the floor by her thighs. Her full-figured frame seems practically dainty when handled by his strength. She wraps her fingers around the thick muscles of the half-orc's neck while sliding a tongue between their kisses, and Viktor groans with excitement. He carries her to the bed, bends at the knee, and places her to sit on the mattress as gently as a pressed flower. "Fuck, you're stunning," he praises. "Never expected that I'd be treated to a sight like you in this city."

She giggles, allowing her heeled shoe to fall from her foot. "Oh? I've never met someone from out of town. The men here are a bore... Where are you from exactly?"

"Me and my mates came here from Hightower, by accident, actually. We got a bit turned around running from a giant, typical guild stuff. It's a big city. I'm sure you've heard of it," he replies, sliding off her remaining shoe. Even her toenails are painted. He watches as they slide from his hands and rest on his pants. Slight pressure, applied by the ball of her foot, massages between his legs until something presses back.

"No, I haven't," she admits, laughing. Her foot falls away from him, onto the floor with the other, but the swell in his lap remains. "You and your friends are quite the spectacle. I've never seen an elf or a halfling before. I thought maybe they were make-believe. And you, you're handsome, of course, but what... are you? When you walked in, my friend said there was a demon at the bar selling tomatoes. I thought she was joking, but then I saw you for myself. Are there more like you where you're from?" She looks him in the eyes while she speaks. Her expression conveys innocent curiosity, though her words sting a bit.

"Heh, don't worry, I'm no demon," he chuckles half-heartedly. "My mother was human, and my father is orcish. It's pretty uncommon, even in urban cities like mine. Orcs tend to keep to their own. Not much for mixing. I was the only one like me growing up with my people in the Dunelands."

She nods as if she's heard of the location. "Was? Did I hear that right?" she says, placing a supple palm on his cheek. "I'm sorry for your loss. My own mother passed away three years ago, and my father a few years before that. I know it can hurt."

"Oh, your loss is sadder than mine, actually. I never knew her. I guess she died in childbirth," he replies, resting his arms beside her hips. "That might be another reason orcs don't mix much. They're a pretty large race of people. It can be dangerous if it's the mother who's not orcish."

"Hmm, should I be worried then?" she wonders, rubbing the side of her foot slowly up his leg.

Viktor smirks, bringing his chin between her knees, replying, "That depends, babe. You plan to have my kids?" He chuckles, genuinely this time, as his lips brush against the smooth skin of her inner thigh.

"Sir, we've only just met," she giggles, untying the charm-adorned scarf at her waist. It jingles as she tosses it aside on the mattress.

"You asked," says Viktor. "But, no. A child isn't really what I'm looking for from you. If it was anything like its mother, though, I'm sure it'd be adorable." He unlatches the fastens over his shoulders and at his sides that hold the breastplate to his body. It's discarded on the wooden floor. The baggy gray shirt he wears underneath is already untied at its lace-up, v-shaped neckline, showing off the hair on his chest, but he further loosens it with his two fingers.

Marsha responds by sliding the strap of her revealing top off her left shoulder with purposeful seduction.

The warrior moves forward to help her with the other but is stopped by her foot that presses down on his chest.

"You can take mine off," she hums. "But I want to see yours first. That's fair enough, right?" Her eyes all but sparkle with mischief.

Wasting no time, Viktor undoes his utility belt, letting it tumble to his feet, grabs the bit of his shirt that puffs out over his pants and lifts it off over his head.

"Now, let's light the lantern," Marsha suggests. "I think I'd be selling myself short if I didn't get to see you clearly."

"As you wish, my lady," he says, standing to his feet to follow her instruction. The room, now flickering with firelight, is tinted in warm oranges that accentuate the soft browns of his skin. He twists his torso to pose for her with one arm resting on the dresser where the lantern sits. Shadows and light mold around his relaxed muscles, emphasizing their sheer mass. His free hand reaches up to tousle his braids and stays there, gripped to the back of his head. "What do you think, babe?" he asks through a cocky smile. "Do I meet your standards, ay?"

A look is all the confirmation he needs. Her expression drips with approval. A wag of the dancer's finger beckons him nearer, and he wordlessly complies, standing over her at the edge of the bed as she repositions to kneel before him on the mattress.

The warrior looks down, watching her hands explore his chest, then his abdomen, and finally grabs the waistband of his pants.

She stops, looking up at him to whisper. "Do these tattoos go any lower?"

"You'll have to find out, won't you?" he answers, cupping her chin with his two fingers. She kisses the brawny thumb hovering over her lips.

"Do they have any special meaning?" she asks, tracing the section surrounding his belly button. "I've never seen anything more than a small, needle-pricked design. They aren't common here."

Carefully sliding the other strap from her right shoulder, he responds. "It's a coming-of-age tradition in my village. Though, in my case, it wasn't quite allowed because of my mixed blood. My older sister thought that was bullshit, though. She took me on a three-day trip to the mountains and did it herself. Things were never the same after that. The elders decided that I should fuck off. Old bastards. The desert never suited me, anyway."

A glint of pity in her eyes dissolves in a moment once he meets her gaze again. Bending her head forward, the dancer skillfully unbuttons his pants with her teeth, causing Viktor to groan and wrap his hand around the back of her hair. She pulls away again, asking, "Your sister broke the rules for you? Is she half-blooded as well? Didn't you say you were the only one like yourself?"

"She did. And, no," he replies. "She's my half sister. Great woman. She fucked right off with me to the city. But forgive me if I don't want to be thinking of her while looking down at you. There's rightfully a conflict of interest."

"Ah, sorry." She giggles. "I wasn't thinking. Maybe I'm just distracted by your manly physique." She lets herself fall back onto the sheets. Her long, dark hair frames the space around her head and shoulders like ocean kelp, frozen in time beneath the waves.

The warrior follows her movement, kicking off his boots as he crawls over to pin her there. The bed frame creaks with their collective weight.

"Should I worry about these?" she whispers, touching the tips of his two tusk-like teeth on the bottom row. His tongue travels to one and licks her red-nailed finger.

"They won't get in the way of what I have planned," he whispers back. "It'd be a shame to leave any mark on this beautiful body of yours. I wouldn't forgive myself." The calloused palm of his left hand slides up the outer side of her thick thigh, hiking Marsha's skirt up to her waist.

She softly moans, nibbling at her lower lip again.

"I don't bite," the warrior teases. "Unless you'd like me to, that is."

Her arms reach up to grip his mountainous shoulders, and she pulls him down so that her lips are lined up with his ear. She whispers, "I'm partial to pleasure, sir. But ask me again in the thick of it, and I may have a different answer. Sometimes my emotions get the better of me when I'm getting it... good."

"What about when you're getting it great?" he growls.

The fit of his pants tightens as the bulge in Viktor's lap swells to full arousal, and the dancer can feel the change between her legs. She hums with anticipation and rolls her round hips against it, inviting further response.

Marsha replies, clearly pronouncing each word, "I suppose I'd be inclined to let you do anything you'd like. If it's great."

"Looks like I'll be having my way with you, then," he insists, kissing an oval birthmark on her neck. "Do you doubt me?"

"Less and less as you keep talking, Viktor," she moans. "I hope you don't disappoint me."

His hand travels under her as she arches her back away from the mattress until he finds the clasp of her top, secured below her shoulder blades. He releases its connection and whispers in his deep, raspy voice, "Let's waste no more time, then. I'll show you firsthand how good it can get."

Chapter Seven

Celest looks down at the bronze room key that Viktor gave him. The number six is etched into its metal. He follows the numbered doors through a choked hallway to the back corner of the building on the first floor.

The room is rather small but comfortable, nonetheless. A four-post bed presses up to the western wall across from a round window and an overstuffed chair that sits against the eastern wall. Once lit, the oil lantern on the corner dresser fills the room with the light of a drowsy, yellow flame. With great care, he takes off his shoes and the outermost layers of his bone-colored robes. He folds them into neat squares and tucks them into the top drawer. The elf sits at the foot of the bed, letting loose his hair bun. The ghostly strands float past his shoulders like egret feathers. They settle on the thin fibers of his flowing undergarment, blending together as both are stark white.

Celest centers himself on an open space of floor and bends to his knees. "My goddess. My divine. Bless me with your witness," he whispers, now bowed over his thighs with palms to the floor. "Amatetra of the eternal light, you who have sheltered me in your radiance, I praise you." A familiar mental clarity is awarded to the cleric, like a gentle breeze after a hot bath. He sits up and crosses his legs while resting his hands palm-up on his knees. Once he straightens his spine into perfect alignment and takes a dragging breath from his nose to his sacrum, the cleric feels an invisible buzzing halo form above his head. Involuntarily, a smile relaxes on his face. "Thank you, my goddess. I ask you again to give me the strength I need to care for this body, sharpen this mind, and honor this spirit. May my actions reflect your divine will. Let me be kind, forgiving, and compassionate to all. Let me extend myself. Let me give all that I can in service to your infinite wisdom and benevolence." He meditates now on gratitude, each breath becoming another reason to be grateful.

Deep into meditation, he experiences more than himself. Set in motion by the aethereal, his hair and undergarment ebb and flow like seagrass beneath the tide. An intangible ray of divinity begins to rekindle Celest's own holy light like the morning sun feeds the flowers. However, quiet, rhythmic thuds from the ceiling snap him back to the confines of his skull. Muffled through the layers of wood, a woman is moaning with long, drawn-out breaths. "Oooh, fuuuuck!" the voice squeals as the thuds quicken in pace.

Celest tries to pay as little attention as possible and continue his devotion, but his focus is broken, and he can feel the moment leaving him. Threads of blessed energy are sucked up by the halo sending a rush of upward force through the top of his head, so the cleric sighs in equal parts satisfaction and disappointment. His prayer has ended.

After a slow rise and light stretching up to his feet, Celest flips back the duvet cover and configures the pillows to his choice positions. He just begins to lift his foot from the floor to slide under the sheets when he hears three knocks at the stained-glass window. The elf freezes. Tiny hairs on his forearms prickle with alertness as his eyes reflexively dart to face the noise.

Familiar red eyes stare back with a stoic expression. "Hello again, Celest. May I come in?"

The elf waits, expecting to act without a will, but to his confusion, nothing happens. "I'm not going to charm you again. I swear it, Celest,

I'd like to earn your trust. Let me show you how reasonable I can be." The memory of the vampire's embrace is inescapably vivid. Celest can still imagine the touch on the surface of his skin. The crimson eyes seem to smile. "I didn't hurt you last time," it says. "And I can tell you'd appreciate a conversation over something more... violent. Am I correct?"

"Y-yes," Celest sputters.

"Good. I believed it to be so." An invisible nail smoothly etches a crescent shape into the glass. "Now, may I come in? Could we have a conversation?"

The elf clutches a nervous fist close to his chest. He's sure the vampire could easily force his will but is now choosing to abstain. If there is a chance for diplomacy, Celest's beliefs guide him to take it. His heart races faster with each hesitant step toward the window, and time seems to stretch as he flips up the latch lock. "If you are willing to reason... come in."

The window opens with a creak. Cold, dark fog floats past him and collects on the foot end of the bed. Celest closes the window and turns to face the vampire, whose form is now fully opaque. He leans on his left arm at the edge of the mattress. The unblinking gaze that fixes on Celest and a wide smile that breaks the unnaturally clean-cut lines of the vampire's face sends a wave of anxiety crashing into the elf's gut. "Very good choice, Celest. I'm so glad you can consider our collective cooperation. I suppose it would be time to convince you of my sincerity." His free hand moves to the bedpost and effortlessly pulls himself to the right. "Would you sit with me?" he asks.

The elf squeezes words through the knot of stress in his throat. "I'd rather keep my distance."

"Very well." Julian lifts his arms as his enchanted cloak slides away from his shoulders and folds itself perfectly beside the oil lantern.

"What are you doing?"

"Making myself comfortable, I suppose," muses Julian. "I wouldn't want you to feel underdressed in that gown." Celest's eyelids flutter with embarrassment as he realizes his lack of full clothing. His cheeks burn deep-red as he tries to remember how little he was wearing the night before. "No need to be upset, Celest. I could take off more if that would make you comfortable."

"No, thank you," hastily replies the cleric. The dark robe under Julian's cloak, semi-loose fitting but tailored to perfection, is sleeveless with a low plunging neckline. His arms and chest look sculpted from marble, free of any color or blemish. Dark shades of red tint his lips and slightly outline the sharp shape of his black fingertips. The sanguine melt of the vampire's irises perfectly matches the hue of the silken sash tied at his waist. And, despite his deadly appearance, the elf finds himself fascinated by the vampire's beauty.

Julian runs his fingers down the bedpost, letting the robe fall from his right shoulder. "You're afraid of me." Celest can't read more than the vampire's dry expression.

"I'm trying not to be," says Celest in earnest. "You seem aware enough of your actions to change them."

"I appreciate the sentiment." A smile pulls at the left corner of his lips. "It's been a long time since I've known someone with kindness like yours. Truly, it feels like a breath of clean air." On the mention of breath, Celest notices that the vampire only takes in air to speak. The stillness between his words is uncanny.

"In your story," whispers Celest. His tone remains calm, but the tension holding his body in place is evident. "You had said that the woman you loved died. How did she pass?"

"Oh... She fell from a balcony. It was raining. She was frightened, and the castle stone was slick. I was there when it happened." He closes his eyes with a pained expression. "I tried to reach out and grab her, but

I wasn't fast enough at the time. It would have been so easy with my current ability. Ironic."

"Why was she frightened?" he asks incredulously.

"I'll choose to ignore your tone. I loved this woman more than anything," says Julian calmly. "She suffered from night terrors. As a child, she came close to drowning and would relive the trauma from time to time in her sleep. I should have locked the windows. It was my fault. I should have been... more careful."

Celest's stiff shoulders soften and fall away from his neck. "I'm sorry." He takes a slight step toward the vampire, who perks up so quickly at the cleric's mitigation that the change goes unnoticed. "You also said you were cursed by dark magic. The vampirism?" Celest, again, stiffens at his own query.

Julian's eyes meet the elf's. "Yes. I tried to bring her back from the dead. Hundreds of years ago." He sits up, allowing the loose robe to fall at his elbow. The entirety of his right shoulder and chest are exposed, thoroughly distracting the cleric from his words. The flawless skin that stretches over his lean muscles is an even moonlight color and appears as fresh as youth could possibly allow.

While unaware of himself, the cleric's eyes linger longer than they should.

The vampire, however, actively watching for details such as this, is acutely aware. "It worked. At great cost. I lost my life and became a monster. I trapped myself, this domain, and her soul, which currently resides in the body of Adinine, in limbo. That's why I've been visiting her. I'm certain she is my Katya. I had been watching her for some time, waiting for her to reach a proper age before I introduced myself."

Celest's expression tightens. His brows pull together, trying his best to appear as authoritative as Sable or Viktor when they dig for information. "What did you plan to do with her?"

"I would break the curse. Reuniting with Katya would release us of our bondage." His eyes glaze over like he's looking somewhere far away.

"If that's true, why did you charm her? Why did you drink of her blood?" Celest's knees begin to quiver.

"I don't just feed mindlessly on the innocents like an animal. While my condition creates an immense… thirst, I'm still a man of discipline. I've learned to resist my temptations. As a cleric, I'm sure you can understand the value of that. In her case, my bite creates a bond. I've been told the sensation is quite enjoyable for those that willingly receive it. It lets me sense her, even when she's not around. I can tell she sleeps now. She seems impaired. Probably wine." The vampire's expression hardens. "As for the charm spell, it's never my first option, but when I'm met with horror, it's for the best that they forget what they saw, especially Adinine. I had to charm her to be able to bond. She would have refused me otherwise… Of course, she would.

"Look at me." In one fluid movement, he stands and stalks forward to tower over the elf. Celest's muscles turn to stone before he looks down to avert the vampire's gaze. "Even now, sweet Celest, every fiber of your being tells you that you're in danger, that you should run as fast as possible away from me."

Celest struggles to find his voice. "N-no. I'm fine," he manages to mutter unconvincingly.

Julian leans in, inches from Celest. "You can't lie to me."

In a meek voice, the cleric asks, "Can you read my mind?"

A wry smile breaks across the vampire's face. "That would make things easier. But, no, Celest. Your thoughts are safely your own. However…" Julian presses a palm to the cleric's chest. The chill of his touch bleeds through the thin fabric of the nightgown, sending shivers down the cleric's extremities. "I can hear each quickened beat of your heart." He whispers each word clearly. "I can smell when you start to sweat." He leans in ever closer. The air, vibrating with his voice, can be felt as he whispers, "And I've noticed that in a panic, you forget to breathe." Celest hadn't realized. He sucks a shaky inhale through open lips, but before he can release the air—

Julian closes the space between them with a kiss.

Celest's eyes open wide in shock, and he freezes. The vampire's icy lips move tenderly over his own. They are firm but smoother than anything Celest has ever touched.

Julian pulls away, allowing the elf to exhale, but only for a moment. Unnatural grace connects their lips again. One of Julian's bone-white hands disappears in Celest's hair to cup the nape of his neck and the other grips onto the nightgown faster than can be perceived.

Celest gasps and jolts backward into a bedpost. "W-what are you doing?" he exclaims. "Why did you kiss me?"

Irritation paints Julian's face. "I'm trying to earn your trust, of course," says the vampire bitingly. "Did I offend you?"

Celest can't think of a response. A confused sound escapes his mouth, but nothing more.

Julian stares scrutinizingly at the cleric, thinking to himself until the two are distracted by heavy thuds from the ceiling and the same moaning that had interrupted the cleric's meditation before.

"Oooh, you beast!" yells the woman. "Harder! Yes!" It sounds like her face is pressed down to the floor above.

"Say my name!" grunts a familiar voice. "Say it! Fuck!" They hear the muffled slapping sound of skin meeting skin.

"Viktor! Viktor!"

Celest bites his lip with embarrassment upon hearing his teammate's name in that context. Julian tilts his head upward and raises an eyebrow. "Sounds like someone has succeeded," says the vampire sardonically.

He looks back at the elf, trying to read his expression. "Clearly, this is upsetting you. Should I go put them to sleep? We could—"

"No! Don't go up there," shouts the elf, scrambling to stand in front of the window.

"Oh?" Julian's interest is piqued again at Celest's haste. "Why?" He takes an unhurried step toward the window. "Is someone up there important to you? Viktor, maybe?" Julian chuckles.

The tipped ends of Celest's ears droop a little as he admits, "Viktor is in my guild. We came here together."

The vampire's face softens. "I see. He sounds like a brute. Is that what you like? Brutishness?" His head cocks to the side as he asks.

"I—we—yes, I care for him," stammers Celest. "But it's nothing like that."

"Oh? Are we certain you aren't jealous?"

"Jealous?"

"Of his companion tonight, that is," says Julian with a wicked grin. He narrows the distance between them as Celest swallows the stress in his throat. "I'll stay down here and leave your friend to his mate," he offers, lifting the elf's chin with two fingers. "But only if you try to relax. I've told you already that I won't hurt you."

The cleric takes a moment to consider the proposal but trying to do so while staring into Julian's enrapturing gaze is almost impossible. Reluctantly, he nods and slides past the vampire's frame to lean on the edge of the dresser. "Fine," mutters Celest, "but before anything else, there's something I need to know."

Julian, blatantly delighted, flies to his side with a swiftness that causes the elf to flinch. "And what might that be, Celest?"

"You are a vampire. You drink from the blood of mortals," the elf whispers, trying to keep his tone level. "I need to know if... this means you have taken a life."

"Ah. How should I explain," says the vampire. He gingerly places a hand on the old oak top behind the cleric's back. Continuing, he says, "If a tree bears fruit each year at the harvest, would you cut it down? No. That would be foolish. Likewise, it would be foolish of me to kill. So no, sweet Celest. I have not."

The elf sighs with relief. "I see... that's good, but even still... I don't know why you're here or what you want." His hands grip the lip of the top drawer, and they firmly squeeze the wood.

The vampire makes an effort to slow his excitement. "I'm here for you, Celest."

"But why?" Question marks wrinkle into the cleric's forehead. With great effort, he looks up to meet the vampire's gaze.

Julian's expression suggests amusement, but his eyes are focused, molten rock.

"Last night when you touched me," says the vampire with a smile. "I've never felt something like that, even as a human—even with Katya. I can't quite find the words for it."

At this angle, Celest can see the tips of his fangs as he speaks. They glisten, crystal white.

"I'd like to understand." He gently reaches for the elf's hand and takes it in his own. "You can help me understand. You may be my very salvation." Suddenly, in one fluid movement, Julian picks up Celest with one arm cradling his back and the other behind his knees, glides to the corner chair, and sits down with the elf on his lap.

A full-bodied tension strangles the elf's bones. "What are you—"

"You said you would relax," Julian whispers in his ear. "So, relax."

The cleric sits up, trying his best to touch as little of the vampire as possible. His hands dampen, his heartbeat races, and he holds his breath like it is his last.

Julian stays quiet, waiting for Celest to soften. Although unnecessary, he begins to breathe in a slow, rhythmic pattern, allowing his chest to rise and fall in perfect time. The rest of his body is absolutely still. Julian waits like this for minutes. Eventually, the elf takes a breath, then another—and another. Warily, the tension begins to leave his body, starting at his chest and radiating outward. With the delicacy of a tailor, Julian runs his fingers down the elf's back and combs through his hair.

In a barely audible volume, Celest says, "I'm not sure I can."

Julian doesn't reply. Instead, he carefully wraps his free hand around the elf's knee and explores the naked skin under his thumb.

Deep within the cleric's mind, something blooms. A memory, shoved to the corner, digs its way to the surface of his consciousness. He was an adolescent when it happened, just under sixty years old. It was a cold autumn night at the Everlight Citadel. Most acolytes were deep in meditation under the silver light of the moon. But Celest, and his playmate Soleil, had snuck past the council room and into the oratory. It was her idea, of course, but Celest was eager to see the plan succeed. The ceiling of the oratory had been constructed of thin, clear glass that let in every drop of sunlight for the morning service.

That night, they lay on the floor looking up at the stars and pretended to sail through space in a magical ship. She confessed to Celest, with brilliant golden hair covering her eyes, that she had waited for them to be alone. Soleil's breath trembled as she rolled herself on top of him. After a stare that seemed to last for hours, she leaned in and kissed him on the forehead. Celest's cheeks were stained pink with delight. He replied with a ginger kiss on her lips. They spent the rest of their time curled up, twisted in each other's arms, and made plans for the planets they would visit in their spaceship.

Little did the two of them know, it would be the last time they would speak. The divine arts maester noticed them missing from Moon Circle and found them shortly after in the oratory. For months, Celest was punished for his disobedience. He was forced to bathe in the searing hot waters of the metal cleansing tubs during the night, and by day he begged his goddess to rid him of his impurity and profane defiance. It was during this time he learned that as an acolyte of the sun and one destined to become a cleric by trade, it was his role to give. To serve the goddess, he had to surrender himself to the citadel, the maesters, and eventually his guild. He was to listen, assist, and stay out of the way. To receive from anyone but the goddess was indecent. To seek pleasure for its own sake was obscene.

The shape of her face escapes his memory. Soleil was sent to an all-female citadel in the far north of the Elvyn Highlands. Tucked away atop Mount Saphyn, the Skyreach Citadel would be her new home. He can barely recall the way her laugh made him giddy with excitement or how soft her sunlight hair felt brushed against his cheek. He missed her more than he thought.

Tears well up in the elf's eyes and wet the vampire's shoulder. Celest, now fully leaning into the vampire's chest, wrings his hands together, trying to stifle the feeling brought up by his memory.

"Sweet Celest," hums Julian. "Why are you crying? Have I made you upset?" He moves his body to further cradle the elf in his arms and tilts his head, trying to see his face. A white sheet of hair covers the elf's expression.

"You've reminded me of a childhood friend," replies Celest as he wipes away the tears. "She kissed me too. We got in trouble for it."

The vampire's grip loosens, and he pauses. "Celest, how old are you?" he asks dryly.

"I... It's my one hundred and thirty-seventh year."

Julian lets out a surprised sound and then bursts into laughter that bounces the cleric on his chest. Celest sits upright. "Did I say something funny?"

"Older than I expected. Is that common for a full-blood elf? For a moment, I thought that you may have been too young for me to hold you like this." The vampire tightens his grip again, sending chills down the elf's back that are offset by a growing warmth in his core. "You're still younger than me by a few centuries, but you must have shared similar company if you've lived a hundred years." Julian sweeps the silken strands of hair from the elf's neck. Starting at the shoulder and gently moving upward, the vampire slides his lips over the elf's golden skin. Their touch is as light as the wings of an insect.

A spirit of rebellion stirs in the cleric's gut as he tries not to react to the pleasurable sensation. "I've never."

"Don't lie to me," Julian whispers. A cold, wet tongue slides over the knife edge of Celest's ear and circles around its pointed tip. A hand glides under the elf's hair and slowly but firmly grabs it at the root, tilting his chin upward. The heat in his chest is back and burning.

"I'm not lying," moans the cleric.

After a heavy pause, Julian says, "Suppose I believe you, Celest." The words drip from his mouth and linger on the name. His breath is sweet like tea, and the scent is intoxicating. Celest inhales it with the deepest part of his lungs. "I suspect that you're excited by something. Tell me, my sweet. Is it me that you want?" asks the vampire in a siren's tone.

The cleric's chest pounds as the burning heat descends into his lap. Without pausing to think the question through, the elf nods yes.

Leaning in but stopping just above a kiss, Julian purrs, "I want you more."

Celest, dazzled and provoked, seals the gap between them. Their lips meld into each other like dark and light candles spilling together into melted gray.

With gentle persuasion, Julian coaxes his tongue inside, filling the cleric's mouth with the taste of honey. A deep, seductive groan rumbles in the vampire's throat, and the insistent progression of intensity leaves the elf limp as a wilting rose. Julian is quick to guide his submission. In a single, smooth motion, he lifts him up and pins him to the bed.

Surprise knocks the air from Celest's lungs, and before he can recover, his mouth is sealed again with Julian's lips. They move like a silken stone over the elf's chin, down the middle of his neck, and pause at the collar of his nightgown. One of Julian's hands grips the center of the dress. He bites down on the frill and tears off the garment, sending buttons flying onto the floor.

The cleric crosses his legs with swiftness, and his hands rush down to cover himself. They are caught at the wrists by Julian's firm grip. "Y-you ripped it!" yips the elf.

"Shh," growls the vampire. "It's of little consequence." Straddling the elf, he takes both wrists and holds them down over his head. Starting at his chest, a serpentine tongue slides to the softest skin on the underside of his forearm.

Another quiet moan escapes Celest's lips as it travels. A dozen feathery kisses follow. The elf bites down on his lip, trying not to squirm.

"You like that?" questions Julian through a wicked grin. The vampire sits upright on his ankles to get a good view of the cleric's blush-pink face. He makes a show of unbinding the scarlet sash around his waist. A muted, swishing sound accompanies its movement. Once free, the sleeveless, black robe slides down his body with the slightest twist of his shoulders. It falls around his thighs, revealing the entirety of his torso, ending at a deep v-shape that tucks away behind the fabric.

Celest does everything in his power to avert his eyes from the marble white of the vampire's skin.

"You don't want to watch?"

The elf's heart beats like a hummingbird as he looks anywhere else.

"Fine then." Julian pulls Celest up to his chest and expertly ties the sash over his eyes as if wrapping a gift for himself. He then takes a few moments to braid his white hair in an intricate pattern with the remaining length of scarlet fabric.

His chest radiates a glacial chill, but it's welcome against the cleric's burning cheeks. Pressing his palms to the vampire's abdomen causes them to cool immediately.

"Your warmth feels like the heavens. Can you see me?"

"I can't."

"How sad for you," Julian whispers.

His voice is barely audible, forcing Celest to listen closely. He can hear the soft crunch of linens as he is laid again on his back. Under the mattress, rope supports creak as he squirms. His own heartbeat seems to boom through his chest. Celest's nerves curl as a hand fastens to the nape of his neck, and its thumb glides to stroke the yielding skin around the corner of his mouth. The elf's jaw relaxes, and his lips part, setting free a blissful sigh.

"Good boy," says a voice alarmingly close to the elf's face. Its deliberate, icy breath trails its way to the pointed peak. "I'll be careful if you let me." Julian gently bites the tip of Celest's ear with his front teeth.

"Aah..." moans the cleric. "That's... sensitive."

"Tell me to stop," says Julian, persisting with the act.

His reply is met with titillating silence, which cues one of the vampire's hands to leisurely descend under the black fabric covering their thighs.

"Wait," the elf whispers breathlessly.

"Wait, isn't stop, sweet Celest." The vampire tests their boundaries and brushes his fingers over the elf's private appendage.

Celest pants as it grows in response to the contact. He bites his lip, trying to distract from the feeling with conflicting sensory input.

"Don't bite too hard, now. You don't want to break the skin." Julian nibbles tenderly on his earlobe, causing a pulsing euphoria to fill the cleric's loins that burn despite the cold touch of the vampire's fingers.

Through airy moans, Celest sputters, "P-please. Ju... Julian..."

"Please, what? How am I to know what you want if you don't tell me?" He moves to tuck his thighs under Celest.

The elf is caught off guard and stabilizes by rising to his knees. He can feel the black fabric covering them fall away. Exposed.

"Mmm," hums the vampire. "You look delicious."

A reminder of fear pings on the cleric's nerve endings.

Just before the elf can squeak a word of protest, Julian lunges his cock forward onto Celest's. His grip holds them both between the curve of his fingers. Uninhibited, Julian smoothly grinds his pelvis while stroking them together.

The touch is cold, but the cleric burns, and the delicate sound of the vampire's fingers sliding up and down their growing erections is maddening. "Oh G-goddess," moans the cleric. Cold liquid drips onto the vampire's hand and spreads downward over his palm, coating their erections in a smooth, slippery film. The sound turns wet, sloshing with each stroke. "This... Hah..."

"This what?" growls the vampire. His free hand twists around Celest's braid and carefully pulls it down, along his spine, to his sacrum. His back arches, and he props himself up by the wrists to stay upright.

The friction buzzes on his nerves like a bard's song touching the harp strings. The elf's blindfolded eyes roll back as he gives up the fight, letting his body fall limp against the vampire's embrace. "Oh... Julian... I've never felt this."

"This what?" asks the vampire through diamond teeth and an expectant smile. "Are you always so vague, or is it embarrassment that binds your tongue?"

Glowing energy emits from the elf in crashing waves like that of a storm at sea. "Mmm... Ooh!" He can barely control a surging need for release.

"Not quite yet, little mouse," says Julian as he slides away from his partner. Celest is left trembling and confused momentarily as Julian repositions himself. "Pay close attention. I'll only show you once." A wet ring slides down the elf's phallus, creating an airtight seal at its base.

"Is that..." pants Celest as he tries to think over the slurps and suction enveloping his shaft, "your mouth?"

After a soft popping sound marks the end of the sensation, the elf is maneuvered off the bed and commanded to his knees by a generous amount of pressure applied to his shoulders. "Say *aah,* and you'll know for certain."

Celest timidly parts his lips, unsure of what's expected of him. One of Julian's large hands cups the back of his head and guides his lips to the tip of his cock. The elf flinches as it makes gentle contact.

"Well then," says the vampire, "go on."

Roses blush on the cleric's cheeks and bridge over his nose as he explores the shape of it with his lips. When he's ready, he opens wider and timidly sucks on the dome.

"Ahh... good boy." Julian slowly presses together his hand and pelvis, pushing deeper into the elf's mouth as his tongue laps against the shaft. "Yes," growls the vampire, "very good." Julian takes control of the tempo, gradually thrusting deeper until the full length of his cock is taken in.

Celest chokes as his throat closes around the foreign object, but Julian holds it there, waiting for surrender. It arrives as expected.

"You're perfect."

Submission comes easily, as it always has to the cleric. Tonight is no exception.

Julian uses a black nailed fingertip to slip the scarlet blindfold up past his left eye, and Celest's sight is quick to adjust to the lamp-lit room. His liquid gaze crawls up the rippled marble of the vampire's abdomen and lingers on the spear-sharp points of his collar bones. It climbs long curtains of dark hair and melts at the discovery of sanguine lips parted as if to taste the sex in the air. Julian pulls his hips back and tilts the elf's head up to witness the captivating authority of his expression.

There's hunger in his eyes. "More," pants the cleric.

The vampire looks doubtlessly pleased, but there's also a touch of surprise. "Certainly," he responds, pulling the elf up by his arm. He moves forward until Celest's shoulders press to the northern wall. "I intend to give you all of it," whispers Julian, "piece by piece."

He slides his cock in the gap between the elf's thighs, causing electric jolts of pleasure to surge up his spine. The vampire positions his arms behind the cleric's knees and effortlessly suspends him up against the wall. "Now, little mouse, it's time to relax."

Celest's panting slows to a dull whisper as he tries his best to obey.

Julian allows the cleric's ass to slide down until it makes contact with the tip of his erection. "Keep breathing," he says, pressing the bone-stiff shaft as gently as possible into the entrance.

Each new depth is met with a pause to acclimate between the careful moments of undulation. Pleasure and pain compete for the elf's attention, neither holding space for long, but building in intensity as they deepen. "Oh, Goddess..."

As Celest's body relaxes, the pleasure grows impossible to ignore. Eventually, Julian thrusts the totality of his cock inside. An instinctual, inhuman sense for the elf's indulgence guides its pace and intensifies. Each deep stroke is accompanied by the sound of his thighs slapping against Celest's golden skin. "Can your goddess see you now?" growls the vampire. "Getting fucked like a grateful whore?"

The answer is yes, the cleric thinks briefly, but he couldn't care less. He is enraptured in the carnal heat of erotic connection, and there isn't a devotion in existence that can compete at this moment.

Julian's kiss connects like a fist, and his tongue finds fast entry behind the other's lips. Celest sucks it reflexively, unable to think past the tremendous building pressure in his loins. "Oh Goddess..." he whines.

"Not yet," groans the vampire.

Celest attempts to hold back the inevitable. "Goddess!"

One of Julian's hands rushes to the elf's neck, grips it, and pounds into him as hard as he can get away with. Celest is bursting at the seams while the vampire's carnal groans reach a crescendo. "Now cum if you want to breathe," commands the vampire.

"God—" The plea is cut short. Julian's grip releases from his neck in an instant to penetrate the cleric's open mouth with his middle and index finger. Unable to chain his pleasure any longer, Celest reaches an overwhelming climax. The excess energy boils at the edge of his skin, spills over, and soaks the starved vampire in its savory warmth.

Chapter Eight

A perfect circle traced on the pale golden skin of Celest's chest rouses him to wakefulness. His eyes flutter open, noticing the heavy clouds backlit by mute sunlight through the window. His head turns away drowsily but freezes as he is caught by the splendent red of Julian's adoring gaze. "My brother, Damion, was also a man of the cloth. I never did understand his devotion. In life, I, too, was a mage. However, I delved into a very different domain," says the vampire casually. "You remind me of him in your temperament. Ignorant, but kind."

Celest, now fully awake, rubs the sleep from his eyes and sits up on the bed. "Did you make me fall asleep?" he asks, confused.

"That was of your own volition. Or, rather, your exhaustion after last night's activities," he replies, giving the elf a tender kiss on the cheek.

The act sends a sincere quiver of gratification to the center of the cleric's chest.

Julian sits up as well, leaning in with his body. "Sweet Celest, may I ask, are all elves hairless? Or, maybe, do you take it off yourself?"

The question burns pink patches of embarrassment onto the elf's cheeks.

"You shouldn't be here," squeaks the cleric. "It's morning. My friends are expecting me." Just as he ends his sentence, four loud knocks pound on the door.

"Hey, Sunshine. We're all waiting in the parlor. We've gotta get a move on," says a voice, rough as sandpaper, through the wood.

Celest's skin prickles like the fur of a startled cat.

"Coming!" sings the cleric, who begins frantically untying the scarlet sash from his loose braid.

In a flash of movement, Julian is dressed in his cloak and robe. He glides back to the bed and lands a quick kiss on the elf's lips before dissipating into a thin, dark cloud.

A whisper of Julian's voice tickles his ear. "See you soon, my sweetest Celest."

The fog floats to the eastern window, and an invisible force cracks it open. It slides through and disappears into the rainfall.

"What's taking so long?" says Viktor impatiently.

Celest finally releases his hair from its binding and shoves the scarlet silk into a pillowcase as the door handle turns. He had forgotten to lock it. The elf rushes to cover his naked body under the sheets and lifts the duvet to his chin as Viktor barges in.

"What the hell? You said you were coming." The warrior stomps toward the bed and grabs the duvet with his wide palm.

"Wait," yips the cleric as the sheets are almost pulled completely off.

"Oh, oops," says Viktor, quickly averting his gaze. "Where the hell are your pajamas? Let's pick up the pace here, alright?"

Celest's eyes dart over the room, remembering the moment his night-gown was ripped off and thrown to the floor. To his surprise, he finds it folded neatly on the dresser, each button perfectly intact. The fabric gives off the faintest scent of Julian's essence. "A mending spell?" he asks under his breath.

"We don't have all day, Sunshine."

"I'm sorry, Viktor, just one more moment." He slips on the under-garment, finds his outer robes where he had last left them, and retrieves his boots tucked under the dresser. Once decent, he walks over to his teammate and touches a hand to his arm. "I'm ready. Thank you for your patience."

"Yeah, yeah. Let's go."

They scoot down the long, narrow hallway and enter the parlor where Sable and the Lasaunt siblings sit, finishing a breakfast of apple porridge. Celest gets a bowl from the daytime barkeep and sits next to Nyx, devoting his full attention to the action of eating. He shovels the food into his mouth and stares down at the spoon.

"Hey, buddy," says Nyx, "don't choke on an oat."

The elf half-chuckles and slows his pace.

"I hope you slept well, Celest. I know I did," says Adinine in a sing-song voice. "A bit too well, considering the circumstances."

"Uh, yes. Very well, thank you," he replies truthfully.

"Good to hear," Sable chimes in. She's as chipper as a bird at dawn. "We'll need the extra bit of energy today. Cassianna and I made a plan to search the woods for the shrine while keeping Adinine safe from the threat. I'd love some help from you, Celest. Is that alright?"

"Oh, of course. What do you need me to do?"

"I thought that we could combine my strongest barrier spell with holy energy," says the witch. "It's my understanding that divine magic has the ability to turn away the undead."

"It... can. Circumstantially," replies the cleric.

"Perfect. Cassianna gave me the idea." The two women share a warm look. "I'm fairly confident my spell alone would do the trick, but the added protection wouldn't hurt. We've never actually tried casting together. It could be fun."

"And I'm coming with you three," adds Cassianna with a toothy smile.

"Which is a stupid idea, by the way," says Viktor, who is polishing his shield.

"I think you should let the brains of this party decide what is and isn't stupid," snaps Sable. "As my newly appointed apprentice, I think it's a lovely idea for her to come along. And as the team leader, I have the final say." A twinkle flickers in her cosmic black eyes.

"We'll see what the guild thinks of your leadership after we return empty-handed from this prolonged sidetrack. I wouldn't be surprised if they assigned each of us to different parties altogether. Three months of good ol' team building down the drain. Whatever. Everyone's done eating. Let's do the magic barrier thing and get on with it," huffs the half-orc. "I wanna get back here before it gets too late. I have another date with the sexiest woman alive."

"Congratulations," she says dryly, then turns her attention to address the others. "Adinine and Nyx. You'll both stay in the tavern today. We'll be back tonight with more information and hopefully a missing girl."

"Aye, aye, captain," says Nyx while flashing a two-fingered salute. Adinine gives a thumbs-up.

"Okay. I'll set up that ward now with Celest. It should let the living through without an issue, but still, please don't leave the building. Oh, and if we don't come back before dark, cover the window in your room. We don't need the possibility of you being seen when you're sleeping and vulnerable. Honestly, I should have suggested that last night. I'm sorry. I don't know how I became so distracted." Her gaze momentarily flitters about Cassianna's face.

Guilt swells in the cleric's stomach as he holds his secret behind closed lips. An internal dialogue debates the idea that he would only be causing more trouble to his friends by telling them. He comes to the conclusion that he'll convince Julian to stay away from Adinine on his own. After all, the vampire's interest have seemingly switched onto him. He had every ability to visit the girl last night, but Julian decided to take him to bed instead. Even so, the protection of a holy barrier is bound to provide some peace of mind for everyone. Celest swallows the anxiety and distracts himself with the task at hand.

The two trained magi spend the next hour and a half synchronizing their intentions to find the runes most suited to their desired goal and another half hour fusing the holy and arcane energy profiles. At the end of their spell, they summon a high-quality barrier made of divine light. The Harvest Tavern Inn now stands behind petal-shaped aether sheets of shimmering gold and purple. A drizzle of rain passes through the dazzling lotus barricade undisturbed. Sable, boastfully proud of their craftsmanship, estimates that it will hold for about six days.

"It's so beautiful," Celest hums. "We should try spells like this more often. I don't remember the last time I've had this much fun casting one."

The halfling stands on her tiptoes to give him a satisfyingly coordinated high-five. Their hands clasp together, and they hold each other in a jovial grasp. "Great job, friend. It's been a treat. Literally. Your magic tastes a bit like lemons. It's delightful," says Sable.

The cleric covers his mouth with his sleeve to stifle a laugh. "Oh really? I've never noticed."

"Never? I've smelled lemon bloom before when you've healed me, but I didn't know it would taste like lemons, too," she replies. "There's also a trace of something else. It's woodsy sweet. Honey?"

Celest purposefully evades the query. "I don't think I can taste magic."

"Well then, good thing I'm around to tell you all about it," she says with a smile. Although usually perceptive of minutia, not a single waft of suspicion touches her senses. What possible circumstance would cause her selfless Celest to hide anything from her? The idea doesn't even occur.

After a thorough check of the perimeter, Sable gathers Viktor and Cassianna, and the four of them depart for the northwestern woods. The northern city gates are bound together by an ancient rust-orange lock and chain. "If I had my fucking axe..." grumbles Viktor before running full force into the metal with his shoulder. It twangs as it bounces him away. After that failed attempt, he begins kicking the chain with his boot. "This is bullshit. We'll have to climb."

"Step aside, fight man. This is a job for a witch," says Sable rolling a tiny piece of bomber's clay in her glove and sticking it to the chain. "Stand back, everyone." A spark of flame flicks on the end of her fingertip and shoots itself into the clay, causing a loud boom to split the gate wide open. The witch twirls into a pompous bow while Cassianna showers her in sincere applause.

"Seems more like it was a job for an alchemist. Unless you made that bomber's clay yourself," teases the warrior. "Come on. We're wasting time. The owl said it was two hours northwest."

"The trail is heading north," says Cassianna.

"Yeah. Looks like we'll be off-roading," replies Viktor, trudging forward through the forest's edge. Branches hang heavy and low, bearing the weight of massive growth-like moss. Swelling black fungi the size of children pucker the sopping ground. The skittering of creatures, unseen in their coverage of leaves, unite the four in collective unease. Difficult terrain makes each step a challenge, causing heat to cling inside their clothes despite the chilled air that numbs their noses. Through the twisted trees, whose commandant roots lord over the soil and pierce their siphons deep underground, they continue on.

"The shrine should be around here somewhere," says Viktor.

"We've been traveling for roughly two hours," adds an out-of-breath Sable. "Part of me is doubting whether or not we should have trusted a bird."

"Can you get up past the trees and scout the area?" asks the warrior to the witch. "If there's a clearing near here, you'd probably be able to see it."

"I could if I had enough coin for a new flying broom," she grumbles.

"There's really nothing else you can do?" ask Cassianna, whose curled hair sticks to her sweat-damp forehead. She hasn't yet complained despite not being accustomed to this level of physical effort. Sable looks at her sympathetically and sighs.

"Well, there is one way for me to get over the canopy, but..." She pauses, shuffling through the plethora of pockets hidden neatly in the deep folds of her skirt, and pulls out a bottle holding a small, glittering powder. "I came across this fae dust in the black markets of Hightower. To be honest, I'm not sure it was ethically sourced, so I've been wary of using it. But even if it works exactly as expected, I'll be floating a hundred feet in the air for well over an hour."

"I know I could use a little rest," says Celest. "You might be able to relax and eat something while you're waiting to come back down. I realize that might be uncomfortable, but this weather could turn sour at any moment, and we don't want to be wandering aimlessly when it does."

Sable, surprised to hear Celest's opinion so clearly, ultimately agrees with him. The four split a bundle of rations that Viktor had been carrying on his back. Sable licks her finger, presses it into the powder, grimaces, then places it onto her tongue. After a burst of shimmery fae magic flares outward, blowing back a whirlwind of fallen leaves and twigs, she begins her slow ascent skyward. The internal effect is giddying levity, but the witch keeps her composure, crossing her legs as if it were a carriage ride.

The others watch through a thin part between the tree branches as the witch reaches a final height of three hundred feet. She stops and hovers there like a bubble reaching the surface.

"She looks fine, right? Up a bit higher than expected, but fine?" asks a squinting Viktor as he tries to make out the meaning of her waving arm.

"She doesn't look panicked," replies Cassianna.

"Yeah, it's fine. Sure," he says, taking a seat on the titan-like roots of a felled tree. The three eat their fruit bread leisurely, occasionally looking up to check that Sable hadn't been swept away by the wind.

An hour goes by, then another. The clouds darken, condense, and begin to rain as the party below grows nervous and waits. Just as the weather starts picking up, Sable begins her equally slow descent back down to the forest floor. By the time her feet touch the mud, she is soaking wet and furious. "Let's get the fuck on with it! Follow me!" she shouts and sprints away in a northern direction. The other three quickly collect their belongings from under a wagon-sized leaf where they had been resting and run after her.

The elf is last to reach the gazebo at the outskirts of the clearing. A ring of white marble stones marks the edge of the wild forest. Inside the perimeter, meticulously manicured gardens and walkways are brought to life by the downpour of rain. Bright orange water lilies bounce on their pads in the center of decorative ponds. Stone bowls overflow into each other like waterfalls off a mountainside. Wet drops glisten and fall down the vine-curled lattice walls, and amphibians croak together as a baritone choir. The garden draws their eyes toward the center of the clearing, where a teardrop-shaped building seems to float on a large pond of rainwater. It looks to be made from the same stone as the perimeter but is also adorned with a lace-thin layer of orange glass.

"Truly masterful," says Celest once he catches his breath. "I've never seen such quality glass smithing. Someone skilled must be here taking care of the grounds."

Cassianna's eyes are wide with curiosity. "Wow. That must be the shrine. The detail is striking," she adds, "so perfect and delicate."

"Looks like the kind of place one might find a new weapon. Axe, maybe? Something with a name like Stormsplitter or Tidalwave," says Viktor, pulling his wet shirt away from his chest and ringing out some moisture. "The best loot is always hidden inside some pretty bullshit like this."

Sable is shivering with anticipation, but after being exposed to the weather for hours, a deeper chill threatens to freeze her to the bones. She sticks her shaking hand into a dress pocket that holds the sandalwood bark and snaps it between her fingers. A gust of arid heat warms the party but isn't enough to dry their soaked clothes. "Sorry," says the halfling, "I just needed to—"

Her words are interrupted by a blinding white light that seems to come in an instant and out of nowhere. Celest flinches with a gasp, nearly tripping over Sable, and Cassianna lets out a sharp scream followed by a string of profanities.

"Oh," the light dims slightly, and a voice like clear crystal hums, "I believe I have guests. I have startled them. Allow me to apologize with an invitation. Welcome."

Chapter Nine

"You all must be cold from the rain. Follow me," chimes the speaking light as it floats its way through the garden maze toward the shrine's entrance. A trail of glowing thread is left along the path it takes.

Viktor straightens his brow, turns to Sable, and asks, "Any idea what the fuck that was?"

"Let me think," she replies. The witch begins inspecting the end of the gossamer thread of light. She slowly swipes it with a finger, but the beam goes straight through her skin undisturbed. "Its magic seems to be extraterrestrial, or maybe even extradimensional."

"Extradimensional?" repeats Celest with wide eyes. "You mean that it could be of the gods?"

"There are other planes of existence besides The Allahquery," offers Sable, "but it very well could. It's my best guess for what appears to be a human-sized star."

The cleric's heart pounds at the possibility.

"I think our safest bet is for you to take the lead here, Celest. Provided that this isn't some kind of trap, it seems... nice enough. Let's follow the light and try at conversation." The elf agrees with a nod. "If anything seems off, follow my lead. Viktor, keep your eyes peeled."

"Aye," the warrior replies, "but if I say fall back, do it."

"Could I help?" Cassianna asks, anxiously twisting her fingers.

Sable steps in close and takes her hand. "You just stick with me," she says with a reassuring smile. "If anything happens, I'll keep you safe and sound." They cautiously follow the path through the garden, making their feet light to avoid squishing the native frogs.

As they approach, light begins to spill from the shrine's threshold. "You all may enter," says the crystal voice.

Celest takes a timid step to the front of the group and replies, bowing his head, "Thank you for your hospitality. My friends and I wish no harm to you or this place. We would graciously accept a reprieve from the rain."

"Certainly," says the voice. The elf takes a deep breath and leads the party inside. Beyond the entrance, the light bounces off the white marble walls and glitters through delicate glass fixtures. "Warmest welcome, travelers. I haven't been treated with guests in quite some time. Is there something I could do for you?" As it speaks, its light radiates impossibly bright. It feels like morning sunlight on their skin.

"Yes, there might be something you could help us with," replies Celest, "but I'm afraid our eyes are too sensitive to look at you while you're speaking. We mean no disrespect."

"Oh! My apologies," says the voice as its light begins to dim and condense into a humanoid shape that floats over the floor. "Your kind are sensitive to my aura. Yes, I remember this." Abstract features that resemble wings sprout from its temples, wrists, back, hips, and ankles. Its face, although difficult to perceive, is a construct of otherworldly beauty that beckons to an ancient corner of their minds. "This is better, yes?" it asks. On its chest, a dark red symbol is contrasted against the light: a sun rising over the water, haloed by three succulent drops of daylight.

The cleric knows this symbol well. A rush of recognition throws him to his knees in reverence.

"Uh," whispers the warrior worriedly, "you okay, Sunshine?"

Celest hears the words but doesn't register them. His mind is racing through his teachings, trying to recall if he had learned how to address a daeva.

Sable steps up as the elf fumbles over his thoughts. "Yes, and well met," she says. "My name is Sable. These are my friends Viktor, Cassianna, and Celest. I notice the symbol on your chest. Would that be the divine crest of Amatetra?"

"Ah!" the being says, beaming. "It's been many years since I've heard her name spoken by another. Yes—peace be upon her eternally." Still floating, the form crouches down to inspect the cleric. "Rise, child. There is no need to cower."

With haste, the cleric complies. "P-pardon," he sputters, "I am a disciple of our goddess. It's an honor to be in your presence. Please, tell me how I may best address you, my daeva."

The last word clicks Sable's suspicions into place but also drags a memory to the forefront of her mind. "You're an angel?" she asks curiously. "I think, in a dream, I read about you."

"Some would call me an angel. Others would call me a daeva, or spirit, or seraphim," it replies with a jubilant expression. "If you wish to call me a more casual name." It tilts its head to the side in contemplation and continues, "then you may call me Morningdew. I shall share the name of the shrine to which I've been assigned."

Celest's eyes all but sparkle with astonishment. Somewhere beyond excitement and fright, the cleric feels like an unspooled string. "That's a beautiful name!" he exclaims. "Have you met the goddess? I have wished all my life to be with her. Could you tell me about her?" Shame follows the questions like a leopard stalking its prey. It pounces, tightening its grip around his throat as if to punish him for speaking out of turn.

"In a sense, yes," it replies warmly. "To describe her company would be nothing in comparison to the experience. You could not conceive of it, sweet child of the waters." Its attention is that of an experienced doula. "Perhaps I could show you a portion of the divine." A delicate hand is placed on top of the elf's head. Wings on its wrists unfurl as a spiraling, white light builds above them. It funnels through the back of the angel's hand like a drill tip, boring into the cleric's energy field.

The party watches closely, waiting for any sign of discomfort from Celest. Untrusting the supernatural, Viktor clenches the fist at his side. His temperance, requiring absolute focus, is in full view of Cassianna, who is positioned at the back of the pack. But the warrior's apprehension isn't urgent enough to take her attention away from the gravitational pull that now surrounds the cleric.

All hold their breath except for the elf, who for a moment, is outside of himself. His body, filled to the brim with euphoric plenty, seems unable to hold any sense of selfhood. Figuratively freed from its skull, his mind flits aimlessly about the expanse. If not for the vague sensation of being an object in space, there would be nothing stopping his spirit from dissolving into the moment.

The spiral gradually slows, thinning until only a thread of light remains. It is then severed by one of the daeva's wings, but before the connection is completely broken, a familiar smell is followed by an indulgent vision. Myrrh and honey, like that of Julian's breath, perfume the back of his throat. It is impossible not to recall the sensation of last night's encounter with the vampire, despite being in the presence of one so holy. Eventually, the vision fades, and so too does the angel's touch.

Celest, completely intact, is almost dripping with tranquility. His eyes are glazed over with a peaceful sheen, and his demeanor is uncharacteristically casual. "Thank you, Morningdew," hums the elf. "I feel like I'm flying..." His voice trails off at the end and turns into a yawn.

"It is my absolute pleasure, child," replies the seraphim. "You are quite the open vessel. It reminds me of someone I knew long ago."

"Well, you've broken him," says Sable as the cleric sinks into a comfortable sitting position on the floor.

Under his breath, Viktor adds, "This is why I don't like calming spells. Look, he's practically drooling."

Cassianna can't help but stifle a laugh.

"So, Morningdew," begins Sable. "Do you mind if I ask you some questions?"

The angel floats to the halfling and lowers its face to meet hers. "You may ask anything you like. If you prefer, I could draw your bath first."

"My bath?" Sable looks down at her rain-soaked dress.

"Yes, child. The center rooms of this shrine contain hot pools. I shall prepare them with rose hip and chamomile," explains the angel. "It is ritual to bathe in the shine's waters. It is also quite soothing to the mortal body and mind."

"Oh, interesting. I thought we may have had an offensive odor," says the witch. "I'd like to ask the questions now if that's alright."

"Proceed."

"Firstly, there is a missing girl. Have you seen a human with dark curled hair and blue eyes?" she asks. "Her name is Briar, age nineteen."

"I have not, for I have been alone longer than she has been alive," replies Morningdew. The angel floats up and over to Cassianna to address her. "You are the first human I've seen in three hundred and twenty-four years."

"So you haven't seen her either?" questions Cassianna. Her hands are behind her back, nervously pulling at a loose string on her waist belt.

"I am afraid not. I hope, wherever she may be, she is safely in the light of the goddess."

"Blessed be," chimes Celest.

Viktor chuckles and rolls his eyes, equal parts irritated and amused.

"Have I said something wrong, fireborn?" the daeva asks, flying to the half-orc.

"Fireborn?" replies Viktor. "Huh, I like that. But no, not really. It's a bit concerning that we haven't found a single lead on the poor girl, though."

"No one we've spoken to has seen her, neither before nor after she went missing," adds Sable. "I'm starting to think the man who told me of her wasn't in his right mind. In any case, I have a few more questions. May I?"

"Please continue."

"There's been some targeted attacks happening in the city. Does that sound like something you know about?" asks the witch.

"How awful." The angel sighs. "I know nothing of the goings-on outside of the clearing's stone borders."

"The locals have tales of a demon with vampiric power," persists the halfling, pressing for more information. "You've been stationed here for quite a long time. Surely, you have some idea of this being's presence?"

"Make note, curious Sable," it begins, gliding toward the center of the room. "For my words are that of history."

She takes the invitation as an opportunity to ready her still-damp notebook and quill. Viktor and Cassianna are likewise attentive, but Celest looks up at the seraphim like a tired child waiting for a bedtime story.

"This fallen kingdom was founded on the back of one, Prince Julian Markov. The castle was built, and the city was rising up from below it. It was only after his younger brother, Damion Markov, had moved here that this shrine was erected. It was a gift from the elder brother to the younger prince. Damion, a fellow servant of the goddess, tended this place and his community with care. Divinity recognized his good work and assigned me to aid him," it continues, arranging its form to create a dance that accompanies its words. "It was a time of plenty. Damion's congregation was likewise growing, but everything changed when a new member of that congregation fell to her death. Her name was Katya. It seemed she was well-liked, for the humans so mourned her. Damion stopped attending the faith daily as he once had. Six days passed where I saw not a single soul, but it was then that Damion came to me in a hurry. He was frantic and asked me to wait in the garden as he cast spells of protection on the inside rooms. I did try to ask what frightened him, but all he told me was to stay alive. That was the last time I saw him. The curse took hold that very night." The angel pauses, allowing its audience time to think.

"Okay," says Sable as she fervently writes down the details. "But what is the origin of this curse? And, what else does Julian Markov have to do with this story?"

"Your questions are precise, child of the harvest. The answer is this: the elder prince mourned Katya, too. So much so that he tore through realms to rip her soul from the grips of death. He succeeded, but something evil slithered from the rift and consumed all lives within its reach. At its center was the prince, whose soul was so darkened that it cast away the sun."

"So that's how he became a vampire," muses the witch, "delving into the dark arts. Do you know of any reason he would be targeting a young woman named Adinine Lasaunt?"

"I know not."

"Understood," says Sable. "One more question, please. How have you survived all these years alone with no congregation to keep you tied to this place? It's my understanding that worship fuels your physical manifestation, or am I incorrect?"

"Your well of knowledge is impressive, Sable. I have not been stimulated in conversation like this for some time," compliments the daeva, as the witch offers an awkward smile. "You are correct. With no following, my essence should have dispersed centuries ago. I have concluded that I am also trapped in the confines of the curse. Although, Julian himself may be able to kill me. If so, I do believe he has yet to figure out a way. Prince Damion's protection seems to still be in place after all this time, yet I am unsure of its nature."

Viktor speaks up, "Any way to stop the curse?"

"I know not, fireborn."

"Thank you, Morningdew," says the halfling. "You've been a great help. I'll need some time to chew on this information."

"I offer again for you and your fellows to use the bathhouse. It will take but a few minutes for the rosehip and chamomile to infuse. Shall I show you to the changing rooms?" asks the angel, unfurling from its dance.

"Uh, we're not the type to share a bath," mumbles the warrior as he glances over at the ladies.

"There are two separate pools and changing areas if you wish to separate by sex," Morningdew assures. "Feel free to stay as long as you like. I find myself very much enjoying the company."

"I think we can do that. It's pouring outside after all, and I may think of another question once I mull it over," states Sable. "Is everyone in agreement?" Cassianna nods quickly with a slight blush to her dusk-honey cheeks.

"Aye," declares the half-orc. "Wouldn't mind the heat, and I'd be lying if I said I didn't need one. Celest could surely use a splash of water."

Toward the end of the daeva's speech, the elf drifts off into a sleepy meditation. He's sitting upright, but his eyes are closed and the hair loose from his bun floats up and down as he breathes.

Viktor nudges him with his knee.

"Hmm?" moans the elf, returning to his senses. "Is it time to leave?"

"Even better," replies Viktor. "We're taking a bath together. It's your lucky day, Sunshine." The warrior grabs his shoulder and helps him to his feet.

"Oh." The cleric yawns. "Okay."

"Perfect!" exclaims Morningdew, brightening as a result. "I shall ready the pools."

Chapter Ten

The party splits up as they are shown to the center rooms. Quick to unbutton her dress, and eager to get warm, the witch is in and out of the dressing room in a flash. Past heavy pink curtains, steam rises from the water. It curves like ribbons through the heavy air and collects into swollen droplets that hang from the ceiling. Gravity pulls them down one by one, and some drip into the sultry, pink waters. The pool itself is oddly shaped, as if a natural spring has been coated with this black-as-night stone. Through fracture-like patterns throughout the room, bright pink light is visible. Upon closer inspection, it appears to be saltstone heated by an unknown source.

As she approaches the nearest edge of the water, Sable's breathing slows, trying to capture the sweet scent rising with the heat. The last time she had a proper bath, she thinks, was a fortnight ago at guild headquarters in Hightower. Since then, she has been getting by with a little prestidigitation and some conjured water, but it isn't the same as an unhurried soak. "I'm getting in," she says in the direction of the attached dressing room.

"Go ahead," replies Cassianna, who's still getting undressed. The halfling notices a new shyness about her and assumes she'd like some privacy. Sable always thought others were overly concerned with modesty. Among many human cultures, it is uncommon for adults to see each other naked unless they are wed. Elves are a fairly diverse group in terms of ideology, ranging from self-righteous celibates to polyamorous nudists. Dwarven practices seem reasonably egalitarian, but Sable suspects it is because less emphasis is placed on the importance of gender in their social orders. The farming village where she grew up was similar in some ways. Bathing was a communal activity for genders and ages of any kind. She isn't sure if that was common in other halfling settlements, though. Her ancestors were of the oral tradition, and the pillaging took not only the lives of her people but their stories as well.

Sable reflexively runs her fingers over the skin on her hands and arms that have been scarred by its fire, but she quickly distracts herself with the lightning cracks of crystal peeking through the smooth black stone. The crystal itself emanates a brilliant heat that keeps the water simmering. She sits down at the bath's lip, lowers in until her feet touch the shallow end, and blows out the air in her lungs. Bubbles rise from her puckered lips as she sinks below the surface. She pauses, dissolving in the still water, then bounces back up to lean on the ledge with her arms.

Her apprentice, it seems, is through changing. She stands between the curtains at the entrance with her hair pulled up high and a towel wrapped under her arms. "I feel like a noble in a place like this," admits Cassianna as she approaches. "I can't believe this gem has been so close to home all this time."

"Ah yes, princess," teases Sable. "Your bath is ready for you. Only the finest aromas, hand-selected by an angel, await your indulgence."

Cassianna laughs heartily, lowering herself into the ripples at the opposite end of the spring with her towel securely attached. Now wet, it tastefully seals to the topography of her form. A curl that escapes her hair tie floats on the pink surface as her eyes close to relax.

"I feel so lucky to taste the life of an adventurer," she mumbles over the water. "I never dreamed it was possible for me, yet here I am, learning magic from a witch and hunting a vampire."

"Strange, isn't it?" agrees Sable. "I've observed that the call to adventure usually isn't voluntary. Rather, it's this force that scoops you up in its wake, drags you along, and tests you all the while. But, even so, I'm glad to be here with you... for however long that is." The sincerity is evident in her soft smile.

"Thank you, Sable," replies Cassianna. "Please teach me all you can."

"Right." The witch winks playfully. "Here's a lesson. Water can be used in spellcraft as a scrying tool, a base for potions, or a medium for transmutation. There's also a spell that uses water as a kind of prison to bind an entity in place. It's basically water shaping in its most powerful form."

"Really?" asks the human. "How could you hold something with a liquid? Are you sure it isn't done with ice?" Her hands wave under the water causing ripples in the surface that lap at Sable's chin.

"You would think," muses the witch. "But it actually has to do with density. No matter. Let's practice something more basic. As I said, water can be used as a conduit for some kinds of energetic magic." Sable finds a foothold in the stone and uses it to climb out of the pool. She sits on the edge holding her feet over the water.

Cassianna averts her gaze away from Sable, staring down into the water instead.

"Oh, does my nakedness bother you?" asks the halfling, sweetly masking her condescension.

"No," assures Cassianna nervously. "I just don't want to stare. Sorry, I guess it's strange if I'm trying too hard to look away." Her cheeks are turning pink, either from embarrassment or the heat of the bath.

"It's hard to look away?" teases Sable, testing the boundaries of their relationship.

Cassianna fidgets with the edge of the towel covering her upper thigh, clearly flustered. "I'm digging myself into a hole here," she laughs. "If I keep talking, I'm finished. Just... tell me more about water magic."

"Alright," concedes the witch. "I got out so that you could get in touch with your own energy. The still water will amplify it. With enough concentration and intention, the water will start to move. Try getting into headspace like we practiced last night."

"Right," she replies, closing her eyes and placing her right hand over her solar plexus. A current begins to churn to the speed of her breath as momentum gathers in her palm with an inhale and flows forward through the base of her rib cage with the exhale. The night before, her body was where the spiraling sensation stopped. But here, it continues, shifting the pool water like a gentle spoon mixing soup.

"Perfect. You really are a natural," chimes Sable. "Now, let's introduce your other senses. There's a new smell to the bath. It will be difficult to discern from the physical fragrances, but it's there nonetheless. On that note, one must be careful when using magic against another mage. If they're paying close enough attention, they might smell or taste your next spell coming."

"Does it smell... bad?" asks Cassianna self-consciously, scrunching her brows.

"Actually, sometimes yes," replies Sable with a laugh. "Necrotic arts can have a particularly bad scent. But don't worry. You'll discover your natural resonance is quite delightful. Focus, and you'll be able to catch a flavor."

She obeys, directing her attention to her pear-shaped nose. The calming blend of chamomile and rose hip selected by Morningdew is obvious, but there is a hint of something warmer. Cassianna mentally guides the faint scent up through her sinuses, then onto her tongue.

"There's a heat?" she contemplates out loud.

"Yes, good," praises the halfling. "You're on the right track. Try to go through the types of heat in your mind and compare them to your resonance. So close."

"It's not pepper. That's for sure," exclaims Cassianna. "It's earthy but doesn't have a sting like horseradish. What is that?" Sable smiles proudly, seeing her student at the precipice of self-discovery. "Oh, it's cinnamon."

"Beautiful," Sable celebrates. "You're absolutely right." Her feet kick up and down in excitement. The left heel accidentally splashes on the surface, sending quick ripples deep into Cassianna's chest. The water stills immediately as if all energy was vacuumed away, leaving her protectively curled over her heart. "Sorry to give you a start. Are you alright?" asks the witch worriedly.

Cassianna is silent for a moment, with the tension in her shoulders almost palpable, even from across the pool. She speaks in a soft, even voice, "I'm going to be honest now... Will you listen to me?"

Sable slides her legs safely onto the lip of the pool and perks up in concern. "Of course. Tell me anything you need. I'll listen as long as you'd like."

She hugs her knees together, squeezing the towel tighter around her form. "My whole life, I've felt like I've lived, I don't know, in chains. It's like I'm trying to stand tall and walk forward, carrying the weight of everyone else's expectations. At first, it's backbreaking, but you survive the day and build up this strength that you didn't ask for. Honestly, it feels less like strength and more like armor. It's a suit that you've been forced to wear, and it's uncomfortable and humiliating, and you wish you could just crawl out of it, but you're stuck." A few falling tears create the only movement in the pool.

Sable waits, giving her space to continue.

A shaky sigh escapes from Cassianna's lips before she begins again. "My mother deliberately ignored my pain until the day she died. I took care of her in the last few months when the end was coming. I half expected... I thought she would face it. Face me. Just once. But she didn't, and I couldn't bring myself to ask her to. You know, it hurts to be treated unfairly by a stranger, but it's so much worse coming from someone you love."

"My spirit goes out to you," soothes Sable. "I'm no stranger to defying expectations. Sometimes it's met with ridicule or violence, but it must be heartbreaking to feel that in the company of your loved ones. That was never the case for me."

Cassianna tilts her head up and glances at Sable, then back to the steam beginning to rise again from the water. "It's different now. Since my mother passed, it's just been Adinine, Nyx, and me. They've shown me unbelievable support. When I'm with them, I feel like I never have to hide or be weighted by their judgment," she explains. "And... I feel the same when I'm with you."

Sable's dark, full lips part into a smile. "I'm glad to hear it," she says. "And yet, you seem quite reserved at this moment. Am I wrong?"

"No..." the human admits. "You're right." She looks up at Sable with an expression that melts the witch's heart. "I'm falling in love with you, and I think you might be feeling the same, but I'm afraid that you don't see me for what I am."

The halfling stares into her eyes and emanates a warm invitation. "I've been drawn to you from the moment we started speaking. What is it that you think I don't see?" she asks.

Cassianna steels herself and says, "I was born and raised as a male. My name is one that I chose. Some days, I wish I could shed my skin and not have a body at all. You might not understand it, but that's... the truth. I just needed you to know."

"Cassianna," says Sable. "I hope this doesn't come off as rude, but your community seems extremely cloistered. In the larger world, it's not unheard of for someone to adopt a different gender. There's another mage in my guild who enrolled at the same time as me. He began his transition into becoming a man shortly before joining the guild. We've discussed it a few times over drinks... and halfling smoke bloom. I've also read that in some ancient elvyn cultures, every individual would experience time as three separate genders and then decide for themself which best suited them. Some were even content to continually change for the entirety of their lives."

The human's brown eyes are wide and shining. "So... are there more women like me?" she asks in sounds colored with astonishment.

"Absolutely, darling," responds Sable. "In fact, I've read quite a bit on the subject since the magic associated with it falls under the category of transmutation. Again, that's my specialty. Nothing you've just said surprises me or changes my attraction. That's what I need you to know."

Cassianna's legs fall away from her chest, opening her posture. A need to process this new information is evident in her expression. "This reaction is beyond anything I expected," she admits.

"Thank you, Cassianna," says the witch, "for trusting me enough with that information. I understand, given your position, how difficult that must have been to even tell me. So, thank you." Sable twirls her wrist, gathering steam into the shape of a heart with her aura. Then, she winks, which sends the puffy heart over to make gentle contact with the human's cheek before dissipating. Cassianna dreamily smiles back at her. "Now, shall we get back to the lesson? Or maybe you'd like to continue professing your love for me?" she asks brightly.

"Yes—wait," chimes Cassianna. "You mentioned people that use magic to change gender? How is that possible? Is that possible for me?"

"Technically, gender is the part of your identity that's a bit amorphous, but we're talking about physical changes to affirm your gender. It's absolutely possible, and in this instance, exceptionally probable," replies Sable. "In humans, as well as other species, the difference between masculine and feminine is a matter of hormones. I know a spell that changes the production of chemicals in your body gradually over a period of time. Elves take to this change rather quickly despite their long lives, but for humans, notable results happen in a few months. As a woman, you may feel more comfortable with feminizing hormones. Mind you, it's not an illusory disguise spell, so it won't entirely change the appearance of your anatomy. Some medic healers do those sorts of procedures, but they usually take place in urban cities like Hightower."

The moment the halfling pauses, Cassianna speaks, "Cast the spell on me. It's everything I've ever wanted. Please."

"You don't have to plead. If that's what you wish, I'd be happy to," she responds with her hand over her heart. "Maybe, once your sister is safe, we could take you all back to Hightower. It's full of opportunity, especially for a fledgling mage and vastly different people of all types that live in relative peace. I think you would feel free to express yourself as you wish there, even if it's just to visit. How does that sound?"

"It sounds like a dream to hear a place like that exists. I'll have to talk with Nyx and Adinine, but if what you say about the outside world is true, they'll be as marveled as I am. Thank you, Sable."

An earnest smile is set on the witch's face as her feet lower back into the pool. "This setting seems better than most. Are you ready to begin?" she asks.

"The spell? Now? Oh. Yes," agrees Cassianna. "How?" Her back straightens eagerly, and her expression reads as excitedly focused.

"Get back into your headspace, and I'll do the work from there. It'll be faster if you're open and relaxed, but there's no rush. We'll take as much time as we need," says Sable in a calming hum.

Cassianna complies by closing her eyes and returning inward.

The water is quicker to excite this time around. However, Sable's energy is distinct and distracting when met with her own. The witch's ankle twirls in the water, creating a counter current that tickles the surface of the human's skin. The waters act as a spinning wheel, weaving together their separate energy patterns into one stronger thread.

When harmony is reached, Sable dips back into the bath, and Cassianna sees clearly, in her mind's eye, every tiny, heavy curve of her form. She feels the witch's spirit connect like a bee landing on a flower, gentle yet invigorating as it nuzzles against the petal-like layers of her aura.

"Shifting spirit, *Alzibeaunin,*" Sable chants aloud as her fingertips crackle with purple beams. "Trust anew, so may it be, in Self to hold what is known. *Alzibeaunin Thehisitt Freay. Alzibeaunin Thehisitt Freay.*" Slow purple lightning crackles from the water's surface, mirroring the pink cracked patterns in the stone.

Cassianna sighs energetically as a tingle vibrates in her nervous system. The sensation feels caught at her scalp, so she reflexively undoes the tie in her hair. As it falls to the water, her curls soak with weight, revealing their true length.

Sable's irises sparkle like a clear midnight sky as she continues the chant. Her words move the human, intangibly but effectively. Energy builds within them, creating a fizzing vortex centered in Cassianna's lower back, until the spell fully connects. Purple plasma bursts from the pool in a dazzling light show that crackles and pops into glittering embers before disappearing altogether.

Sable leans back, resting her arms on the ledge, and gathers her breathing. Her student's eyes reopen slowly and then fix on the halfling. "Is that all?" she whispers. "I don't feel much difference."

"It's a gradual change so as to not shock your system," she replies. "My peer from the guild told me that it gives your psyche some time to process the change, as well. That's only his account, of course, so I couldn't say for certain, but I hope this spell does for you what it did for him. He said it saved his life."

Just then, a bright light appears behind the changing room curtains. "Is everything alright?" sings an angelic voice. "I felt a burst of arcane energy."

"Uh, yes, quite alright, thank you," stutters Sable awkwardly.

"Everything is perfect. Thank you, Morningdew," reaffirms Cassianna.

"Yes, just making certain. Please continue to enjoy yourselves," it says before the light dims and then disappears, leaving them alone again.

Chapter Eleven

Cassianna stands and walks across the pool to be beside her companion. As she sits on the stone that Sable is standing on, she sighs and lays the back of her head on the pool's lip. A wet curl falls to the side, brushing over Sable's arm.

"I think that's enough spellcraft for now," says the witch, gently combing the curl back into place. The halfling catches the other's eyes trailing quickly over the scars covering her arms, but then she looks away as if not to stare. "Are you curious about them?" asks Sable, calmly.

"Oh," mutters Cassianna. "You don't have to. I'm sorry."

The halfling extends her arm in front of them, twisting it around at all angles. "It doesn't bother me, but the story of it is quite sad. I used to live with my family in a small farming village. I was always an ambitious child, dreaming of a life far grander than the one I had. I remember having to beg the village elder to teach me to read." She laughs to herself before continuing, "I quite resented the peaceful life that I had, so I'd spend my days escaping it. I would skip my chores and go hide in the hills, reading and teaching myself novice spellcraft. One day in my adolescence, I was doing just that, but then I heard a commotion from the cottages. I ran back to see what was the matter, and when I got within eyesight, I found my village being ransacked in a goblin raid."

Her gaze is directed at the ripples in the pool, but her eyes look far off as she imagines the violence that took place. Resting her temple on the human's smooth shoulder, she continues. "They stole all they could, rounding up the livestock, shoving grain into their wagons, keeping my people back with the tips of their spears. No one in the village was versed in the art of war. We made our living with fair trade and spent the evening with song, dance, and smoke bloom. I watched, paralyzed with fear, as the ones that did fight back were felled. The raid had numbers on us, three for every one, and all were armed with weapons.

"Once they had taken all our supplies, they bound the rest of my people in rope and rounded up each and every one of them into the main barn. As if that wasn't enough, they sealed the barn doors, set flame to the wood, and finally left. The barn was filled with dry grasses for the animals, and by the time I reached it, the screams had begun to quiet. I received these burns clawing at the burning wood, but it was no use."

Tears drip into the bath, creating sorrowful, circular layers outward from the impact point.

"Oh, darling," whispers the witch as she wipes them from Cassianna's cheek. "Don't cry on my behalf. I've long since accepted my misfortune. Fate can be cruel, but who knows where I would be now if my life hadn't taken that turn. If it hadn't, I might have never been able to follow my dream. Or, have gotten the chance to meet someone as lovely as you."

"That's absurd," responds the human, attempting to collect herself. "A tragedy like that can't just be rationalized with gratitude."

"Maybe you're right," concedes Sable. "Or maybe... I've just gone mad!" The witch's cosmic eyes open wide, and her mouth pulls to the corners of her teeth in a silly smile. Despite herself, the face makes Cassianna laugh.

"Well, you are certainly strange, to say the least." The human giggles.

"I've had enough talk about gloom and doom. Maybe... we could continue our other conversation?" hums Sable. Cassianna sighs with her eyes closed and brings a hand to meet the halfling's small fingers that are still woven through the human's hair. She holds it to her ear and leans in. "The conversation where you were falling in love with me," Sable continues in a whisper.

"Oh? When did I say that?" Cassianna asks with playful sarcasm.

"It was right after you told me how smart, and funny, and charming, and witty I am," she replies in kind.

"Hmm, I definitely don't remember that," teases Cassianna. Sable laughs and tosses the human's hair a bit in half-hearted punishment. "But," she continues, "it all sounds like something I would say." A jolly smile is framed by her full, honey-colored lips as their faces meet at eye level.

Sable lets a silence grow, turning the still air between them into a force that pulls them closer together like magnets. "Say it then," she offers. "I want to hear it again, whispered in my ear." The witch stays put, leaning on the pool wall, but her posture is inviting. While standing, the water laps at her chest, barely obscuring her dark nipples beneath the ripple of waves.

"I've got a better idea," whispers Cassianna before planting a ginger kiss on the lower corner of her cheek.

Sable tilts her neck so that their foreheads meet. The two stay like this for a few moments, breathing in each other's air and steam that is caught underneath their faces. Sable inches forward. Her companion's lips tremble with excited breath as she plants a slow kiss. They linger gingerly together, molding each other, each set full and pillowy.

Sable pulls back, leaving a sliver of space between them. "I want to hear it," demands the halfling playfully. "That you can't get enough of me."

The human smiles, trying not to giggle. "Then maybe I'll keep it. Like a carrot on a stick," she replies, bringing a hand to the witch's chin. They kiss again quickly, and Sable moves forward to stand on either side of Cassianna's lap. She presses her body to the towel that separates their skin, wiggling her hips enough for it to loosen. Cassianna's focus is concentrated on the tip of her tongue that now meets the other's own. She is barely aware of her towel sliding down her chest but does notice a movement of the witch's tongue that tastes of longing so sweet that she pulls her kiss away so as not to dilute the flavor. Sable goes in for a third time but is stopped by Cassianna's index finger. "You want more?" she whispers flirtatiously.

"Does a toad want the monsoon season? Yes. I do," replies the witch with a low moan.

"And, what if... I made you work for it?"

Sable's eyes roll back half-heartedly. A huff of air leaves her nose before she answers, "Please. At this rate, you won't be able to keep your hands off me."

Cassianna holds back a smile, clasping her hands around her head.

"Try me," she replies with a sly gleam in her eye. The shift of her arm to stop Sable's advance is enough for the towel that has been covering her to fall at her waist.

The witch, excited by the challenge, presses her chest onto the other's bare skin. Her breasts are soft and yielding under the water like river soil. They contour to Cassianna's chest like dewdrops on a petal and glide smoothly over her skin as Sable rolls her shoulders, shifting their weight flirtatiously. The witch's night eyes glitter behind sultry black lids.

However enticing, the human manages her composure and keeps her fingers locked behind her head. She purses her lips in victory, but her heavy, wanting gaze betrays her. Sable catches this tell and decides to tease at it.

"You can't hide it," says the witch. "I'd bet all the coins in my pouch you're thinking of nothing more than how I'd feel in your hands."

"You can't prove that," she retorts, clutching a section of curls between her fingers.

"I think I can." Sable backs away, swimming to the shallowest ledge of the pool. Slowly, she rises from the water, allowing it to stream down her shoulders and dribble from her plum nipples. Her hands are placed gingerly on her neck but then begin to wander down and around her wet, naked body. "You wish," she continues rubbing gentle circles on her bosom, "these were your fingertips... or maybe the flick of your tongue."

Cassianna's face reddens in the cheeks, and the witch suspects her apprentice is close to conceding this game of theirs. Her lips are parted slightly, and her breathing is heavy and slow. Her eyelids, with their thick lashes, flutter like a hummingbird anticipating a drink from the bowl of sugar water placed on a windowsill.

"You don't have to resist me," she offers, confidently sliding out of the water to lean back erotically at the pool's lip. Her short legs are spread wide, bent in at the knees as her position is held in place by her full, round bottom and the tiny palm of her left hand. The right, however, is exploring the supple folds of skin between her own legs.

Cassianna, captivated by Sable's one-woman performance, sinks absentmindedly into the pool until the surface rests at the glistening depression just under her nose. Like an alligator, focused in its attention, the woman stares at her mentor. This person, she thinks, has a brilliant mind and a power unencumbered by her petite frame. Her heart is radical, worn on her chest. Sable is like no one else she's ever known, and Cassianna is ready to treat her as one in infinity.

Sable begins to moan between dragging breaths. Her two fingers find a rhythm that leads her to an escalating paradise.

Cassianna breaks as Sable's midnight eyes roll slightly to the back of her head from pleasure. She wants to be a part of it, the cause of it. The water parts, leaving a wake behind her as she walks along the bottom of the pool and kneels in the shallows before her quivering paramour. Still silent, the human's hand surfaces from the pink pool, and her middle finger daps along the two-petalled ridge of her vulva.

"Couldn't stay away?" moans the witch.

Instead of words, Cassianna replies by kissing her plush inner thighs that smell of the rose she's soaked in. The human's finger wriggles cautiously at the entrance, then slides inside to the first knuckle. Sable bites her lip, continuing the circular strokes over her clit, as Cassianna's lips reach the sensitive underside of her ass cheek. She begins to suck and press with her tongue on the skin there, and when she pulls away, a shimmering gossamer of spit remains. Sable sees this and twists it around her pointer finger before returning to slide the film around her swollen pearl. They moan together this time, and Cassianna's breath between Sable's legs is even hotter than the steam that fills the room.

The halfling asks between wet breath and slick teeth, "Do you want a taste?" She spreads herself with two fingers and positions to the very edge.

"How do I... do it well?" asks Cassianna dreamily before exploring the folds with the tip of her tongue.

"Ah, mmm." Sable giggles, instructing: "Imagine it's a peach, ripe with juice. Pretend you're eating it. And there, right there—where you are now, yes. That's the pit you can suck on—Ahh... ah..." She trails off, allowing her presence of mind to focus on the slippery suction.

Cassianna's middle finger moves almost instinctively, wriggling deeper and shallow again with the tempo of their collective breath. She laps attentively at her partner but quickly realizes that flicking and sucking at the pearl garners the most animated quivers and moans. Occasionally a shiver of pleasure escapes her nerve endings, causing an equally physical reaction in the other, like they are connected somehow in immaterial space.

"I'm getting close," Sable whines. "Tell me how you like it done. I want you to feel as good as I do."

Cassianna slows her pace and looks up longingly into the other's eyes. "I do feel it. I've never felt it so clearly," she replies in a daze.

"I mean—love, what do you like when you're alone?" she asks. "Tell me, and I'll make it be." She whispers something more under her breath, accompanied by an intricate wrist motion. A handful-sized glob of water rises from the pool, outlined with Sable's signature glittering purple aura. "Tell me a shape, tell me a texture, tell me a movement. That is, of course, if you're comfortable with me pleasuring you. I would very much like to."

Cassianna exhales and bites her lip in anticipation and embarrassment. "Can you make it smooth... like a broomstick?" she murmurs. "Shallow... here." Her finger slides, wet with film, down to the witch's bottom hole and circles it.

Sable tries not to smile too suspiciously while molding the water into shape and then dragging it slowly down her back. She fails to contain her amusement and jests, "You had no idea you were a mage, but this whole time you've been riding a broomstick? It's a classic, really. Tale as old as time." The halfling giggles at her own joke.

"You shouldn't mock me, being as exposed as you are," she teases back, then continues kissing her pink pearl. The halfling moans, trying to maintain the hand movement required to hold the enchantment. It descends back into the pool, but Cassianna can distinctively feel the spellbound water pressing between her cheeks. It begins to vibrate with a curl of the witch's finger, feeling unlike any sensation that the human has experienced on her own. She leans forward, dipping the small of her back and spreading at the knee. Sable watches her dazzled eyes as the enchanted object inches in and out of the entrance. "Ahh—that feels good," she whimpers, yet her mouth is still fully occupied. "That's just right. Mm—go faster?"

"That's right, darling," Sable moans. "You want a quicker pulse?" Her delicate fingers articulate in perfect rhythm, causing the vibration to increase steadily and Cassianna's eyes to widen with pleasure. The sound of little gasps between suction and moans makes Sable curl up at the toes. "I'm going to finish," she says. "I'm so close. Don't stop."

The human complies while penetrating with her middle fingers for added engagement.

The space around them crackles with invisible energy as Sable reaches a climax that leaves her legs trembling. After a moment to catch her breath, she slides back into the pool and kisses her apprentice with a fiery passion. Her focus is now keen on the other's pleasure. Every shiver is an inspiration that helps the halfling bring her partner closer to an epiphany. Every moan acts as a tuning fork, furthering their harmony.

"Oh, Sable!" she gasps. "Fuck me faster. It's so good."

"Yes, love. I want to leave you quivering," she replies. "Cum for me." The witch guides the other's head down with her hand. Cassianna's chin touches the water's surface, her face at the same level now as Sable's breasts. The witch shifts her shoulders, sliding her nipples across the human's drooling lips until she latches on one and begins to suck and roll her tongue around the deliciously smooth areola. Her eyes are closed, yet her expression is so wanton that it appears almost pained. With the free hand, Sable pets her head and murmurs, "You deserve it, darling. Every ounce of it. It's all yours. You deserve everything, love."

Her attentive words send Cassianna over the edge into a release that feels more like a revolution.

Chapter Twelve

Inside the adjacent bathing room, Viktor and Celest are relaxing in the perfectly warmed pools. The elf is snuggled up with a wet towel in the shallows while the half-orc stretches his stiff muscles in the deep end. The water and its temperature aid in flexibility. Viktor takes full advantage of the opportunity, reaching high above his head and bending over gradually at the hip to touch his ankle, which rests on an underwater shelf. He does this for a few minutes, sighing and groaning like an elder from the pleasurable pain.

"Grrrr," mocks the cleric, giggling to himself. "Urrg. Mmph."

"Hey, I know you're having fun, but shut it over there. Stretching is important. Maybe if you tried it, you'd snap out of that holy-high of yours."

"I stretch every day," hums Celest, "without making any silly noises. Heh—silly, silly, silly. Is that a real word? Silly?"

"The more you say it, the less it sounds like one," replies the warrior, moving over to lean on the side of the pool. "Don't mess with me. You heard the angel. I'm a fireborn. If you don't shut it, I'll burn you to a crisp." He doesn't make an effort to bolster his joke with any sort of performative machismo. Viktor feels quite relaxed, and in fact, is thoroughly amused with Celest's inebriated antics. Since he's usually so prim and proper, this is a welcome change of pace.

Celest giggles again, turning to face his teammate, and says, "You can't burn me. You're not a mage, and that's not what Morningdew meant... Silly." His hands paddle at the water, entertaining himself with the simple movement.

"Pff—maybe I'll drown you instead," he chuckles. "What do you mean that's not what it meant?"

Celest grabs the bath's lip and uses it to pull himself closer to the half-orc, asking in return, "Don't you know the story of life on Nem?" He clumsily sits next to his friend and stares, wearing a sloppy smile.

Viktor grabs a dry towel placed on the ledge and wraps it around his neck to act as a pillow. "I wasn't there. How should I know?" says the warrior. "In my village, the story was that a volcano burst and orcs rose up from the lava, but I guess that story only half applies to me. I suppose your version has something to do with the goddess, right? Tell me."

The elf bounces from side to side, making ripples in the water that lap onto Viktor's chest like tides on a beach. "Mhmm, in part, yes," Celest replies. "The sisters, Amatetra, Hesheik, and Nemvysi, came together to create mortals to worship them."

"Hewhat and Nemwho, now?"

Chuckling, he answers, "Hesheik is the goddess of the moon, and Nemvysi is the goddess of our world. That's why it's called Nem, of course. You're so funny, Viktor. You never learned this?"

"Yeah, laugh it up," teases the warrior. "But, what's that got to do with my new nickname?"

The elf is transfixed on the heat coming from a crack of glowing salt stone under his foot.

"Sunshine," he barks to recapture the cleric's attention.

Celest perks up, looking at his teammate in alert confusion.

"Fireborn. You were telling me a story."

"Oh, right," sings the cleric. "Anyway, the goddesses made six races together using each of the world's elements. From soil, they made halflings, dwarves from crystal, elves from water, humans from—uh—wood, fae from the air, and orcs from fire. That's why Morningdew calls you fireborn. Maybe your volcano story is a reference to that."

"Mhmm, interesting," hums Viktor. "I don't usually believe in any of that crap. I mean, sure, your goddess is real and all. I know gods exist. Where else would you be getting your power from? But stories are twisted when they're told. Over time they're nothing like what really happened. Plus, there are twelve races of people. Your story misses half of 'em."

Springing up from blowing pouty bubbles below the water's pink surface, the elf retorts, "It's not just a story, Viktor. It's history. The citadels have kept detailed accounts for thousands of years. And that's not the end of it. I just told you enough to answer your question. So, there were originally only six races, but as time passed, Hesheik got jealous of her older sisters. Mostly, the six races preferred the sunlight and woke during the day only to rest at night when she could spend time with them. Nemvysi lived among them, Amatetra was favored, and Hesheik was lonely. She went behind her sister's backs and made her own nocturnal races to exalt her using the same six elements." Celest pauses, trying to remember which race corresponds to which element.

In the middle of arduous thought, Viktor playfully splashes his face with water.

"Hey!" protests the elf.

"Pop quiz," teases Viktor. "Say 'em all, or I'll dunk you. No mistakes."

"Uhm, uh—well, sirens were obviously made from water, giants from fire, goblins were from soil, pixies from air... And... Oh, moonkin are made from wood, and gravelins form crystals!"

Despite his accomplished expression, the warrior lunges over, takes him by the shoulders, and pushes him under the water. Pulling him back up after only a second of time, the warrior roars with laughter.

"Why?" Celest whines. "I got all of them right."

"Yeah, well, how am I supposed to know that," snickers the half-orc. He again lounges on the lip after having fun.

"You didn't know any of it," responds the cleric. "That's the whole point of me telling you this, is it not? Because you're dull, and you don't know anything?" He wraps his arms tightly, pouting like a child.

Viktor's glare would appear ruthless if it weren't for a slight smile dug into the corner of his mouth that hints at his true feelings. In the short few months of knowing Celest, he's never been able to rile him up. Any prior attempt was met with awkward prostration, but high-as-all-hell, he's finally biting back, and the warrior wants to keep pushing. "Since it's usually me that's drunk off my ass and saying shit they don't mean. I'm gonna give you one pass, Sunshine. Watch your mouth." He slaps the water's surface with his hand spread wide, sending a tidal wave that splashes the elf with the force of an ocean.

After a moment of tense silence, Celest counters with a doublehanded splash of his own, followed by a mocking tongue spat out at his teammate.

"Oh, you little shit—" snaps Viktor, grabbing the cleric by his arm and dunking him under the water again. A wrestling match ensues.

Although mostly one-sided, the cleric, while flailing under the rose water, manages to grab a chunk of the half-orc's braids in his left hand and pulls them down enough that Viktor joins him under the surface. The scuffle turns the pool inside out as globs of water are sloshed over the sides with their movement and ends with the cleric in a headlock, cheeks squished between Viktor's bulging bicep and the thick mat of hair that covers his chest.

"Mercy, mercy," squeaks the elf. "I yield." His hands tap meekly at the arm around his neck. When released, he gasps for breath, clutching to the bath's lip as if it were a lifeboat.

"That's right, you yield," huffs the warrior. "No way I'd lose in hand-to-hand combat with a twig." He relaxes back in the tub and places the towel over his eyes as Celest calms down.

The elf's breath slows to a normal pace as he returns to a seated position. After a moment, he begins to observe his teammate. His gaze falls from the full peaks of his chest, down the vertical line of hair on his abdomen, to the front of his legs that are spread casually apart for comfort. Water from the bath, still wobbling from their brawl, sloshes gently over his thighs and between them. An itching compulsion to stare at the private part of him is acted upon. Celest stares at its soft length as it's jostled over the equally large ovals underneath it. Empty-minded, his mouth starts to wet. A swelling in his lap does nothing to break his focus. "Viktor," the cleric quietly pants.

The half-orc lazily removes the towel from his face to find Celest holding tightly to his own torso with a fevered look on his face and fully erect beneath the pink water. Astonishment strikes him first, followed by a jittery concern. "Cele—what are you doing?" His eyes narrow in disbelief as the elf's mouth parts with a wanting sigh. White, stringy hair partially covers his face and chest. He's pretty, like a girl, shy, and welcoming. A nervous blush burns on the warrior's cheeks. "Are you coming on to me?" he asks, too stunned to move.

"I feel hot. Can I see it?" His eyes slide over Viktor's pelvis, then look timidly away.

The warrior stands abruptly, swinging his towel across his waist, and secures it.

"What the *fuck*. No."

Disappointment hangs from the elf's lips.

"Uh, okay look... I don't care what they taught you at the citadel. When we get back to Hightower, I'm taking you to an undercity brothel. I have *never* in my life met someone who so desperately needed to get laid. Come *on*. A wrestle in the nude with *me* did it for ya? Yeah. No. I'll find someone nice to show you the ropes. Not me. So—ugh. I'll chalk this up to the drugs. And I'll forget this ever happened." He sighs deeply with a hand on his forehead.

The idea of Celest that Viktor had built in his mind is immediately shattered. No more is he the untouchable saint. The image is replaced with that of a man with a desire and thirst of his own, a person like any other. The pedestal has cracked, and the warrior physically shakes off the shock. "So much for a relaxing bath. Hell, maybe that sobered you up a bit. Come on, let's get out of here and move on with our lives. We've got more important shit to worry about." Viktor actively avoids unnecessary contact while scooping up the cleric, but out of the water, he struggles to find his feet. With the support of a wall, Celest manages to stay upright, and the two head back to the dressing room to change into their clothes.

After the not-so-sedating soak, the boys are guided by Morningdew and shown to a lounging area at the back of the temple. Just like the natural design of the pools, the lounge has cushions and seating nooks strewn about the room in ordered chaos. It seems like the type of place one could spend hours curled up with a book and, snugly contented, not realize how much time has passed or that a world outside the strangely curved walls even exists. Brightly colored throw pillows and blankets are neatly tucked into any available corners and atop one stack of three plush quilts, a fat, black cat is sleeping. It stirs as Viktor throws his shoes on the floor, yawning wide and flaring its crinkled whiskers.

"Ooh, there's a kitty in here," hums Celest as he stumbles over to it, still feeling the effects of the blessing that Morningdew inflicted him with.

Slumping onto the largest bench cushion he can find, Viktor mumbles, "Don't touch that mangy thing. The last thing I need is you getting your eyes gouged by a stray."

The angel, mechanically mirroring the warrior's casual posture on another seat, chimes, "Oh no, that is no stray, my fireborn friend. Gluttony is my pet, you see. He keeps great company, I can assure you. He was given to me many years ago. We've since grown as close as two beings are capable. I feed him and clean his messes, and in return, he sits on my physical body and vibrates with a sound from his chest. It has become my favorite of pastimes."

"Gluttony?" chuckles Viktor. "Yeah, he looks like a glutton. You might be overfeeding him, mate."

"He has always been quite round. Nothing much has changed over the years aside from his playfulness. He is certainly friendly, though, holy child. Feel free to indulge him in scratches upon the head," the angel explains. The elf coos in delight, petting the fur between its ears as the cat begins to purr. Lured in by the softness, Celest curls up on the quilts and joins it in a nap. After a few moments, his heavy breathing develops into a quiet snore.

Still flushed from the heat of the pool, Viktor lays back, letting his bare feet rest on the pillows. "Hm. You said the cat was a gift. I thought you hadn't seen anyone in years. Or did you just say that to guilt us into spending time with you?" he asks dryly.

"It would never be my intention to inflict anyone with guilt. You simply misunderstood my choice of words. I stated that it had been many years since I had met with a human, you see," replies Morningdew. "Julian was the one who gifted Gluttony to me, and he is certainly not human anymore."

Viktor's eyes open wide, and he lunges to a seated position. "The vampire?" he chokes. "You're friends with the vampire and failed to mention that? What in the bloody fu—"

"Again, you misunderstand," interrupts the angel, "I would not consider our relationship to be friendly. In fact, he is often quite hostile toward me. Julian has tried many times to take my life, but each time I resurrect. For some reason, death doesn't quite take. Gluttony was one of the very few acts of kindness he has ever bestowed on me, although I know not what motivated his action. I have not seen him since that meeting. It has been eight years and thirty-five days."

Pinching the bridge of his nose in frustration, the warrior murmurs a profanity under his breath. "Well... have you fought back, then?" he questions. "Do you know of any weaknesses that he might have? Vulnerabilities? Anything else of dire importance you feel like telling me?"

"I have not. My nature is that of a pacifist. Though I do try and defend myself, my attempts have always failed," replies Morningdew. "Secondly, unholy creatures of all kinds have a vulnerability to silver, as it is the purest of elements. Then, of course, in the case of vampires, there is a weakness to sunlight. They will burn if exposed to it for more than a few moments. Unfortunately, the nature of this land's curse has cast out the sunlight since its inception."

Viktor's head falls into his hands as he sighs. "I don't suppose you have any silver on you either, then?"

"I do happen to possess such an item. One moment," hums the angel as it floats out of the room in a flash. Returning, holding an ornate candelabra, it chimes. "I present you with this gift of silver, fireborn. May it bc of use to you and your fellows in your battle against the wicked forces of this land."

"Oh shit," says Viktor, accepting the offering. "Sable might actually be able to make a weapon out of this. Thank you." He sets it beside him on the bench and fidgets with the edge of the cushion as the daeva looks upon him with a semi-perceivable smile. Its face is abstract like a reflection in moving water which makes observing it for an extended period of time almost uncomfortable despite its vague sense of beauty. "Where is that little witch, anyway?" the warrior huffs. "They're sure taking their sweet time."

"My senses indicate that they have been having intercourse," says Morningdew, as nonchalantly as any other phrase that it speaks.

Viktor stutters, choking again on air and staggering upright, "W-what? They're fucking in there? For the love of hell, now is not the time to be bumping uglies." His attention turns to the sleeping Celest. "What in the world is the matter with you all? Something in the water." His thought trails off as he considers the elf's actions in the pool.

The angel floats above him, arms waving as if to calm his spirit. "Fret not, fireborn," it hums patiently. "It would appear they have just moved to the changing room. I will go to collect them and bring them here. Your wait will soon be over." Morningdew glides like the seed of a dandelion out of the lounge to fetch the ladies.

Chapter Thirteen

A few minutes go by before the light of the angel's form returns to brighten the lounge room. Behind it, Sable and Cassianna follow, and as they enter, Viktor recognizes an aggravating ease about their manner. "Have a nice bath?" he grumbles.

"Huh, not even an angel's pampering can lighten your spirit," mocks the halfling. "Well, thank you for asking. We had quite a lovely time. Right, darling?"

Cassianna smiles warmly while nodding in agreement.

"Yeah," Viktor scoffs. "I bet you did."

Sable's eyes wander over the room, and noticing the cleric remarks, "Celest sure does sleep a lot for an elf. I was under the impression that they didn't need as much as the rest of us. Maybe once we're back in Hightower, we should take him to see a medic."

"I think it's from whatever Morningdew did to him," offers the half-orc. "He's been fucked up on it this whole time. It's not permanent, right?"

"Oh, no. Of course not. He should be back to normal by tomorrow at the latest," chimes Morningdew. "My apologies. He is quite the receptacle. He soaked up a bit more divinity than I had intended."

"Yeah, thanks for that," says Viktor sarcastically. "It'll be annoying to try and get him back to the tavern while he's like this, and the rain has only gotten worse. Ugh. I bet the path we took is all but flooded at this point."

"You're right. It would be a bother. It's almost evening, too. I guess I may have lost track of time in the pools," muses Sable as Viktor rolls his eyes and groans. "Maybe we should stay here until morning. The Lasaunts are safe inside the barrier, so there is little to worry about on that front. Do you mind that, Morningdew?"

"Please, stay as long as you would like," it sings. "I am happy to share your company." Sable smiles in reply as she and Cassianna remove their shoes and join the others to lounge on the seat cushions.

Cassianna unfolds a thin, periwinkle blanket and wraps it around her shoulders like a shawl before cuddling into the pillows to the right of Celest. The expression she wears is one of total security.

The witch moves to join her, but the seat is a bit too high off the ground. Cassianna extends a helping hand, pulling the little witch up to her side. "Thank you." Sable sighs. "The struggle is constant for a halfling navigating furniture proportioned for the taller races." She turns to face the angel, sitting cross-legged and leaning back on a round, tufted pillow. "Morningdew, I realize that I have failed to ask you if you have any firsthand experience with the vampire, Julian Markov. If you could share anything that might—" she begins but is cut off by the half-orc.

"Way ahead of you," says Viktor, flipping the silver candelabra into the air and catching it by the stem. "Apparently, the vampire has tried to kill our angel friend here a few times. It hasn't stuck, though. He keeps reviving. I asked him if he knew any weaknesses from the encounters, and he gave me this candle thing made of silver. I figure you could make me a sick little dagger out of it, and I'll slit the monster's throat."

"I am not male, fireborn," explains Morningdew. "Nor am I female. My being encapsulates the entirety of gender expression. The pronouns of they or it would be more accurate."

"Uh, sure. *They* gave me this candle thing," replies Viktor, correcting himself. "You know, you're the second person who has been particular about that since we've got here. It's confusing to my tongue."

"I am not exactly a person either. I am more similar to an amalgamation of persons."

Viktor sets the object back down on the seat and grunts, "Okay. Yeah, yeah. Tomato, *tomahto*. I'm not trying to get all philosophical now."

"Anyway," says Sable, diverting the conversation. "Silver. That's perfect. I'll fashion it into a weapon, but are we safe here? I assume since you are bound to the shrine that the vampire came to you?"

"As I have told your teammate, it has been many years since he last came here. It would be highly unlikely and coincidental if he decided to return tonight of all nights," comforts the angel.

Sable hears its words, but her eyes are now fixed on a framed artwork on the west wall across from them.

A sense of familiarity itches at the back of her mind as she views the painting's depiction of yellow flowers, an orange sun, a solitary tree, a wooden swing, and children. Then, it clicks. She has seen this image before. Bouncing to the floor and running closer to the piece, she asks, "Morningdew, could you tell me about this painting, please? When was it made? By whom? Do you know who these children are?"

Cassianna tilts her head to the side and inquires, "What's the sudden interest? Is there something wrong?" Sable offers a disarming glance in lieu of an answer, then fixes her stare on the angel, awaiting its reply.

"Are you an admirer of the arts, harvest child?" it hums, gliding over to meet her. "This piece was made by the younger prince, Damion Markov. It's quite lovely, isn't it? He used to teach painting classes to the congregation from time to time. This one was made on one of those occasions. It depicts him and his brother in their youth, a simpler time for the both of them perhaps."

"Does it have any special significance?" she asks, absorbing each detail in hopes of finding some kind of clue. "Is the location it depicts relevant in any way?"

The angel floats up to the frame and pauses with it at eye level, although Sable gets the impression that its perceptual vision is omnidirectional. "I have never before seen this location. However, I would assume it is a place that existed in the prince's memory. The brothers were not born in Markovia, nor did they grow up here. Julian's ambition built this city from the ground up. Before the curse debased this land, all was new and modern."

"Would you mind taking it off the wall for me?" she requests. "I had a dream two nights ago that drew me to this shrine, and now, this painting. If I could just see the backside of it, there might be... something there. I'm not sure. A note, maybe?" The angel does as she asks, lifting the frame up and away from the wall. Behind it, etched into the stone, is the divine crest of Amatetra.

"Ah, intriguing," hums Morningdew while touching a hand to its grooves in the marble stone. "This symbol appears to be spellbound. I am unsure of its nature, but it indisputably carries Damion's magical signature. Curious. I've never noticed this before. Perhaps his spell also concealed its presence from me. Here you are, harvest child." The angel hands her the painting that is barely light enough for her to hold.

She promptly flips it over, sets it gently on the floor, and discovers a single word written in elvish on the bottom left corner of the canvas.

"Viktor, wake Celest. Bring him over," she demands, not once looking up from the word.

The warrior obliges, shaking the cleric by the shoulder until his eyelids flutter open.

"Hu?" groans Celest as the cat at his side stretches over to the open space on Cassianna's lap. "Are we leaving?"

"Not yet," says Viktor. "Sable needs you for something." He hoists the cleric to stand and half-carries him across the room.

Celest's feet stumble underneath him like a drunkard, and the smile he wears looks equally as inebriated as his stride. When they reach the witch, he slumps to his knees beside her and blinks a few times as if to bring her into focus.

Sable points her gloved finger to the canvas and asks, "This is elvish, correct? I'm unfamiliar with this word. Could you tell me what it says, Celest?"

"Hmm?" he sleepily hums, following the line of her finger. "Burn. That's the symbol for burn. The action, not the... injury. Yes?" His attention drifts to the angel above him. Through his warped perception, fractal rainbows emanate from its form in wonderous patterns like heaven's light dispersed through a crystal.

"Burn," thinks the witch out loud. "An instruction to burn?"

"Your friend is correct. And it appears to match Damion's script. He would often ask me to help him practice his elvish. He picked it up as a second language a few years before his passing," adds the angel as it descends to inspect the word.

Sable's skeptical eyes move from the crest on the wall to the painting, then back again as her palm twists, building a spark of energy between the space there. *"Ignius,"* she commands. A flaming speck is shot from her fingers with a snap at the wall, but nothing seems to change as the heat hits the marble, then disappears with nothing to ignite.

Addressing Morningdew, she asks, "How would you feel if I destroyed this artwork? It seems distasteful, but I believe it to be the solution to dispel the magic emanating from the crest. I admit I don't know why I have received the premonition that drew me here and to it. But I can assure you, regardless of the outcome, I intend to do whatever is necessary to protect these people and rid them of their vampire menace.

You can trust me and my party with that. I swear it." Her brows pull to the center, displaying the utmost sincerity.

"I have no need for material possessions, child," chimes the angel. "Thank you kindly for your consideration, but it is unnecessary. You may do with it what you will."

Sable nods in response and casts the flame spell again, this time at the canvas. The moment it finds contact, a glittering gold aura crackles from both the painting and the etched symbol. The crest itself begins to glow like sunshine, and the wall around it mimics the canvas, falling away to ash as the fire feeds itself on hemp and oil paint.

Celest softly applauds this display like a spectator in the theater as the rest watch with curious silence, waiting to see what is being revealed. As the last bits of fiber burn away, the crest disappears, exposing a shallow, square shelf in the marble. A vitreous orange stone, the size of a currant berry, is placed inside. Though small, it radiates a generous amount of white light, similar to the angel.

"All that fanfare for a rock?" questions Viktor as he plucks it from the shelf. "It's kinda warm. You know what this is, Dewy?"

After a moment of silence, the angel replies, "Ah, you have simplified the name that I chose. How clever of you. Yes, fireborn, that gem in your hand is a sunstone. It possesses the innate properties of sunlight. That one, in particular, belonged to Damion himself. He used it to enhance his clerical abilities." It pauses for a moment, considering a possibility. "It may be the reason that I am trapped in this place. Perhaps it assists in my regeneration. If so, please, do me the favor of taking it with you. There is nothing that I desire more than to return to my service in The Allahquery." For the first time since meeting it, the angel's presence is almost frightening. Lacking any mortal mannerism, or gentleness, its request is presented as demand.

"Uh—yes, thank you," stutters Sable. "We'll take it. Thank you."

Morningdew softens again as its wings stretch outward in relief. "That is good to hear," it says. "Pardon me. Time doesn't hold much meaning to a being like myself, but the centuries spent here have been far less than pleasant. I simply long for purpose and reconnection to my goddess. Although I feel her light within me, I yearn for her presence and instruction. Here, my ability is wasted. I'm sure you all can understand my plight. This state of being is quite unnatural, even for a supernatural being such as myself."

"Yes, indeed. That makes perfect sense," replies the witch as she stands to her feet.

The angel zips around her, collecting the ash on the floor and placing it neatly into the newly formed shelf. It then takes the empty frame and hangs it back up on the wall around the square hole. "There," it says. "This will be a memento of the time that you've spent with me, a new piece of art to admire."

As night draws nearer, the four mortals and their immortal host make the most of their time chatting and relaxing in each other's presence. Sable manages to transmute the candelabra into a fine-pointed silver dagger, Morningdew indulges Cassianna's inquiries about life in Markovia before the curse, and each one has their turn entertaining Gluttony with attention and affection. Even Viktor, who is hesitant at first, eventually succumbs to the cat's charm and finds its companionship amusing. By late evening, their stomachs begin growling, so the angel fixes some herbal tea with rainwater and offers them bitter root vegetables from the garden outside.

Cassianna, practicing her taste enhancement spell, successfully manages to boost the sweetness enough for easy consumption.

By the time the meal is finished, Celest has regained half of his wits and can hold a conversation without drifting into oblivion. "This is a what?" he asks, holding the glowing stone like a fragile creature in his palm.

"A sunstone," Sable explains. "Apparently, it will magnify your holy magic. Undoubtedly, that will come in handy when facing off with the vampire. I know you aren't well-versed in offensive spellcasting, but I'm sure a few full heals on Viktor and I would go a long way in a fight. So, hang on to that. If you lose it, it might cost us our lives. Understand?"

The cleric grips it tight and shoves it into an empty pocket on his garb. "Y-yes," he replies hastily, still grappling with sobriety. "It's important. I'll keep it with me."

Sable pats the pocket twice for assurance. "Good. Breathe easy, Celest. You are very much needed, but we've got your back," she advises with a wink to assuage his tension.

The elf chuckles unenthusiastically, wringing his forearm. "But how will I know how to use it?" he questions.

"That, you'll have to figure out for yourself," she answers. "It could be very useful or a total waste of pocket space, so let's not rely on it. Exhaust your resources and use the skills we have practiced before trying something new if it comes down to a fight. I don't need you getting flustered and fiddling with something you aren't familiar with. We trust you, but I'd rather we play it safe, tried, tested, and true."

He nods his head in understanding, then excuses himself to a low cushion in the middle section of the room in hopes of waiting out the comedown of the divine blessing he received. The other mortals begin to ready themselves for sleep, each finding a suitably sized bench or cushion to lay on and deciding between the multitude of pillow and blanket combinations.

"I suppose my aura would bother you all while trying to sleep," says Morningdew, gliding to the archway that leads to the hall. "I shall be in the entrance room if you need anything at all. Enjoy your slumber, my friends. The morning will arrive soon enough. It always does."

The cleric stands and slightly bows his head in reverence. "May I join you, my daeva? To share your company is an honor. Perhaps we might meditate together? I'm plenty rested," asks Celest before sputtering, "T-that is if it's alright by you."

"That's a lovely suggestion, my seaborn child," it sings in reply. "Follow me, and we will leave the rest of them in peace."

The warrior perks up and points a calloused, leery finger at the both of them. "Hey," Viktor barks. "No more fucking with Celest's head, yeah? If I wake up and he's seeing rainbows and shit again, we're gonna have a problem."

"Viktor, how dare you speak to a—" Celest begins but is overlapped by the angel's humming concession.

"Of course, young fireborn," it says. "You will need him to function at maximum capacity upon your departure. Fear not, for I understand this." With the reassurance taken care of, they say their good nights and spend the next several hours nestled in the comfort of the sanctuary.

Chapter Fourteen

Viktor awakens the next morning to find Sable and her apprentice wound up in each other's arms. At some point during the night, the witch moved from the spot she initially chose in favor of resting her head on the human's chest. They look peaceful in their sleep like two fawns curled together in a bed of tall grasses. The warrior quietly scoffs but ultimately leaves them be. He stretches upright and heads down the curved hallway to the entrance room. Backlit by the gray morning haze through the doorway, Celest and the angel are visible. They mirror each other's posture, right leg bent with their foot resting just below their opposite leg's knee, spines perfectly straight, and hands pressed together in prayer over the center of their chests. The two float a short distance above the ground, surrounded by an aethereal ebbing current, and are completely silent in their focus.

"Morning," disturbs the half-orc. The two heads turn in eerie synchronicity, revealing a golden light pouring from the cleric's eyes and slightly open mouth. "Fucking hells," loudly chokes Viktor. "Uh—if you're love-drunk again, I'm gonna kick your holy ass, Sunshine." The two descend to the floor in tandem, and the elf's features return to normal. He looks more alert than usual and possesses a liveliness to his manner.

"Good morning, Viktor," sings Celest. "I'm in my right mind. And look, the rain has softened. It's only sprinkling now." He gestures at the open doorway to the outside garden. "Did you sleep well?"

The warrior sighs and cracks his neck on either side. "Yeah. And, good. We should get going as soon as we can. Thanks for making us feel at home, Dewy. We do appreciate everything you've done."

The angel nods and clasps its hands together. "It was my pride and pleasure to host you all. If the fates allow it, feel free to return at any time. And, if not on this plane, may we meet again somewhere in the great beyond. I shall hold you all close in my memory and will it to be so."

Sable then emerges from the hallway, followed by Cassianna, who is rubbing the sleep from her eyes.

Sable groans. "We heard a shout. Is everything okay?"

"Yeah. Rain has let up," replies Viktor. "Let's get our stuff and head back to the inn. The longer we take, the more Nyx and Adinine will worry."

Cassianna agrees. "Yes. Staying here was an unexpected treat, but I'd like to let them know we're still okay." The party then collects their belongings from the lounge room, exchanges their gratitude and goodbyes, and continues on their journey back to the Harvest Tavern Inn.

Although the path they took through the woods is fresh in their memories, the drenched, soppy soil makes travel more difficult than it had been the day before. During the trek, each traveler, save Viktor, takes a spill that lands them face-first in the muck and soils their clothing down to the innermost layer.

Celest, naturally the clumsiest of the four, can easily be mistaken for a bog druid by the time they reach the dirt road. Greenish-brown sludge sticks to his robes, skin, and hair as if he crawled up from the swamp to forage for a meal or scare away trespassers. His eyes water from a mix of filth and shame. "I can't go into town like this..." he whines. "Sable, please. What if you conjured water, and then I used my purify food and drink spell? Do you think that might work? I can't be seen like this."

The witch sighs, looking down at her soiled dress. "Well," she says. "I guess we can give it a try. I'm going to need to summon quite a bit of water for all four of us."

"I'm fine," Viktor asserts. "One of us knows how to keep his balance. I'll just wash my boots in the street gutters or something."

The witch pulls together her focus, calling forth the element of water to collect in a globular sphere beside her. A few minutes pass, and she begins to sweat. Total control is required to keep the water's form as it grows larger and larger. After a few more minutes, the mass is finally large enough for the three to fit inside. "Alright," huffs Sable. "It's all up to you now, Celest. Let's try it."

The three take in a gulp of air, hold it, and enter. The moment they do, Celest shakes around, causing his foulness to diffuse in the liquid. He then motions a symbol with his finger, directs his intention, and hopes for the best. The glob shimmers for a few moments, and slowly the grime in the water fades back to crystal clarity, washing them as it does. Sable then drops the spell, letting the conjured water splash to the ground.

"Very good, Celest," she says, catching her breath. "That's a neat little trick we've uncovered. Thank you for suggesting it. I guess there's no need for a bathhouse when you've got a witch and a priest. You should tell us what you're thinking more often. Who knows what other great ideas you've kept locked away behind those prayers."

The elf laughs at the compliment as Sable snaps one of her last few pieces of sandalwood to dry them, and the party continues down the road, past the rusted gate, and reaches the cobbled streets of Markovia.

Just as the four tired adventurers round the corner of New Arbat Street, they are accosted by Adinine and Nyx. The siblings run hand in hand out of the tavern and through the barrier toward the party.

Adinine shouts, "Hey! What took you so long?" The two reach them and slam Cassianna into a tight hug. "Ugh, we were so worried. We've been at the window, waiting all morning. Here, let's get you all inside." Adinine escorts them the rest of the way, asking, "Are you hungry? Some fishermen came by last night with a catch from the river to sell, and the chef made fish stew."

Inside, the entire parlor smells of the savory meal. The scent wraps around their stomachs and pulls them taut, causing Viktor's to growl like a bear. Situating themselves around the hearth, Cassianna begins to explain yesterday's events in colorful detail. She recounts the trek, the shine, the angel, and even the cat to her siblings, who hang on her every word. The barmaid attends to their food and drink, all opting for the stew and wine except Celest, who simply asks for some bread and tea. They partake together, continuing to relay the events between warm bites.

"Again, sorry to worry you both." Cassianna sighs. "Sable had to keep reminding me that you would be safe inside the barrier, but I couldn't help but consider the worst. I guess nothing bothered you last night, though?" She sets her bowl on the raised bottom lip of the hearth, unable to eat another bite.

Nyx answers, "We stayed inside, kept the curtains drawn. Even got a pinch of sleep. I'd call that a win." They bring the bowl to their lips and use the spoon to shovel the last bits of stew into their mouth. "Real question is, what's the plan from here? You guys got a dagger and some magic stone, but is that gonna be enough to kill this thing?"

The elf's chest tightens at the thought.

Kill Julian? Kill the man with whom he shared his bed? Kill the one who occupies his every free thought, who he gave himself to just two nights prior? Logically, the cleric knows the vampire's presence is disruptive, and he has great empathy for the fear Adinine and her siblings feel, but to consider taking the life of the person he offered his most vulnerable self to is an unacceptable demand. Julian is forceful and perhaps, Celest thinks, out of touch with mortal sensibilities. But he is capable of reason, not beyond persuasion, and hasn't lifted even a finger to harm him. Upon first meeting the vampire, Celest echoed their trepidation. The way Julian moved like liquid stone and his eyes, which were as red as the blood that sustained him, were terrifying. Yet as he spoke, gently and with such charm, the elf became wet clay. He molded to the vampire's words, his touch. Even thinking of him now, Celest's jaw loosens. His quiet breath wavers. His hands yearn for the chill of his skin. But this, too, is unacceptable.

Smothered between his duty and his desire, Celest mutters, "Might there be another way to fix this?"

All heads turn to him in confusion as if the words he spoke were in a foreign tongue. Viktor is first to register the question and replies sarcastically, "Oh yeah, Sunshine. *Sure*. We don't have to kill the monster terrorizing these folks. So, what do you suggest, then? Should we befriend him? Ask nicely for him to stop? Maybe we can all get together in a big hug and realize that this was all a misunderstanding. What the fuck are you on about?" His reaction stabs a stinging pain into the center of the cleric's chest.

Celest grips tightly onto the cup of tea in his hands and stutters. "Uh—no. Well, I mean, maybe?" This is met with a bark of a laugh from the half-orc. "All I mean is," he continues, "maybe there is a way to cure the vampirism itself without having to harm anyone. Is that so outlandish? We don't even have proof that Julian has taken a life, and yet we wish to end his? I don't think I'm the unreasonable one here."

The cleric tries to read the faces around him, hoping for a glimpse of understanding but instead finds a mix of disappointment, agitation, and bewilderment. All of which are most painfully present in Adinine's expression. She excuses herself from the group, and Cassianna follows her to a table at the far end of the room where they can discuss in private. Celest chews on his lower lip, internally berating himself for causing her discomfort.

Sable moves from her position across from him to kneel at his side on the bearskin rug. She gently takes his hand in her own and says, "Celest, your heart is in the right place. I know your character. And, I know the work that we do can sometimes be draining on someone as empathetic as yourself, but you have to understand that this person you're worried over isn't even a person anymore. It's undead, meaning it should have died already.

"Have your holy teachings not specified that to be an affront to life itself? You, of all people, should understand this. Celest, you are lovely and kind. You don't have to change a thing about that, just trust me to lead us." The small thumb in her glove strokes the back of his hand, and she offers up a concerned smile. "In any case, don't worry. When have we ever made you responsible for a killing blow? It'll be just like those wolves in the cave from our last mission. All you have to do is stay alive and help us do the same. We'll handle the rest."

The elf's brow scrunches together, frustrated with his inability to find any more words to convince them.

"That's right, Sunshine," adds Viktor as he picks up the empty bowls and glasses around them. "And remember, it isn't murder if they attack first. That's just called self-defense."

He walks away to return the dirty dishes to the bar, and Sable releases the cleric's hand and sighs, knowing the warrior's condolences caused more harm than good.

"Right..." says Nyx. "I've gotta say, it's a bit disheartening that you guys aren't on the same page with this. I guess that answers my question, though. No plan?"

"Sorry, uh," replies the witch. "Celest means well, but he's... sensitive. And we love him for it. Nevertheless, the shrine's angel confirmed your suspicion of Castle Markovia being the vampire's home. And we know they're nocturnal creatures, so we should have a better chance of striking during the day. If we're lucky, we'll be able to catch it by surprise while it rests. Obviously, you and your sisters will be staying here where it's safe. Cassianna is picking up my lessons quickly but is nowhere near an offensive level of the craft. At the break of dawn tomorrow morning, the three of us will go to the castle and finish this mess."

"Thank you," sighs Nyx, stretching their chin to the ceiling to release some tension. "Also, I know you've said you're helping us just 'cause it's right, but once this is done, we want to reward you. Adinine and I have already agreed. There is a safe back in our house."

"Let's discuss that after all is settled," she replies. "I believe, too, Cassianna has some future plans to run by the both of you, but I'll let her tell you all about that."

Nyx stands from a crossed sitting position and extends their metal walking cane. "Do you mind showing me to them? I mean, I'd find 'em eventually, but, you know."

"Oh, of course. They're right over here," Sable complies, reaching up to take Nyx by the arm and guiding them away.

Celest is left alone by the fire to suffer in silent anguish. He stares into the flames, watching the wood peel away from itself and dissolve into the glowing pile of ash on the brick base. He feels like the logs, burning up slowly, engulfed in wanton discord but unable to move away from the flame. If only he could voice his dissent in a way that couldn't be argued, but he fears the repercussions, not only from his teammates but the guild. And far worse than either, he dreads what would happen if a report got back to the citadel. The last thing he wants is an audience with the Sunsaints to confess his defilement.

The cleric swore an oath of purity and piety under the teachings of his goddess. What he did is explicitly forbidden. He can't imagine a punishment worthy of sleeping with a demon, yet his deepest desire is to turn from his oath and taste that pleasure once more. For some time, he had been curious about it, giving oneself to another in that way. It seemed that everyone else was, aside from his fellow clerics from the three citadels, which were the only institutions training holy workers for the guild. Each time his curiosities piqued in the past, he had been able to resist it, distract himself, and remember that punishment awaited him if he indulged. Julian's advances, though, were the first to have been so forward. How, Celest wonders to himself, could he have resisted the vampire in all his impossible beauty and unnatural allure? He can't summon an answer.

A sudden crack of the logs startles him back to reality. Groaning, he presses his palms over his eyes and realizes he's been forgetting to blink. Abruptly, he stands to join Viktor, who has ordered himself another drink at the bar. Celest sits on the stool next to him without looking up to meet his gaze and remarks, "Sable says we're staying here tonight and going to the castle at daybreak."

"No shit," spits the warrior. "We came to that conclusion last night. Guess you were too fucked up to remember." Celest now notices a sour grimace set into Viktor's features that weren't present a moment ago.

"Is something wrong?" asks Celest. "Are you upset with what I said by the hearth?" The elf drops his head again in shame.

"No, that's not it. I expect all that bleeding-heart bullshit from you. That's fine," he replies, lazily attempting to manage his volume. "I asked the barkeep when the dancers will be here, but she said they only come on certain days. Yesterday. Not today." He chugs the rest of his drink, belches, and motions for a third. "Ugh," he grunts. "Here I was, looking forward to seeing Marsha again. So, fuck me, I'm aggro. It's not your fault."

"Fine," mutters the elf dryly, then gets the attention of the barkeep as she hands the warrior his wine. "Could I have a room key, please?" She grabs one hanging on the wall behind her and slides it down the bar top to Celest. He takes it and wordlessly gets up to leave.

"What," scoffs Viktor over his shoulder, "not gonna offer to calm my nerves?"

"Why would I bother? You'd just say no," Celest snaps, walking toward the staircase without looking back.

Viktor chuckles in disbelief at the cleric's tone. "Well, shit, somebody's pissy. See you bright and early then, Sunshine," mocks the half-orc, but the elf ignores him and continues up the steps.

Chapter Fifteen

Celest spends his afternoon pacing around the room, stopping often to obsessively check the brightness of the sky. It's the clearest it has been since they arrived in this city. The sun still refuses to shine, but the cloud layer is thin as if exhausted from yesterday's downpour. He stares at the alleyway, past the purple and gold barrier of light, and waits. A few times, he catches an impression of movement but is immediately disappointed upon discovering that it's just another stray animal sniffing at the ground. Hours pass like this, and eventually, the sky turns black with night. With his elvyn vision, the bit of lamplight from the adjacent street is enough for Celest to still make out the shapes outside.

Each moment he stands there, his anxieties grow, wrapping around his throat and chest like chains, until finally, he sees a glimpse of what he's awaited. Dark fog rolls around the corner of the nearest building and curls at the barrier's edge. Celest frantically unlocks his round window and flings it open. His pale golden hands grip the wooden sill as he watches the vapor condense in the alleyway into Julian's silhouette. From the second story, looking down, the elf is confronted with the height, but the bricks making up the outer walls are uneven enough to be footholds, and to his right, a storm drain stretches to the ground.

The elf collects his courage and shimmies out of the opening. Its circumference is just wide enough to fit his slender body through. He finds a solid grip on the drainpipe, tests its stability with a tug, and decides that it can hold his weight. The elf then takes a chance, shifting the weight of his left foot on one of the bricks. It holds. The other foot follows as he grips the pipe with all his strength. Though old, it's solidly attached. Slowly, he descends, carefully finding his next foothold and ever so gently shifting his weight.

The curtain on the window below his room is open wide, but luckily, the inside is pitch black and vacant. Celest slides past it, trying his best not to make a sound. About two feet up from the ground, as he lowers his left foot to another brick, the one under his right foot crumbles. He instinctively grips tighter to the pipe, but gravity pulls him down to the ground. A metal pipe strap holding the drain to the wall gashes his hands as he slides, and he releases them in panic, falling a short distance onto his bottom. Blood wells up through his stinging palms, and he acts quickly to stop the bleeding. The cleric casts a heal onto himself which causes the blood to seep back into his hand and seal itself under newly threaded skin. He stands up hastily with embarrassment and turns around to realize that Julian hasn't moved an inch.

Celest advances toward him but pauses at the barrier. Through shimmering gold and purple stands the vampire, whose form melds into the shadows of the alley. His eyes, pronounced in the darkness, glow a liquid red. The gaze scrutinizes the elf like a puzzle, piecing together the subtext of his body language. Celest is tense, but his posture is complying. It suggests timidness rather than uncertainty. "Will you come to me?" asks Julian dryly.

Celest replies softly, "Yes, I will." He takes a half step forward, then pauses again. Part of his forehead peeks through the protective light.

Julian remains still as the night. "You've made it this far from your bed," he remarks.

"Yes. I will meet you," says the cleric. After a breath, he finishes his movement and leaves the safety of the spell.

Immediately, the vampire stands before Celest and envelops him. An instant embrace is followed by a dazzling kiss that stuns the cleric in place and sets the fire in his chest that he's waited for. Julian looks down at him, searching through his dewy, yellow eyes for intent.

The elf stares, nervous but in awe. On instinct, he hugs him back, burying his face into the black robes that cover the vampire's chest. Julian's forest-sweet scent hangs on the fibers of his clothing. The cleric takes in its essence through his nose and sighs as relief washes over him. "I couldn't stop thinking about you," confesses the elf in the safety of the fabric's folds. "Each time I closed my eyes, I saw you."

"I'm here." Julian combs his chilling fingers over the back of Celest's neck and down between his shoulder blades. "But where were you?" he questions. "You left me alone last night to wonder."

The vampire's words travel with a wave of energy that tightens the cleric's open palm into a fist. This tension, however, doesn't come from himself. Celest turns his chin up and catches a sour twinge in the vampire's expression.

"You're upset with me, oh, of course, you're upset," stammers the elf. "Of course. I'm sorry. I had no intention of worrying you. I swear it." He backs away sheepishly and bows his head. "I apologize."

Julian's face flattens. "I'm impressed you managed to hide from me in my own city," he replies. "And this?" He gestures at the barrier. "What am I to think? My sweet Celest is so afraid that he uses magic to cast me away?" He turns his head in betrayal, but the bold shapes of its silhouette reveal a new facet to his spellbinding beauty.

"Please don't believe that," says Celest. "The barrier exists for Adinine and her sibling's peace of mind, not mine. What I feel toward you isn't fear."

"Then, tell me, what is it that you feel?"

The elf juggles with the answer, struggling to keep balance on solid ground. "I care," begins the cleric, "about your pain. I wish to heal it. And your pleasure... I wish to attend it." Celest bites his lip, trying to override the shame that attaches itself to his brazen speech. "I've put my trust in you," he says. "Is that not enough for the favor to be returned?"

The space between the two dissolves again as the vampire advances to cradle the cleric's cheek. His crimson gaze is saturated with curious interest. "You've put your trust in my hands?" he asks.

"Yes," declares Celest without a drop of trepidation to his tone. "I have."

"I see." Julian takes another step forward and turns to the right, causing the elf to stumble backward onto the gray brick walls of the alley. The vampire pins him there with his stone body. His left hand, secured to the brick, keeps the elf face-forward as the other travels around the white robes at the cleric's hip. "And you wish to attend to my pleasure?" he adds in a siren's voice. Celest's mouth moistens as if anticipating a meal, and he grows ever more aware of Julian's thigh filling the space between his legs.

"I believe so," insists the elf. "You can tell that I do. Why do you ask if you already know?" Celest relaxes his head on the vampire's wrist and nuzzles against the absurdly smooth skin. His heart pounds in his chest, fueled by the magnetic charge of attraction.

Julian smiles warmer than ever before. "You've done it again," he says, pushing in ever closer. His eyes close for a moment as he tenderly kisses Celest on his lips. "I'm not used to being the enchanted one," he admits. "Yet, it seems I'm under your spell." He kisses him again.

This time the elf responds with an open mouth, eager to taste the honey steeped on the vampire's tongue, but Julian doesn't take the bait.

"Will you repay me for my lonely night?" he asks.

"How can I?" Celest searches his mind for something to give. "I could sing for you?" he offers. "I only know the hymns of the citadels, but the maesters often said my voice was pleasant." An ache of self-conscious embarrassment follows his words, and he adds, "Well, you probably wouldn't be interested in that. Never mind."

"I would love to hear you sing, sweet Celest," whispers Julian adoringly. "I would also very much like to take you somewhere that isn't a rain-soaked alleyway."

The elf looks about, noticing his surroundings for the first time since seeing the object of his desire through the window. At best, the view is unappealing. Fuzzy, reddish mold flourishes between the cracked alley stones. The smell of its spores and the piss of the drunk is close to nauseating once perceived. His face puckers in disgust.

"A place like this would be unworthy of your performance. I can assure you that. I'm also inclined to remind you that my senses are heightened. To breathe this air is absolutely vile, but it is required for speech."

Celest winces empathetically at the thought but struggles to imagine its intensity.

"You're right. It's much less than comfortable," says the cleric. "But I can't take the barrier down. You can't come inside." His tone is almost weepy.

"I do trust you, Celest," he replies.

"Uh—thank you," sputters the elf.

"And I have somewhere different in mind," asserts Julian. He reaches into the inner pocket of his robe and takes out a small mirror, the back of which is ornately decorated in blue gemstones. "Would you like to see the best view in all of Markovia?" The sky seems to part at his whim, and he angles the mirror to catch a sliver of moonlight that escapes through the clouds.

The gems appear to ripple as an image projects from the mirror's surface. An oval shape, outlined in glittering lapis lazuli, reveals a clean, black marble patio overlooking the city. Sparse lights from the streets below mimic stars reflected in the sea. Fog acts as the rolling waters, and the image is accompanied by a fresh wind that chases away the back-alley smell. "My home is quite clean and undisturbed," says the vampire. "If I leave this mirror nearby, we have a portal right back to this very spot. We could enjoy our time together in luxury, and you can be back before the morning comes. How does that sound, my little songbird?"

Celest's cheeks blush at the pet name, but partially out of embarrassment. "I'm... hesitant," he replies earnestly.

"I understand," says the vampire. "Yet, trust sires trust, doesn't it?" He effortlessly reaches the eaves of the closest building and places the mirror on a strip of moss growing there. "I've done nothing to harm you. In fact, since we've met, I've done everything to pleasure you. You trust me enough to climb down from a second-story window and meet me, unarmed, in a dark alley. Isn't that right? You freely express your interest in me, and yet you are hesitant to accept an invitation to my home? Forgive me. Maybe I don't understand."

The elf's eyebrows pull together in worry. "You're right," he murmurs, trying to cast away the feelings of apprehension. "I'm contradicting myself. I want to say yes, but in truth, I feel so guilty."

"Why is that, sweet Celest?"

"My friends," he begins. "If they knew I was meeting you in secret, they would be furious with me, but how could I tell them? You've shown yourself to me as a person of sound mind and...open heart. But, what you've done to Adinine—"

"I wish it weren't so," Julian interrupts. "I believed it to be the only escape from my damnation. As I watched her grow, I had planned to win her love, not simply take it."

"You would win her love?" asks the elf. A twinge of jealousy marks his words. "You bit her. She's terrified of you."

The vampire slides him a chilling glance and replies, "The plan wasn't met. Not all living creatures are as accepting as you and try as I might, there is no hiding what I am. She feared me on sight. I've told you this. My only other option was to create a blood bond and force away the fear in our moments together. She would have been fine if we hadn't been interrupted the last time we met."

Celest straightens up and fills his chest with air from the open portal. "And now?" the cleric demands. "What are your options now?"

A microexpression flashes across the vampire's face but gives way to a relaxed demeanor. The elf is indefensible against Julian's gentle eyes. "Now I hope for something more," says the vampire. "You have shown me that there are holes in my understanding. I believed that relief was impossible, but you relieved me. I believed that my pain was infinite, but you lessened it."

Celest, moved by the sentiment, clutches a hand to the robes over his chest.

"So, sweet Celest, I wish to return the favor of your trust. Let me treat you like royalty as a guest in my home." Julian bows in front of the portal, inviting the elf to step through its gem-blue threshold.

The elf takes a deep breath in and closes his eyes. One self-defiant step after another leads him through. The wooden soles of the cleric's boots tap against the marble. His eyes open as he exhales, realizing that the partial vantage of the portal couldn't compare to the sweeping view before him. "Ahh," says Celest, pleasantly surprised. "This is incredible." He scurries to the balustrade to lean against it like a traveler at the bow of a ship.

Julian is close behind him, and the portal shrinks and disappears once he passes through it. In awkward haste, and before Celest can reach the edge of the balcony, his balance betrays him, but Julian catches the elf as soon as he slips on the slick surface. With the same movement, he glides forward and pins him securely to the railing from behind.

"Careful," commands the vampire. He leans forward, guiding Celest to bow at the waist over the balustrade. "It's quite dangerous to lose your footing." From here, the elf can see that they are on the third floor of the castle. Further down, a sheer cliff face plunges to a spiked moat far below. Color drains from the cleric's face, and his knees lock in place as he confronts the height. "No need for fear, Celest," says Julian in his ear. "I'd never allow you to fall."

"Ah—yes, you're very fast," replies the elf shakily. "Thank you." He relaxes his knees, but the caution is not so easily dismissed. It reminds him of the sight just before washing up on the gray stones of the riverbank. Instead of being forced to the edge by a club-wielding giant, he is here of his own accord, seeking the company of a charming vampire. The thought churns his stomach into butter.

"Isn't it captivating?" Julian asks in a tone that's more statement than question.

"Yes, captivating." The cleric thinks about the word. The view is captivating in the way of a whirlpool, ever pulling into itself and swallowing anything that gets too close.

Julian, noticing Celest in deep thought, pushes his body to fit the curves of the elf's backside.

The attention is distracting, and the motion quickly becomes the only thing on the cleric's mind. His breathing slows as he pushes back against it, leaving no room for misinterpretation.

Julian continues, releasing one hand from the railing to grab the elf by the chin. The friction of the fabric warms the space below his tailbone, and he leans into the sensation as it wraps around his thighs. His hot breath mixes with the mist in the air and collects in droplets on the elf's rosy cheeks as he softly pants in desire.

Celest speaks on instinct, "Will you take me here?"

The vampire hums in delight, sliding a thumb onto Celest's tongue. "Is that what you wish of me?" asks Julian in a sultry whisper.

The cleric looks down again, but fear is the subordinate emotion when contrasted against the lustful ache in his loins. Swiftly, the elf is spun around and lifted to sit on the top rail of the balustrade. The vampire's expression is ravenous as one hand grabs him by the robes over his chest.

Celest gasps, rushing to hold on to the arm that stabilizes him.

"Right here on my balcony?" he growls. "Seems a bit risky. One slip of my finger could lead to a rather gruesome end."

"Not here!" squeaks Celest. "I'm sure the inside of your home is just as lovely, yes? Inside?"

Julian stares blankly for a moment, savoring the emotion in the elf's eyes, then pulls him off the railing and onto his feet with a mischievous grin. "I'm kidding, of course. I leave no room for error," he says confidently, "and I had no intention to ravish you outside like a dog, but I must admit it's inciting to watch you beg."

Celest turns green with embarrassment. "Oh—goddess. Oh my goddess," he repeats, pushing on his temples with the ridge of his palm. "I'm acting like a nymph. There's something wrong with me."

"There's nothing wrong, little bird," says Julian, adopting a posed position at his side. "I'm glad to know how badly you want me." He takes his arm and waist like a ballroom dancer and leads him away from the edge.

Behind them is a fountain adorned with sculpted stone in the shape of joyous young maidens dancing in the water. Celest, finally noticing the portal's disappearance, looks at his host anxiously. "How will I get back?" he asks, feet stopping in place.

"No need to be so wary," replies Julian, guiding him around to the opposite end of the fountain. "Do you see the mirror there?" One of the marble figures crouches down to touch her fingers to the water. The other hand holds a looking glass at her ankle, and sure enough, the Harvest Tavern Inn's round, orange windows shine through its surface. "It's all set for when you're ready to leave," he assures.

"Oh," says the cleric. "That's good." The tension that holds his muscles stiff begins to ease. His stride finds its pace, following Julian's rhythmic lead to a pair of iron doors set into the castle wall.

Chapter Sixteen

The vampire's cloak slides away from his body of its own volition and opens the castle's patio doors as if it were a seasoned steward. Celest responds by nodding politely at the artifact, unsure of its level of sentience. Then, stepping through the threshold, they enter a large, stately room. In its center, a long table is set with white flowers in clear vases placed on a dark purple table runner. Ornately carved cedar chairs are tucked precisely in place, and on floors polished to a shine, quatrefoil rugs mark the flow of foot traffic yet somehow look as though they have never been touched by a shoe. "Is this your dining hall?" he asks.

"Yes, one of them," replies Julian wiping away the condensation on the elf's cheek. "You're a bit damp from the fog."

"Oh," he responds, drying the rest with his sleeve. "I hadn't even noticed."

"Why don't I draw you a warm bath," suggests the vampire. "I can tell you're not entirely comfortable. You can take some time to settle your nerves before enjoying our night, don't you think? I insist."

Celest already feels indulged. "I suppose a bath would be nice," he murmurs bashfully. He does feel like the dirtiest thing in the room, after all.

"Good," replies his host. "Follow me then." Julian takes him to the end of the room past another set of doors. He guides the cleric through hallways decorated with elegant purple tapestries and portraits of royal lords and ladies painted over backdrops of garden flowers. Many faces share Julian's features. A handsome older woman with berry-red hair, framed by a bed of lavender, has the same sharp cut of his jawbone, and most that look like him exhibit the pattern of raven tresses and moonlight complexion, which comes as a surprise to the elf who had assumed Julian's skin color was a result of the vampirism.

"Were you close?" asks Celest. "To the ones in these paintings, that is?" The piece closest to them depicts a girl of about fifteen years in front of lovingly painted blue cosmos. She is also pale and shares his cupid's bow, but her thick locks spiral into tight ringlets that fall past her shoulders.

"To some, yes," answers Julian. "This was my cousin, Illyce. She spent a few summers here at the castle. As I recall, she would follow my brother around the grounds like a chick, always chirping at him about one thing or another. This particular painting was scrapped a few times. She couldn't sit still." He chuckles to himself, but that fades into a silent stare. "I keep them up to remind myself of the way things were... A few years after this was made, she was married to an established southern lord. I often wonder if our lineage continues. She is certainly dead, but what of her descendants? I may never know."

The cleric pays his respects. "Illyce. I hope her journey was one of fulfillment," he says. "You mentioned your brother. He was a mage? And what of your mother?"

"Ah, yes. That's true. He was also a painter. These are his works," replies Julian. "In the few years before this castle was finished, he was studying as an acolyte abroad. He saw me succeeding in my own arcane arts. I presume that's what sparked his interest in the first place. He was always caring and gentle. Priestly magic was well suited to him. As for my mother, she died shortly after arriving here due to illness and age. She had no such talent for magic. Neither she nor my father sought anything of that sort while they lived."

"My condolences. What happened to him? Your father, I mean," Celest asks as they continue down the hall.

"I've been alive for four hundred and forty-eight years," says the vampire with a bitter inflection. "They've all turned to dust. He's one of the few I don't miss."

Celest considers reaching for more insight but feels worried to pry. Weighted with the consequence of unasked questions, he frowns, and his ears turn downward.

"There's no need for that expression," Julian asserts. "I've learned not to dwell on the thought. Come now. There's a bathtub here to the left." He opens the door to a quiet, dark room. It has a large bed, two dressers, and lounge furniture surrounding a small hearth. A thick sheet of tinted glass separates a space beyond the lounge. With a flick of his wrist, the wick of each lamp in the room catches flame. "Behind this glass is a bathing area. I've already heated the water for you."

"Did you expect me to come here tonight?" questions the elf with sincere confusion.

"Perhaps I'm a gracious host prepared for any occasion," purrs the vampire. "Or perhaps it's an evocation spell… I'll leave you alone to wash. Although it's tempting to stay, I'd like to set up a meal for you in the dining hall. I do, however, have one small request." The left corner of his lip is angled into an expectant smile.

"What can I do?" asks Celest, looking up at the vampire through his eyelashes.

"There's an outfit in the bottom right drawer of the vanity," Julian answers. "It would please me if you wore it tonight." His baritone voice crawls over the elf's scalp, resulting in a pleasant shiver. "Tell me you will."

The elf nods obediently. "Yes, I'll put it on after my bath."

"Very good, Celest," praises Julian.

It's enough to make the cleric's inner fire pull to the boundaries of his chest once again, but the elf yearns for much more than his name to be articulated on Julian's tongue.

"Do you remember your way to the dining hall?" he asks.

"Oh, yes, there was only one turn," he replies. "I could follow the paintings in any case."

"Yes, meet me there after you've changed. In the meantime, make yourself comfortable and enjoy the water's warmth. I'll see you again soon, my sweet." The vampire glides backward out of the room, gently touching his palm to the doorframe. His eyes hold to Celest's as he carefully kisses the dark wood above his hand before sliding out of sight. The door clicks shut.

Alone now, the elf investigates the back portion of the room. He half expects to find something haunting behind the glass divide but is relieved to see a normal bathing room with all the essentials organized in a stately manner. A porcelain clawfoot tub is set against the blueberry-colored wooden wall paneling, and a lighter paint extends from it to the ceiling. An ornate, orange vanity is highlighted against the blue. Its mirror is fixed in place with the same style of glass smithing that decorates the shrine in the woods. Celest wonders if they were made by the same craftsman while taking off his boots. The floor rug in the middle of the room is soft to the touch and compresses to the curves of the cleric's feet as he approaches the bath. Its still and steaming water is as clear as a polished window. He dips into the surface, testing the temperature with his pointer and middle finger. It's quite hot, but the elf is no stranger to heat. The burning is pleasant compared to the searing waters he had grown accustomed to at the Everlight Citadel.

Celest leans on the side of the tub, grabbing the lip as steam rolls over his face. It gathers in the pockets of his sleeves and rises up his arms, easing the thundering thoughts in his mind. After a moment, he moves to the vanity, untying his wide cloth belt as he walks. He folds and sets it on the shelf in front of the mirror, but the familiar reflection within its borders seems off, foreign to the eyes. They are just as sun-yellow, but the glimmer of a solar flare caught in his iris hint at the discord beneath. He lets his hair down and unfastens his outer robes, sliding them away from his shoulders.

As he goes to fold them, he feels something small and hard in the pocket roll over his knuckles. The cleric inhales sharply as he remembers the holy stone that Sable had entrusted him with. He hastily folds the garment, making sure the sunstone lies hidden in the innermost layer. In his excitement and the gleeful fog from the day before, he had nearly forgotten its existence. He turns away from his reflection to reject the self-judgment scrambling his brain before unbuttoning the final under-garment. After setting it neatly beside his robes, Celest uses a squat stool to step into the tub.

The heat instantly sedates him as it swathes every bit of skin below the rippling surface. His eyes close habitually before holding his breath and submerging entirely. Snow-lace threads of hair float at the top of the water, slowly soaking until they are heavy enough to sink. Given generous room within the tub's walls, Celest sways gently, causing satis-fying prickles of pain to wave across his body until he rises for air. After finding equilibrium and an empty-enough mind, he fetches the soap off a nearby shelf. Hoping to sample a scent, he sniffs the bar in his hand, but surprisingly there is no distinct odor. In a home like this, the elf had expected an expensive fragrance, but he quickly dismisses it and finishes cleaning himself.

The towel, which is hung on a bronze rack, is luxuriously absorbent. As he wraps it around himself and steps out of the tub, it warms momen-tarily, drying off the excess moisture from his skin. This startles the elf, who yips in surprise at the spellbound object before realizing the nature of its enchantment. It seems Julian truly has thought of everything, despite him saying so in jest, and that makes Celest all the more eager to see what kind of outfit he has planned. He returns the towel before walking to the vanity and finds a pretty black box upon opening its deep lower drawer. Resting on top of which is a postcard. It reads in perfect script, "May each thread be a reminder of how I wish to cover you."

He smiles, setting it on the stack of his clothing, then takes the box from the drawer and opens it. Inside, a thin, gold bracelet lays on a glossy, crimson garment that feels like it is made of the same material as Julian's waist sash. He places the jewelry on the table and holds up the silk, letting gravity unfold it. It's dress shaped, tight in the bodice with a high neckline and open back. It also sports a salacious slit on one side of the long, flowing skirt. His cheeks flush even before trying to wear it. This piece is something far from his zone of comfort, but he can't help himself from bashfully admiring the sleek design. He steps into it, slipping the luxurious fabric past his hips and over his shoulders. It's a close fit in the torso, but the open back makes putting it on easy enough.

His own reflection, for the first time, is fascinating. He slides his left leg out from the center, allowing sun-kissed skin to part through the skirt's slit while running his fingers over the fabric on his chest. "Radiant," he whispers to himself, truly glowing with an unaccustomed self-confidence. Checking the box for a second time, he notices a pair of golden sandals and an ornate hairbrush at the bottom of the box. Despite his skepticism, they fit his feet like they were made for them. Even so, the slight heel makes him nervous.

As he brushes his long hair straight, his anxieties pique again. He continues, imagining each tangled strand as an insecurity to release, and after a few minutes, his hair and emotions have smoothed. He ties it up neatly into his signature bun, then picks up the thin gold bracelet and slips his right hand through it too easily. It's too wide to wear properly, but he unfastens the clasp, loops the chain around his wrist once more, and fastens it again.

"There," says Celest, taking in the fully assembled outfit before placing his cleric's garb into the box. He isn't sure what to expect from tonight but, with newfound confidence, is as prepared for the occasion as he'll ever be. Finally, before exiting the room, he casts his purify spell on the water in the tub, and the sudsy liquid becomes clear again. He's ready.

Celest walks down the hallway, passing the portrait paintings, and stops a few paces from the double doors to the dining hall set in the wall to the right. They are open, allowing warm, orange candlelight to pour into the darker hallway. Wondering if Julian could already hear his approach, his pace slows before stopping entirely. He compulsively looks down at his outfit one last time before finding the courage to make his appearance in the doorway.

"Celest. Welcome," greets Julian. The excitement in his eyes turns them into twinkling garnets. He stands behind a seat at the head of the dining table, beckoning with a wave, but the two are not alone. Three new faces, possessing a similarly unnerving beauty, are seated in chairs next to his host.

To the left, and closest to Julian, is a small woman with short, black hair that is cut into points reaching just past her chin. Her face has a childlike roundness that is accentuated by her heart-shaped lips and owl-like, monolid eyes. Another man, as dark as Julian is pale, has his arm around her, resting on the crest rail of the seat. His steely, black hand is gripped slightly to her shoulder, appearing to be a casual touch.

The sculptured expression he wears is inscrutable, and looking away from its mysteries would be nearly impossible if it weren't for the most glamorous woman Celest had ever seen sitting across from him. Her sunflower blonde hair curves into voluminous bulbs that reach just past her chest. Their shape mimics the rest of her form, from lip to bosom. Even the tilt of her eyelashes resembles the beginnings of a divine spiral. The four, all poised around the table like the muses of some divine sculpture, seem like a fantasy that the cleric has stumbled into by mistake.

Chapter Seventeen

"**W**hy don't you all introduce yourselves to our honored guest?" suggests the vampire.

Wordlessly standing at the doorway, Celest tries to react while actively navigating the sensation of free fall that quickly turns into a weightless panic. Just as Celest's eyes begin searching for the escape of the fountain portal, past the balcony doors, he finds Julian at his side. "Must I ask again for you to set aside your fear and trust me?" he whispers to the elf.

"You... you ask too much of me," chirps Celest. "Why am I being met with strangers? What could you possibly want to happen tonight, dressing me as I am? Tempting me as you have? I thought we—"

"Let me explain, little bird," interrupts the vampire. "Firstly, you look phenomenal. I'd dare you to try to convince even yourself otherwise. Secondly, these aren't simply strangers. Just as you have your party, I have mine. Unlike you, however, I'm not ashamed to present my fondness for you to them. Do you think I would bring you here just to put you in danger? No. You are important to me, and thus I'd like them to meet you." Julian brushes the elf's cheek and adds, "They are sure to enjoy your company as much as I, but first..." The vampire releases the tie in the elf's hair and burns it up in the nearest lantern.

He opens his mouth to complain, but Julian kisses it before he can utter a sound. Celest swallows his concerns momentarily, in shock by the public display.

"I prefer it down. Now," says Julian leading him to the seat between the head of the table and the blonde. "Please welcome our guest."

A set of plates in front of the empty seat is filled to the rim with meats, cheese, pastries, sweets, and fresh garden offerings. Its full scent pulls on the pit of his stomach despite his fear's best effort to hold each deep muscle in place.

The three extend a greeting in harmony, each set of their vigilants sanguine eyes fixed on his own. The elf looks down at the table and notices that only his plates are set. "This is all just for me?" he asks. "You all... you all don't eat."

"We may drink with you if you wish," says the dark man, his voice a low, almost vibrating bass.

Celest's heart rate begins to flicker. "Drink? D-drink of *blut*?" he chokes. "I mean, drink of what?"

"Wine, of course," chuckles Julian, wearing an arrogant smile. "Iliya, be a dear and fetch us some from the cellar. Make certain it's from a favorable year."

"Certainly, my lord," responds the blonde before fluttering out of the room. Her aqueous movement is practically dancing.

The elf shyly sits in his chair. "I wasn't aware that was something that... your kind could do. Pardon my ignorance," he mutters.

"Yes," insists Julian. "Fortunately enough, such pleasures are still attainable in this state. It's a consolation prize at best." He pushes in Celest's seat and goes to take his own. "This is Seong, and that's Zoan," he continues, gesturing to them in the order of closest to furthest. "I've told them a bit about you already. The other's name is Iliya. She's been by my side for quite some time. Zoan was next to join me, and Seong—well—she has been part of this house for almost twenty years now."

Celest fiddles with the napkin, placing it gingerly on his lap. "It's a pleasure to make your acquaintances," he replies. "I apologize for my entrance. I wasn't expecting to meet you all."

"That's all right," assures Zoan. "Our lord has a fondness for surprises."

Julian rests his elbow on the table while he strokes his chin with the ghostly fingers that Celest has learned to yearn for. "Is that so?" he contemplates half-heartedly.

"Boredom can get the upper hand on even the best of us, my lord," Zoan responds. The statement is met with a decisive glance that strips it of all validity.

Only moving her lips, Seong comments, "Our lord said you are an adventurer, but you don't look strong enough to fight. Your wrists might be thinner than mine."

Celest stammers at the insult before Julian interrupts, "That's no way to speak to a guest, now is it? Apologize."

"N-no, it's fine," assures the elf. "I'm not much use in a fistfight. My role is as support and healer. When my friends are injured or, uh, afflicted in spirit, I can help. I also have... um... utility type spells."

"I'm sure Celest is a very capable ally. Apologize. Now," Julian commands.

"Sorry," she says while looking at the doors to the hallway. The elf follows her eyes and sees the one named Iliya appear in their frame. She holds two large bottles in either hand.

"Did I miss any of the fun?" she asks, popping both corks open effortlessly with her thumbs. The cleric quietly sighs in relief, now knowing that fun could consist of him still unharmed and breathing. She pours Julian the first glass and then reaches over Celest to fill his. The dress she wears is low cut in the front and falls away slightly from her chest as she bends forward, casting a mild perfume of star anise in the cleric's direction.

She is close enough to touch when she asks, "What's it like being raised by elves, hm? My father was an elf." She flips her yellow hair back, revealing a pointed helix, not nearly as elongated as Celest's but just as sharp. "He left before I was born," she continues, "so my mother raised me alone. She was the village tracker, so we had food at the table and a warm place to call home, but I've read stories about the elvyn kingdoms. I used to dream that I'd get whisked away to one and live my life in luxury. My lord has given me the life I've always wanted, of course." She kisses him on the cheek before moving to the other side of the table to pour the others their drink. A painful twitch of jealousy in the cleric's chest tries to distract him from the question.

"It's fine, no better or worse than any other, I'd imagine. I was raised by The Order of the Sun, and we don't have family structures like most other cultures do. We are all children of our mother, The Goddess Amatetra. Not literally, of course, but in spirit," he answers, pauses, then continues. "In all honesty, I have my fair share of grievances with my upbringing. Tradition is strict in the highlands, despite its propensity for decadence."

Julian chuckles and sips his wine after remarking, "Was that a negative opinion, sweet Celest? I wasn't sure if that was possible coming from you. Though, I'm not complaining. Gossip all you'd like."

"Could we be cousins, perhaps?" asks Iliya as she fills her own glass and sits to his left. "According to my mother, my father was from a place called Springwood."

"No, not likely," he replies. "If I recall, Springwood is the territory of forest elves. It's located in the Fae Wilds, north of Port Moran. They usually live in tandem with nature, worshiping the goddess Nemvysi. I doubt the reality would be much like the places you've imagined, and I heard that they've been at war with the pixies for a few decades now. My maesters would often caution us of pixies. According to them, they're vengeful by nature, but I can't say for certain as I've never actually met one."

"That's interesting. I never pictured my father living in a forest," she concedes. "Maybe the life that I spent with my mother wasn't as different from his as I had thought."

"Celest," calls Julian, arresting the elf's attention. "Please, eat. Drink. Enjoy this feast that our Zoan has so keenly prepared for you."

The cleric obediently begins cutting into a pastry that spills open with glossy orange filling. He quickly forks a piece into his mouth, and his posture immediately softens from the taste. A hushed sigh passes from his throat.

Zoan smiles, showing off a row of milky, white teeth. "That one's spiced peach. It was my sister's favorite," he remarks. "It's not often that anyone gets to eat the food I cook. Try the tart to the left. I was always partial to that one. Tell me what you think." His fangs are visible as he speaks, but his expression exudes warmth.

Complying, he samples the delicacies one by one and is introduced to flavor palates he's never known. The elf compliments each with unique care, leaving the vampire, Zoan, beaming and even more beautiful in joy.

"I'm pleased to know you appreciate my work. It's a passion of mine that is all but wasted in my current state."

"How did you learn to cook so brilliantly?" admires Celest as he is further disarmed with each bite.

"In a past life, it was my occupation," he replies. "My family ran an inn, and I was working as its chef. Baking has always been my true obsession, though. I would stay up all night crafting a new recipe or testing techniques by candlelight. Thanks to my lord, I've had time to sharpen my skill beyond comparison. And, although I can no longer taste my creations, the scents and ritual of it all bring me comfort."

The elf dabs his mouth with the napkin. "It's an honor to partake of. Thank you. You truly have a gift."

Seong, on her second glass of wine, comments, "You've yet to touch your pheasant or boar. I was tasked to slaughter them myself. Perhaps it does not *meat* your standards?" This elicits an aethereal giggle from Iliya, who covers her mouth to do so.

"Oh, pardon my rudeness," he replies. "I don't partake of, um, animal flesh. It's forbidden for my people and goes against my moral teaching. But truly, it looks delicious. I'm sorry. If I had known you would go through all this trouble just for me, I would have told you beforehand, but again, I was kind of... blindsided."

"That's quite alright, little bird," comforts Julian as he leans forward to wipe a speck of food from the cleric's cheek. "You're welcome to eat as much or as little as you'd like." A blush settles over the flat bridge of Celest's nose as he thanks his hosts, and the meal carries on. With one appetite satisfied, and conversation slowing, Julian asks for the song he was offered earlier in the night.

"No, I couldn't possibly embarrass myself in front of new friends," Celest pleads. "To be perfectly honest, I don't even feel all that comfortable wearing this outfit, let alone performing in it. You've all been so welcoming, but I wouldn't want to ruin your impression of me."

"Please," counters Julian. "You look resplendent." He licks a stain of wine from his lip. "Dangerously so, might I add. Except," he says, rising to his feet and hovering over Celest. "I just realized you're wearing that necklace on your wrist. I must have been too distracted by the rest of you to notice. May I?" He unclasps the chain without waiting for a reply, pets Celest's white threads of hair to one side, and fastens the adornment. It's just loose enough as to not be uncomfortable but is a tight fit regardless.

"Absolutely," Iliya agrees. "I've never before seen a mortal so comely as you are. I wonder if it's not a feature of your elvyn lineage? I, too, was once quite the prize in my birth village among humans. What do you think?" She leans in from her seat and slowly traces her fingertips down the cleric's forearm, exciting the skin and raising its tiny hairs.

He stutters in response, "Y-you are a beauty to behold, Miss Iliya. Uh, elvyn people, like all others, possess a range of features and unique temperaments that determine... attractiveness, I suppose."

"Hm. Do you not realize your own beauty, Celest?" adds Zoan. His wide jaw rests quizzically in the palm of his hand. "It seems resoundingly clear to us. Right, Seong?"

"I'd like a close-up view to be sure," she suggests plainly. "It's hard to decide from across the table."

"Silence," commands Julian in an even tone. "I wish to hear him sing."

"But—"

"What could be making you uncomfortable, my sweet?"

The cleric folds his hands together in his lap and sits up mannerly as if not to be reprimanded. He quickly thinks up a new excuse. "I suppose..." he whispers. "This all feels much too formal for me to ruin it with a floundering performance. I'm experiencing a sort of... stage fright."

"Let us erase formality then," murmurs the vampire in his ear. Suddenly the chair is forcefully slid away from the table and pushed onto its back. Julian catches the ridge of Celest's skull in a cradled hand as it clatters to the ground, and the elf yips in startled fright. Over him, he whispers, "I've come to know that shyness can often be fixed by a well-meaning slap." Both hands now hold the cleric's head, and he continues in a growl, "You are not simply a guest at my home, and I am much more than a noble hosting you. Let's no longer pretend that you're more than a little mouse cornered by a glaring of cats, eager to play." The scent of his breath is hypnotizing, reconstructing fear into excitement in the elf's chest against his will. "Eager," he mouths onto the skin on his neck, "to have our fill."

"Of what?" he gasps.

"You, of course." Julian's grip tightens, pulling his hair. Without making a sound, the others have all moved to the cleric's side of the table. Their eyes dart in perfect sync with every twitch of the elf's movement, like reptiles tracking a catch. Julian releases him and takes a step toward his kin, commanding, "Take him to the room. I'll need a change of clothes." His hand, bigger than Seong's entire face, grabs her by the cheeks oppressively. "And, you. Don't touch him. Do you understand?"

"Yes, my lord," she replies as Zoan and Iliya gently advance to the elf's side. Zoan's muscled arm wraps securely around his shoulders, and Iliya takes him by the hand, giving it a gentle tug.

"Come now, Celest," she hums while pulling him along. "Don't be frightened. I do hope to hear you sing. A little change of scenery might well do the trick."

"That's right," Zoan's voice, so close to him, resonates in deep vibrations. "All will be well if you let it be. It's best not to question our lord, after all. He just wants us to take you to a bedroom where you might be more comfortable."

Celest considers protesting, but this familiar touch from the two is more intimacy at once than he has ever received. He's taken by it. Being attended to in this way overwhelms his ability to react. And so, almost involuntarily, the elf follows their lead.

Chapter Eighteen

The two vampires lead Celest past the dining room doors and into the hall. Seong follows a few paces behind. They take the path that Julian had shown him earlier, turning the same corner and arriving a few doors past the chamber that he had previously explored, which contains his holy garments.

Iliya uses her free hand to open the door before them. Extremely dim light from a hidden source in the ceiling douses a room that is colorless from corner to corner. It feels like standing in a void.

Celest blinks to adjust his vision, then notices a colossally wide bed set seamlessly with black linens. As they enter the room, three sets of their steps begin to clack on the marble flooring, black as the castle itself.

Seong's slender hands close the door behind them, and in the illusion of space, the guides release their hold.

Celest is left to twirl about, searching for answers, but only finds a marble bench at the foot of the bed. It's covered with shining black furs that span its length, wide as the sprawling mattress. There's also a gilded, wing-backed chair along the south wall. Celest orients himself with a blade of hallway light shining under the doorway and considers taking the single seat. But standing is more convenient if he happens to be forced to run.

Without seeing her jump, Seong lands on the middle of the bed and rolls onto her stomach. The elf looks above her and notices a large mirror on the ceiling that centers over the bed, surrounded by smaller diamond-shaped ones. Each is ever so slightly backlit by a hidden source of light. He notices too, reflected in the mirror, an intricate lace fabric that she wears as stockings up to her knees. Her dress is shorter than the others in the room, suiting her height. It hikes up her thigh as she kicks her feet through the air. "What happens here?" Celest asks, backing up until he hits the west wall.

"What will happen here?" coos Iliya like a dove. "Or what has happened here? Or maybe what is happening here? You'll have to ask a more specific question for us to give you an answer, darling."

Zoan sits back on the furs, spreading his knees for comfort, and Iliya takes a poised seat at his side.

"Uh, what will happen here?" he questions again.

Zoan responds, "What do you wish to happen is a more interesting question." In this light, the shape of his tightly coiled hair appears as horns crowning his head. "What did you come here for?"

"I... I was invited." His heart rate rises in response to the evasiveness of his answer.

"Sure," growls Seong softly. "Do you think we believe you to be so naive? We've heard plenty about you, cleric. I think you know exactly why you came."

"No, I-I thought," he begins.

She interrupts, "You chased your desire to this room, didn't you? Why deny something so painfully clear?"

"Seong, you're frightening him," soothes Iliya. "Why don't you come take a seat with us? Touch is how you heal, isn't it? Touch me, and you might be relieved."

Conscious denial has been creeping up in his mind, only to be distracted away. His suspension of disbelief, however, is wearing too thin. Iliya shifts her weight to cross her legs together as properly as a royal while shaking back the perfect, blond bulbs of her hair behind her shoulders. "Sing for us while we wait. Our lord won't take much longer, as your company is too precious to waste, but even still, we wish to hear it."

He sighs, stumbling to the bench on the other side of Zoan, a safe distance away. "How am I to sing when I'm so... confused? The last thing I want to do is make a fool of myself in front of you all."

"Maybe if you choose a slow song, it would help to quiet your mood," she suggests, snuggling herself against Zoan's broad arm. "How about a sweet lullaby, hmm? A song that might put a babe to sleep in the cradle."

The elf swallows a lump in his throat. "Will it... please you all to hear me? Truly?" Celest mutters.

"Yes, it would," booms Zoan. "Indulge us, Celest, as we have indulged you. I'll take it as reciprocity for the meal." His voice is so deep that it's hard to get used to and equally persuasive.

Celest sighs again in defeat while stimulating his fingers through the furs. Pressured under their watchful gazes and weighted by their words, the elf concedes. He swallows his nerves, clears his throat, and hums a few notes in practice before gathering the courage required to perform. Then, finally, he begins to sing.

"Hapless yawning

Mother, come back in the morning

'Till the summer

Everlasting

Wakens me

Wait for dawning

White light, and golds, and blue

Meanwhile, I'll bide my time

Because the night is cruel

Sleepless longing

Dreams that are ever deforming

Bind the sanctum

Unless you break them

Set me free

Guide my way through

Help me find you

Across the swirling, idling, airy sea

So that I might be of some use to thee."

The cleric stops, overcome with embarrassment. "The bards used to sing that to us during our moon circles," he adds awkwardly, tensing his hands into his lap.

"Your voice is sweet, like your manner," compliments Zoan.

"Mmm, yes. It's gentle," purrs Iliya. "I did, though, expect to hear your elvyn tongue."

He looks up from his lap to see the contradiction between inviting smiles and sharp teeth. The danger of their scarlet-red irises, too, is offset by each individual's magnetic gaze. Julian's pair are stunning enough, but the three unblinking sets that aim at him now are just as immobilizing. Despite an anxiety that is almost crippling, the vampires draw him further like a moth to the flame.

"The bards at our citadel were exclusively human. Most didn't speak the language... I believe the maesters didn't want us to get too wrapped up in the hobby while learning under them. After all, we were not to be bards. Only children under the age of sixty were allowed to participate in the choir," explains the elf.

"Children?" Seong scoffs. "Sixty years is well over a full life." Her feet fall to a pillow as she perks up onto her elbows in realization. "Are you my elder, cleric? Am I the youngest?" she asks in disbelief.

"M-maybe?" he stutters. "I'm one hundred and thirty-seven... Age seems like an important topic among other races. I'm constantly asked these kinds of questions by them."

"We are no longer afflicted by most human curiosities," says Zoan, creating a barrier between Seong and Celest with his arm resting on the bed. His movement is slow yet exudes authority. "When you've witnessed human life for as long as Iliya or I, you will discover it's all very predictable," he continues, low and unhurried. "Seong's inclination is to be stubborn. Though our lord tries to teach her, she refuses to culture herself. It's quite sad, actually."

"I don't like to read," she growls. "It's a waste of my time." Her anger permeates the room, empathetically affecting the elf. It pulls focus from his nervous stomach down to his feet which subsequently grounds him. This feeling is preferred, and the singing-induced nausea is finally gone.

"Careful," chimes Iliya. "Our lord should be here soon, and he wouldn't want to see you acting like this."

Seong steams quietly, crossing her arms, and lays down her head. "Celest," she pivots. "I'm intrigued by your culture. Elvyn people grow slowly and live long lives, no?"

"It's only in comparison to humans," says Celest. "Some creatures are so old that they've witnessed the world turn to dust and be restored again by the gods. And, the gods must witness all of time. Compared to them, my life will be a short moment."

"Yes," replies Zoan. "The lives of most are restricted by perspective." His posture shifts to further encroach on the elf, who leans away but ends up backing into the arm that encircles him. "You're certainly peculiar among mortals, though. Most wouldn't be able to sit here making conversation with us. I can see why our lord Julian has taken an interest." His voice shakes the air between them as the beating of a drum would to its musician.

And, to Celest, the closeness is stifling. With eyes pulled wide and nowhere to run, the words in his throat are as trapped as he feels. The elf catches a change in his peripheral vision before he can organize himself.

Black fog collects over the floor, virtually invisible if not for the sliver of lamplight under the door. Then, as if aware of themselves, the hallway lamps extinguish. Again, Celest is left alone in the dark as Zoan backs away from him. Julian's clear voice is omnipresent in the room. "You have a beautiful voice, my sweetest Celest," it says in a ghostly whisper. "But I sense you are still distraught." The fog crawls up his skirt, chilling the skin underneath like cold water. He can feel it soaking him, but the vampire's honeyed, myrrh scent is potent in its ability to disarm his objection. "There, I'd like you to be calm," it says as the vapor near his face molds into a hand. Julian manifests before the elf, bent at the hip to face him, and holding the back of the cleric's neck commandingly. As he pulls away, Celest notices the thin leather gloves covering Julian's hands. They tuck into a dark, bell-sleeved shirt that would have been tight-fitting if it weren't unbuttoned almost entirely. His ensemble is complete with red silk pants that match the cleric's dress and polished leather shoes. "You may speak," he permits.

"You..." mumbles the elf. "Um, you look very nice." Iliya stifles a laugh from the other side of the bench.

"Yes, I'm aware," Julian replies.

Celest remains still, waiting to be prompted, but the silence begins to deplete his momentary sedation.

"Have you enjoyed your company tonight?" the vampire finally asks.

"Yes, of course. It's been a pleasure to meet—"

"Who pleases you the most?" he interrupts, casually pulling his right glove tighter with the other hand.

Celest's forehead heats up as he considers the question. "Oh... I couldn't possibly answer something like—"

"You will answer my question," he cuts him off again. "Whose company do you prefer out of the three new friends you've made?" Four vampires stare into him, awaiting an answer that Celest doesn't have. He darts his eyes to the left, catching the amusement in Zoan's expression, and sputters another evasive answer. "Celest, I'm surprised that you dare to defy me in this of all moments. I believe your sense of self-preservation might be terribly skewed. I will not ask you again," he growls.

"Z-Zoan," cracks Celest. "He has cooked the most delicious meal I've ever eaten... However, I'm grateful to you all for hosting me. I don't get to attend parties often..." The sting of jealousy buzzes from someone in the room, but the elf can't tell from who as his glance jumps from face to face.

"It was my pleasure," Zoan whispers, leaning close again.

"Good, Celest... next question," Julian continues, leaving no room for the cleric to reconstitute. "Who do you find most attractive?" The elf chokes on nothing. He opens his mouth to try speaking, but Julian continues, "Do you prefer the slight, feminine figure of Seong to the voluptuous Iliya, or will you again choose Zoan? His masculine form is akin to mine in its perfection."

"This is absurd," exclaims the cleric. "We've only just met."

"That didn't save you from me," reminds Julian. "But you might need some urging to inspire a decision. Zoan, you first. Show Celest how gentle you can be. I think he likes that sort of thing." A mischievous grin is carved on his face.

"Gladly," replies Zoan, slowly advancing toward Celest. The back of his hand strokes down the elf's arm causing him to retreat to the edge of the bench. His ability to deny the situation for what it is quickly fails.

"Wait," he squeaks. "This... can't be right. I agreed to come here with you, Julian, but this is more than I expected. And—"

The protest is stopped short by a finger pressed to the speaker's lips. "Shh," hushes Zoan. "The easiest course of action is for you to remain agreeable." He takes a wide stance over the elf, who backs as far as he can onto the foot of the bed. The vampire follows, leaning in with a knee on the bench to hover agonizingly close to the shivering cleric between his legs. "How's this?" he asks in a voice like gravel, loosening both sleeves and untucking his shirt. Grabbing it by the bottom seam, he pulls it above his head. Dim light from the ceiling highlights the deep browns of his skin tone, and each muscle, cut in perfect symmetry, is defined from the next. His chest, similar to Viktor's, is especially broad. Zoan's shirt slides up and off his arms before dropping to the floor. He crawls over the elf to bar him on the bench with little room for opposition. "Do you like what you see?" he asks. Cold, steady arms cage Celest in place, stealing the rising heat coming from his exposed shoulders, and the vampire's face stops just shy of his own. A breath steeped in elderflower tickles the cleric's cheeks, whispering, "If you enjoy my lord's company, imagine now the both of us. You won't even have to lift a finger. We'll handle it all."

"I'm sorry," pants the elf, "I don't know what you mean."

But, Zoan hears the insincerity in his voice.

"He's lying, my lord," says Zoan to Julian. "Yet, even his lies are coated in sugar. Could I have a taste, Celest, of the fiction still dribbled on your chin?"

The elf tries to respond, but his mouth is sealed with a kiss. Zoan's full lips guide the movement, parting his own and persuading their compliance. Its assertive nature allows Celest to momentarily release his foreboding thoughts, and unwittingly he follows until Zoan pulls away.

"There we are," he whispers. "Surrender. It's clear you'd like some more of me. Why fight it?" The elf begins to break a sweat as the vampire backs away. Zoan then poises himself with his legs crossed widely on the chair near the south wall. "I think I've just won again, my lord."

"You've done well, Zoan," Julian replies. "Sweet Celest is speechless. Certainly, you've got his heart racing, but the others have yet to have a chance to compete. Seong. It's your turn. Be very gentle."

"Yes, my lord," she responds, already kneeling behind the elf. She takes his hand as gingerly as possible. "Will you join me on the bed?"

Celest's pulse beats at the rate of hummingbird wings through his veins. "I shouldn't," he quivers. "I should leave."

"This night isn't over, little mouse," reminds Julian. "Go on, do as she asks."

The vampire's influence is unyielding. Each command breaks the cleric's judgment bits at a time, like a chisel to the stone. Fully aware of his actions now, the elf gives in a little more. Shyly, he lets her lead him onto the bed.

"Very good," Julian praises. "What is next, my temperate Seong?"

She stops for a moment in consideration. "Let me take off your shoes," she says, awkward in her conviction. "It will... comfort you." Her delicate hands unhook the ankle clasps in just four quick movements.

"Slowly," commands Julian as he reclines on the arm of the chair where Zoan is seated. She complies, restraining her supernatural speed, and slides the golden heels from his feet as if he were a princess being readied for sleep.

Iliya takes the shoes and sets them aside on the floor before joining the audience at the south wall. Their red eyes pierce through the cavernous void of the room like predators that stalk the shadow of night.

Seong's too, share a similar danger, but her expression is demure and innocent.

Though it's clearly not a way she is used to behaving, the effort is charming. Celest finds himself partially disarmed. Endearing awkwardness aside, she's idyllic in a kind of beauty that is treasured by his culture, like a gentle morning incarnate, like the goddess in his storybooks. He tucks his feet under him to mirror her seated posture, although the slit in his skirt allows for much more movement.

"Seong, please, I don't think I should be here," he whispers. "I'm not one to partake in... anything like this."

"But I need your help, cleric," she says, ignoring his appeal. "I bit my tongue. It's bleeding. It hurts." She sticks it out, revealing a drop of deep-red blood on its tip. Taking his hand again, Seong adds, "Our lord says you can heal with just one touch. Heal me."

"Your fangs must be sharp to have done that." He sighs. "I... yes, I can help. Just keep your mouth closed, and I'll mend it. I'll have to touch your face so... pardon me."

She leans her chin closer with hands pressed to the sheets, mouth closed, and Celest does as promised, covering her lips with his warm fingers. They glow over her soft skin, and the light soaks into her tongue. He just begins to feel the wound's sting when her lips slide open. Seong licks between his middle and pointer finger, and erotic interest leaves Celest frozen in place to delight in the feeling. He can't bring himself to pull away from its pillowy, wet play on his fingertips. She sucks on them while looking sheepishly up at the elf, trapping him further in fascination. A quivering, lustful moan escapes him after a drawn-out moment of silence.

"Yes," affirms Julian, like an all-seeing presence in the room. "Give in to this, Celest, if you truly wish to abide by my pleasures."

The elf can hear the words articulating through a smile.

"That's enough, Seong. You've done surprisingly well. Let us give Iliya her opportunity to convince him." The dainty vampire stops, leaving his fingers wet and trembling, and retreats in a flash to sit on the floor next to Julian's feet.

Iliya then slides away from Julian's side and approaches the bed, swaying her hips like a panther. Dance, it seems, shapes her form without any extra effort on her part.

"I'm not one to assert myself, Celest," she hums, falling onto the duvet. "It's far too unbecoming, you see. I'd much rather you take me. To be desired, well, it's infatuating. But you've already learned something about that, haven't you? From what I understand, though, you've not yet tried the role of pursuer. Perhaps, once you do, you'll never want to stop."

Her arms reach over her head, recumbent and gorgeous on the pillows. "Oh, it's a bit cold, isn't it? You'll come over and keep me warm, won't you?" She poses again, gripping the dress lying over her thighs. The fabric drags upward and stops just shy of revealing it all. The low-cut neckline, too, scarcely covers her chest, and with a ceiling mirror above, there is little to be left to the imagination.

The elf, against all better interest, is transfixed by the sight. He feels himself leaning in, wishing to touch her skin that looks smoother than melting ice.

"Fear not, sweet songbird," purrs Julian. "Simply take what you desire."

"I am afraid..." whispers the cleric. "I don't know what it is that I desire."

"Your heart rate says otherwise," Iliya responds. Her mouth stays slightly open as she pulls down the puffed sleeve of her garment off her shoulder. Blonde bulbs of hair gather at her neck as she turns to face him, and the expression she wears is irresistibly inviting. She beckons. "Touch me."

Celest risks a glance toward the chair that the others watch from, and the pressure mounts as they stare back expectantly. And so, the cleric concedes again. His breath skips out of time as he crawls toward her. "Okay," he whimpers.

The elf carefully maneuvers to lean over the immortal while trying to keep a hold of his constitution. Most of his weight rests on the hand to the left of her head. The other, reaching over her waist, stabilizes him. Lengthy strands of Celest's snow-colored hair drape around her face, creating a veil of privacy that shields them from their audience. "What now?" he asks in an almost inaudible hush.

She responds not with words but with the tender bite of her lower lip, followed by a sigh that smells like licorice when it reaches his nose. A sense of nostalgia reminds him again of his childhood friend, Soleil. He remembers the look in her eyes as he was pinned beneath her. They ached for affection as Iliya's do now. Celest imagines what it must have taken for Soleil to act on her feelings, considering the kind of lives they endured. But, hovered over this otherworldly beauty, it's easy to ignore the weight of the doctrines that bind him. Celest leans in to kiss her on the cheek, his action feeling more like a dream than reality. He floats on a manic wave that follows his more familiar sense of helplessness. He kisses her again on the curled corner of her lip.

Iliya responds by sliding her hands around his waist, moving up to the skin exposed by his dress, and scratching lightly down his back with the sharp tips of her nails.

A shiver tickles the elf's skin leaving rings of tingling nerves around his skull and the midsection of his thighs. It's a euphoric sensation that he's never felt before at this level of intensity.

She lets go of another elongated sigh, perfuming the air with her spiced breath.

Celest slides his chin to the right to catch her in a proper kiss.

She lets him lead the moment but also combs her fingers across his scalp, which causes a second surge of endorphins that makes him gasp in satisfaction.

Julian's voice purrs next to the cleric's ear, "I love that sound."

Celest, with his limited attention, had almost forgotten the others. He's taken aback by it and begins to flinch away, but Julian halts him by holding a heavy hand between his shoulder blades.

"Don't stop," he commands as his grasp guides the elf to the salacious neckline of her dress and pauses there.

Iliya follows her sire's lead by slipping the sleeve even further down her arm. The hardened tip of her pink nipple escapes the fabric's cover inches away from the elf's face, and his breath races.

Seong's voice huffs from the chair, "she's cheating." Zoan quietly shushes her.

"Go on, Celest," allows Julian, lightening his grip. The cleric, with cheeks burning, complies with his instructions. A kiss begins at Iliya's sternum and makes its way to the right until reaching her plush areola. Instinctually his lips part, and the kiss turns to a lick, then a suckle. She moans like a heavenly spirit in response. The sound fevers him to quicken the motion, but Julian pulls him back before his excitement can escalate any further.

Instead of stopping his passion completely, though, the vampire plants his own lips to the elf's as if to siphon the sexual energy that's been building. Their mouths move zealously in tandem while Iliya's hand slips under the slit in Celest's skirt, but when it reaches the exposed skin at his lap, he remembers himself and pulls away from the both of them. But, regardless of his better judgment, rejecting the two inhuman beauties comes with a sting all its own. Conflicting inclination nearly rips the cleric to pieces.

Chapter Nineteen

Shame eats at his budding desire like fungus on a fallen fruit. "Oh, goddess," he pants, backing away from the vampires. "I'm so sorry."

Iliya fixes her sleeve as Julian strokes the elf's shoulder. The leather of his glove cuts down the chill from his hand underneath. "Still feeling shy after all of this?" he asks through a haughty grin. He kneels onto the bed and encircles the elf, ending up behind him, and pulls him to fit the space between his thighs.

Although the embrace is that of a vampire, there is a sense of security wrapped in his arms. He feels swathed and safe.

"Be still, sweet Celest. You're doing fabulously," he mouths. "Tell me who you choose."

The cleric is catching his breath as he responds, "Everyone is... so lovely..."

The vampire nuzzles into Celest's neck and tugs at the chain, which adorns it with his pointer finger. The sensation triggers an immediate enthrallment. "Choose," he directs.

The fever in the elf's chest softens as he reaches a conclusion in his mind. Tenderly clinging to the arms that hold him, Celest utters the words, "I choose you. I can't help but choose you."

He can feel a smile develop over the supple skin on his neck. Then, moving to the elf's ear, the vampire whispers, "A perfect answer, my sweet, but not the one I'm looking for." He grabs the elf by the chin and turns his face up to meet the rest of them, who have unobtrusively joined Iliya at the head of the bed. "Which of my beloved pets suits you?" he asks.

They lean on each other, Iliya under Zoan's arm and Seong draped around his neck. Still and statuesque, they await the reply.

The resistance left in Celest has been all but extinguished by the vampires' persistent advances. "I don't know," he begins, burying himself deeper into the cold chest at his back, "I suppose... Seong." A whisper of irritation is evident on Iliya's face, but she is the only one to outwardly react.

"Why is that?" asks Julian as he twirls a finger through the hair over the elf's temple.

"She seems," he whispers, "less experienced, like myself. I feel... a kinship in that. Um, of course, you are also beautiful, Seong, like a princess." He trails off at the end, uncomfortable with speaking candidly.

"Isn't that sweet, Seong? He thinks of you, of all people, as royalty," scoffs Iliya.

"It's not my fault he favors you least. That must be embarrassing for you, considering how hard you tried to win his attention," she strikes back. "I didn't even need to take my clothes off. Maybe he thinks you're too easy."

Celest tenses as they argue and tries to mend the rift. "Oh, no, please. I didn't mean any offenses. Iliya's beauty is breathtaking. Each of you is beyond any—" Julian's hand covers his mouth like a seal on a jar.

"Quiet, both of you. Can't you see you're causing him unnecessary stress," asserts Julian. "But on the topic of undressing, Seong, since it was you he chose, why don't you reward him by showing off what's underneath that gown of yours?"

She nods and unties the black ribbon around her neck. As it loosens, she unhurriedly slips the dress up her thighs, stomach, and head. Her slim body, now bare save for the lace stockings clasped to a garter belt at her waist, is on full display. She twists and poses for the elf, using her arms to squeeze together her small breasts into a semblance of cleavage.

Celest couldn't bring himself to speak even if he wanted to, with Julian's gloved hand caging his lips, but the huffed breath funneling through his nose is loud enough to convey his feeling. Likewise, his eyes refuse to shut. They scour her skin, absorbing every detail of her slow, deliberate movement.

"Zoan," says Julian. "Get her started. I believe Celest needs to be educated in the ways of treating a woman. Selfishly, too, I must admit that the warmer he gets, the more it delights me to hold him here. Iliya, be a dear and play support."

"Yes, my lord," replies Zoan. "I'll show the cleric how it's done." Seong lays back on the pillows and spreads her knees, revealing herself entirely. The petaled folds between her legs are tinted a color slightly darker than the rest of her complexion. Her hands rest on either thigh above the cuff of her stockings.

Zoan moves in, laying on his front just below her, yet not obscuring the elf's view. His middle finger slides up and down its length a few times before stopping near the top portion. Zoan makes slow, tiny circles with the finger over what Celest would describe as a spherical pebble of skin.

Julian whispers to Celest, "Have you ever seen such a pretty little pussy? It must be your first time, no? Do you see how his rubbing there is causing her toes to curl? It's important to pay special attention to that, the clitoris. It's very sensitive. You can think of it like a small version of this…" His pelvis pushes into Celest's backside, bringing attention to his hardened organ as it rubs through his pants and the elf's skirt.

The cleric scarcely notices himself moaning under the gloved grip, but the vampires are acutely aware.

Iliya makes her move, carefully choking a bit of air from Seong's throat. She looks down into the other's eyes, seeming to enjoy her squirming.

Despite the mounting pleasure between her legs, Seong glares up at her. Her lips start to form the shape of words, but Iliya is quick to silence her by sliding a pointer finger into the other vampire's mouth. Seemingly pacified, Seong closes her eyes and begins to suck it.

Celest is enwrapped by the sight. He notices a glistening wetness between the inner petal folds, which Zoan, too, makes note of. His finger moves to spread it, wetting the rest until it all but sparkles. His hand then twists, palm up as his finger enters her. It curves, rubbing upward as if to beckon her indulgence.

Zoan then leans in to kiss and suckle where he had previously been circling. The elf's view is now blocked by the coiled black hair on Zoan's head, but the fluttering of Seong's eyelids effectively communicates the sensation it brings.

Blissful waves of emotion crash empathetically through the elf as if, just by bearing witness, he is the one receiving such pleasures. A swelling in his loins grows hotter, listening to the wet sounds of Zoan's tongue met with Seong's reticent whimpers.

Her eyes roll back, and she then shutters deeply. The release is accompanied by a rolling wail of a moan that causes Celest to finally break. The vampires' persistent efforts have succeeded. His shaking hands grasp at the fabric of Julian's pants as if he'll fall otherwise.

Julian responds by biting down on the elf's earlobe just enough for it to sting slightly. Through his teeth, he asks, "Is this you telling me that you wish to partake with us? Have you given up your hesitations?"

Celest pants a muffled agreement and nods his head.

"And you'll do as I command," Julian continues, now whispering into his ear, "without a question of my authority?"

Celest turns his head to look back at the vampire, and Julian allows the motion while keeping his grip. The elf's sun-yellow eyes are liquid and compliant. Without Celest having to make a sound, Julian can see that he's won him over absolutely. The cleric nods again.

"Good," he purrs, slowly releasing his hand from Celest's gasping mouth. "Iliya. Come here."

"Yes, my lord," she replies, crawling over to face the two of them. "Shall I begin with a kiss?"

"Yes, my pet. But, be sure not to neglect his aching desire," instructs Julian.

She whispers, "As you wish," before planting her bulbed lips to the elf's mouth. The kiss is full, fervent, and wet, possessing all the pleasures of biting into a perfectly ripened grape.

Julian's hands brush down the elf's arms until reaching his wrists. He cuffs them in his grasp in a way that demands stillness.

Distracted by Iliya's tongue playing on the tip of his own, the cleric barely notices her hands lifting the skirt of his dress up past his thighs until her cold fingers wrap themselves around his swelling shaft. He gasps, and his arms instinctively twitch to cover himself, but they are held in place by Julian's stone grip.

The vampire shushes in his ear and begins kissing at the nape of his neck to soothe him while Iliya gently strokes its length. Her hands are that of a ceramicist in their motion, yet the skin of her palms is even smoother than dampened clay. He is released from this kiss after a moment, but Iliya proceeds to use her mouth in another way. Rivaling the satisfaction from her fingers, she leans down to kiss and lap at the domed head of his cock.

"Oh, goddess," the cleric whines as a shiver vibrates up his spinal cord. Instead of simply hearing her moan in reply, he can feel it as her mouth envelops him. She slides down deeply to reach the base where her fingers hold then shallows again with a slurp. The sensation is sublime.

"Are you ready to feel what it's like to be a man?" growls Julian as he grips tighter to the point of pain.

"Ah—what?" gasps Celest, confused and wholly distracted.

Julian ignores his question and instead addresses the others. "Iliya, Zoan. Enough. I believe our two younglings are warm enough. Let's let them have their fun together," he says. The two comply, making way for their sire. He guides the elf to hover over Seong. "Go on, my sweet. Carve yourself inside her, and allow yourself the pleasures of men," he commands.

Celest hesitates, but her arms draw him close.

"Take me, cleric," she insists. "Let us please our lord with what he asks. Come. I'll help you." With two fingers, she spreads her petals, and her other hand guides him to the opening. Seong's wetted entrance makes it easy to slip inside, but even so, the walls are tight around his shaft. Her eyes glint with momentary ferocity. "You're so very warm," pants the vampire.

In a forceful tone, Julian asserts, "Let that not distract you, my dear. Temperance. You know what will happen if you fail to keep your composure."

"Yes," she moans as the elf begins a gentle thrust.

Celest drops to his elbows as Julian backs away and reclines on his side, watching the two of them. "How does it feel, Celest?" he asks through an impish grin.

"Aha... It's good. It feels so good," moans the elf. His face and shoulders are pink with blush, and so too are the tips of his ears. Their long points droop down toward his spine, and he shivers slightly with each new depth of his thrust. The other vampires join their sire in a voyeuristic lounging and watch as Seong crushes the duvet between her fingers with a supernatural grip.

"I'd like to see... more," Julian muses. "Zoan, rid him of the gown."

Dazed and preoccupied, Celest hears the request in the time it takes the vampire to snap the straps over his shoulders and tear the seam at his side. He is exposed, but it changes nothing. The final ember of his defiance has already been extinguished under Julian's leather-gloved palm.

"That's better." He sighs. "Iliya, get behind him. Make use of that succulent mouth of yours, hm?"

"Of course," she replies, gliding from the pillows to enfold Celest from behind. He pauses to look back at her, sweat glistening from his cheeks. She unbuttons her dress from the front, allowing her bosom to burst forth from the garment, and then slides off her sleeves. "Don't stop, darling," she coos. "I'll match your pace."

"Eyes on me, cleric," utters Seong, weaving her hands through his long hair. "Pay her no mind."

"That'll be impossible," Iliya responds. Her hands stroke his backside and gently push him to continue. When he begins again, her lips meet his tender skin like morning berries that have been chilled by the air of night. She then persists with her tongue. A high-pitched gasp escapes him as it finds his soft entrance and wriggles there, but the feeling is euphoric and somehow induces a deeper slip into the disassociation between his bodily pleasures and sentient mind.

To the right, the male vampires spectate the performance before them. Julian's cool amusement is in contrast to Zoan's eager tension, but both are roused with interest in their own way.

Without breaking focus, Julian takes the tip of his leather glove between his teeth and slides his left hand free. It falls to the sheets before he reaches behind him to slice through the side of Zoan's trousers with the razor-sharp tips of his nails. "Join them, Zoan," whispers Julian. "Take your pick. Surprise me." In a flash of movement, the vampire is undressed and kneeling to the left of Seong's head. He takes her by the hair and urges his erection past her lips. For a moment, even she is taken aback but yields to sucking on its length as he guides her.

Celest is awestruck as he watches it pop from her mouth and hang between their faces. "Go on, Celest," chuckles the vampire voyeur. "Help her devour it."

The elf obeys, leaning down to brush his lips across its side. The scent of Seong's lily breath is soaked on the skin. Each vampire is like a flower in bloom with sweet perfume and beauty that draws him further to their nectar. Like the glittering leaves of a sundew plant, they lure him to quench his thirst, but now he finds himself stuck and writhing between their beguiling grasp.

Zoan lifts Seong's head to reach his shaft from the other side, and the two work alongside each other. Their tongues meet occasionally, echoing the sentiment of a kiss. The satisfaction is immeasurable, and Celest trembles as the heat in his loins further builds.

Noticing this, Julian is quick to pull him away from the action.

He drapes the elf over his lap. One hand controls his chin as the vampire licks and nibbles at the chain around his neck. The other hand presses the elf's throbbing shaft onto his lower abdomen as if to calm its passion. "I can't let you get too excited before I've had my fun," Julian growls. "You are excited, aren't you? My nymph." Celest peers up at him, panting, with eyes like citrine gems.

"Yes," the elf concedes.

"Yes," repeats the vampire. "Keep saying yes, and I'll give you my whole world." Julian gorges him with affection, pausing only briefly to let Celest catch his breath while the other three continue among themselves. Their focus, however, remains latched to the warm-blooded mortal in their midst. Regardless of their salacious revelry in each other, the scent of life pulsing through his widened veins draws out from them a lust of a different kind.

"Iliya," Julian mutters between slippery kisses. "Come here and get me wet." She rolls over off Seong, allowing Zoan to take the spot on top of her, and crawls over the sheets to unfasten the buttons on Julian's pants. The vampire moves his right hand away from Celest to clutch the hair on the back of her head. A sloshing sound leaves her mouth as he forces it down over his shaft. Iliya's blonde bulbs fall over her flawless face, which bobs at Julian's command. Pulling on Celest's golden chain with enough strength to leave a mark, he asks, "Are you ready to serve me again, my sweet Celest? To indulge in what you've ached for since our last meeting?"

The cleric fails to respond, lips quivering, but his eyes again tell a story of submission.

Julian releases Iliya and flips the elf prone while undressing himself. It only takes a moment before his wide, ghostly hands are holding Celest at the hips like a chalice.

Iliya advances toward the cleric but is stopped by Julian growling, "Wait. I'll have him to myself."

As the vampire finds his tender entrance, Celest stifles a gasp by pressing his face into the sheets. "Ah!" he moans as his body molds to fit the penetration. "G-goddess!"

He receives a sudden, punishing slap to the side of his bottom that startles his pointed ears to their upright position and leaves a stinging red print on his skin. "Enough of that," says Julian. "Think *only* of me."

"You're so gentle with him," pants Seong as Zoan slows his pace inside of her to mirror Julian's. They both are lying on their side, Zoan behind her, to watch their lord assert his sovereignty.

"It'd serve you well to learn my restraint," he replies. "I do not wish to break him."

The vampire's speed increases as Celest stretches wide enough to take him. His hands latch awkwardly to the duvet, unable to summon the proper strength in his grip. His knees tremble like a newborn lamb, and his eyes roll to the upper lids as if he is drifting from consciousness. This, however, is far from the truth. The cleric is entirely aware, emancipated, in the vampire's binding embrace. Not a single thought is wasted on oath, nor shame, nor doubt. It is only himself, only pleasure, only Julian. His body vibrates like a tea kettle heated to the point of whistling, and an involuntary golden, white light beginning at his core emanates across his skin. It casts long shadows throughout the room with its dull glow.

While the three vampires watching are stricken with surprise, Julian's angular face is marked only with overt euphoria. The warm light soaks through him so deeply that it reaches a soul, binds to it, and connects them both in ecstatic rapture.

"Aah-" he moans. "This bliss! Celest. Fuck." His voice cracks as tears from each of his sanguine eyes streak down his cheeks and then drip onto the elf's back. His thumb touches the droplets like fragile, precious gemstones. "What you do to me..." he whispers. The vampire then takes him by the arms, restraining them behind his back, and forces him upright onto his knees. "Calm yourself, Celest," he coos. "I wish to share you, but this feeling shall be mine, and mine alone."

The elf takes a sharp inhale and releases it as slowly as he can. "I... will try my best," he pants. Conscious effort is required to tame the magic that escapes him, and Julian, not once pausing his motion, makes that infinitely more difficult. Eventually, though, the light recedes, and the room is dark once more.

"Good," says Julian. "Perfect. Ladies, be kind hosts and help our guest reach his highs. And, Iliya. Watch her."

"Yes, my lord," they hum in tandem, crawling on their knees to face him. Iliya is first to touch the elf, trailing her icy fingers down the center of his abdomen and then wrapping them around his swollen shaft. She laps with her tongue from base to tip, looking up at him with smoldering ruby eyes under curled lashes, then offers it to Seong, who mimics Iliya's form.

"Careful," she orders as Seong opens her mouth to suck it. Daintily, the vampire encircles his cock and slides her heart-shaped lips forward and back around its length. Iliya trails downward with her tongue, lapping at the sensitive skin that hangs below it.

"A-aah... t-that's..." Celest begins but fails to complete his thought.

"That's sensitive? Yes?" hums Julian before craning his head down to suck on the skin at the nape of the elf's neck. For a moment, his eyes meet Zoan's, then flick to Iliya and back to him.

He understands the wordless command, positioning himself behind the other, and slides inside her. One hand grips her by the ass cheek and spreads while the other reaches around her thigh and begins to tease her clit. She moans in a siren's tone that reverberates through Celest's nerves, prompting him to join in harmony.

The cleric's temperature continues to rise as he watches their passion, feeling it course inside of him. Each thrust of Julian's hips is enough to make him weak with splendor, but the three sets of lips on his skin draw out lust from within him that can barely be contained. "Ah! Nngh!" he whimpers. "F-fuck!"

"Oh," chuckles Julian, quickening his pace. "It seems we've made him curse. That's not very godly of you, my sweet. We might be a bad influence."

Celest reaches his tipping point. Unable to control himself, the elf swells with pleasure and then releases it all into Seong's gaping mouth. She pulls away, cum dripping from her chin, and freezes. But something inside her shifts. Pupils dilated in a wild frenzy, she lunges forward with a guttural hiss but is caught by Iliya, who wraps around her waist and squeezes a tight hand over her mouth.

"Hold her," growls Julian. "Don't let her ruin this. Zoan. Come here. Fuck me."

"With pleasure, my lord," he replies, kneeling behind his sire to attend to the demand.

Julian controls the pace, as he continues to maintain every piece of his unquestionable control.

The cleric, however, is spent. Falling forward, he quivers like a bow-string having been shot, but the vampires vigorously continue.

Julian releases the elf's wrists only to grab hold of his crested hips and forces into him with ferocious intensity.

"AA-Hah!" screams the elf in ecstasy. "Julian! Fuck!"

"I'm close, Celest," he growls in reply. "I'm close." Julian's black nails dig into his flesh just enough not to pierce the skin. As they go, even the quiet Zoan can't help but moan through his teeth in a low, predacious bass note.

"*Please*," the elf begs, unable to handle the beating for much longer. He braces himself, biting into the sheets until the vampire's final thrust loads him with thick, pearly ropes of cum. He then feels Zoan's climax splatter onto his ass and dribble down his thighs to the crevice of his knees. Celest collapses with an exhale, exhausted and dizzy, but Julian is quick to console him with a shower of kisses on the forehead.

"Shh," Julian whispers. "You're okay. You are perfect." Involuntary tears soak through the duvet under the cleric's face as the vampire strokes his back and wipes him dry with a shirt that Zoan offers. "It's alright," he soothes, brushing the hair off his cheek. "I'll take you to the bath again. We'll get you clean and sorted. Everything is perfect, my sweet. Do not fret. Just give me one moment. Zoan, comfort him for me."

Obeying his orders, Zoan moves to cradle Celest's head in his ebony hands and extends whispered praises into the elf's quivering ear.

"You," mutters Julian, glaring deeply into Seong's eyes. At his will, fog collects over his right hand, silencing it in a vacuum of space. He strikes her across the cheek without a sound. She had already calmed from her frenzy and had been released from Iliya's restraint, but Julian's current discipline drains all remaining vitality from her expression. She stares at the wall with a distant detachment. He continues in a hush too quiet for the elf to hear, "That outburst very narrowly risked every fraction of trust that I've built with him. Be ashamed of yourself, for now. And later I'll decide what you're worth to me alive. You should hope I feel forgiving." Julian finds his pants, grabs a fur from the marble bench, wraps it around the elf, and carries him out of the room without another word.

Chapter Twenty

"Julian?" whispers Celest as they exit the dark bedroom.

"Yes, my sweet?"

"I... is there a bathroom that I could use?" asks the elf. His eyes are still swollen from tears.

"I am taking you back to the bath, yes."

"No... I mean... A place where I could—"

"Oh." The vampire comes to a stop and then turns in an instant to walk down the hall in the opposite direction. "It's been so long. I might be getting out of touch," he admits as he drops the elf off a few doors down and waits a distance away. Once finished, Celest reemerges into the hallway, cloaked tightly in the black fur. Julian glides to his side and picks him up once more.

"I can walk," whispers the elf, resting his cheek on Julian's stone chest.

"And I can carry you," the vampire rebuttals. Shortly after, they enter the bathing room, and Julian closes the door behind them with his heel. He approaches the tub, slides away the fur covering, and gently lowers the elf into the still-warm bath. Celest's eyes close as he sinks down to rest his chin just above the water. Julian kneels at the edge, situates his arms on the lip, and runs his fingers along the water's surface.

For a few moments, they idle in silence. The elf repositions to lay his head across Julian's forearm, and the vampire responds with a kiss between the part of his hair. With tender ease, Julian rubs his hand slowly up and down Celest's back. It's comforting. Under the water's warmth, the chill of the vampire's touch is nullified. Aside from its perfect grace, the caress almost feels like that of a mortal. "Julian?" whispers Celest, breaking the silence.

"Yes?" he acknowledges.

"I haven't known you long, but the way you pamper me... Your company is like none I've held before." The elf looks up at him with brows curved up toward the center in concern.

Julian meets his gaze. A composed adoration is the only feature visible in his expression. "I know," he replies.

Celest's hands reach up to grip the tub's lip as his face tilts down toward the water. He continues, "I don't quite know how to say this. I'm in a bit of a bind." The elf focuses on the stillness of the bath's surface and attempts to voice a confession. "You know my intentions. I want to help end this curse that torments you. I don't know how, but I'm sure there is a way. There has to be a cure."

The vampire places a hand on top of the elf's head and pets his hair. "You are kind," he purrs. "Perhaps, to a fault. The quality is rare."

"There's a problem, though," he mutters, fidgeting with the edge of the tub. "I haven't told my guildmates the truth about me meeting with you. I've been doing every bit of this in secret. They have no idea what you mean to me."

"That is no surprise," soothes Julian. "I expected as much. How would you tell them that you've become enamored with the demon that haunts the city? In their minds, I am sure they believe that I'm waiting for my opportunity to attack that poor girl and end her." He hooks a finger through a section of the elf's dove-white hair and brings it to his lips.

Celest again meets his gaze. "It's not only that," stresses the elf. "I tried to change their decision, but we—they… plan on coming here tomorrow at daybreak. They intend to vanquish you. We've been tasked by the Lasaunts to strike you down for the purpose of Adinine's protection." Celest is suddenly startled by a roaring laugh from Julian. Instead of the worry that the cleric is expecting, the vampire looks tickled with amusement. The smile he wears is wider than Celest has ever seen it.

Julian restrains his entertainment but maintains an air of presumptuousness while looking down his nose at his companion. "Listen," he begins. "I don't mean this as an insult. I'm sure your team is quite capable, but there is not a chance that they could best me. Even before vampirism took hold, I was a master of spellcraft. I'm certain that even at their current best, they have not the skill, nor the power, to fell me. So, fret not, my sweet. Let them come. I swear to you, I will bring them no harm. You have nothing to fear." He lifts Celest's chin with two wet fingers and plants a persuasive kiss on his lips.

When Julian pulls away, the cleric asks, "Do you really think it won't be an issue? Can you convince them that you're not the monster they think you are?"

"I could convince them of anything," he replies smugly. "Do you doubt me?"

Celest sheepishly curls his knees to his chest. "I… suppose not." The sentiment makes him uneasy. Julian is gloating. The elf, for the first time, considers a possibility in which his own actions have been swayed under false pretenses. The thought tightens his chest, but he squashes it under a torrent of justifications. Julian, it seems, truly is enamored with him. Why else would he cry in relief at his touch? Why else would he leave him unharmed? Why else would Julian have taken him to bed if not because he adored him? If his feelings for Celest are true, how can he possibly lie about the rest?

"Suppose?" the vampire queries. He appears unsatisfied.

"N-no," stutters the elf. "I don't doubt it. I trust you. Everything will be just fine."

"That's better," he purrs, moving his hand to grab the elf's hair at its base. The vampire uses the grip to tilt Celest's head to the side, exposing the smooth, golden skin of his neck. His tongue travels leisurely from his clavicle to the round curve of his jawbone, just under his ear.

A shivering sigh leaves the cleric's lips.

"I prefer it when you yield to me," he whispers. "You prefer it, too." Julian sucks on the skin, lightly at first.

A vapid longing flushes the elf's mind of further thought, and he pants as the suction escalates to the point of pain. It pulls his blood to the surface, blushing and bruising the skin. Although feeling like a lamb pinned between the jaws of a wolf, he can't bring himself to panic. And, however absurd, he hungers for the bite.

Julian produces a lascivious, guttural groan that stands Celest's hairs on end despite being soaked in warmth, then pulls away. He, too, is panting. "You don't know what it's like to resist you," he growls. "You smell like heaven. You taste like the sunlight that has been denied me."

The elf's eyes are glazed over, their lids hanging heavy across his yellow irises. "You smell like wild honey and myrrh," he offers in a hushed reply. "It's intoxicating."

Julian's lips pull back into a smirk. "Is it?" he purrs.

Celest nods, pulling himself forward, and kisses the vampire again.

"My sweetest Celest," whispers Julian.

"Yes?"

"I'm inclined to inform you that the time is well past midnight."

"Oh," mutters Celest. "And?"

Julian chuckles. "I should be returning you to your mates. After all, the lot of you are planning to storm my castle at daybreak. We wouldn't want you to be late for the show now, would we?"

"Oh... y-yes. That's right," agrees the elf as Julian takes him by the shoulders and lifts him to a standing position. He grabs the plush towel from the rack and holds it for a moment. Deep-red waves of arcane energy pulse through its fibers before he wraps it around Celest, scoops him up, then sets him back down on the rug. It quickly dries him again, exactly the same way as last time. "Thank you, Julian. I can meet you in the hall once I've dressed," says Celest.

"Nonsense," Julian replies. "If I only have your company tonight for a few minutes more, I will have each second of it. Your clothes are in the vanity, I assume? Allow me." Only an instant passes before the vampire slides open the larger drawer, places the black box onto the counter, and flips off its lid. He resumes, "I wish that I could send you off in a properly flattering outfit. Again, I mean no insult, but this garb truly does the most to hide your figure. I prefer a mo—"

The vampire stops mid-sentence. Upon picking up the cleric's outer robes and shaking them loose, the sunstone jiggles free of its pocket. Liberated from the fabric's folds, its twinkling light brightens the room as it falls and lands between the two companions. A flash of recollection is evident in the vampire's eyes before his expression turns to anguish. His arms rush to cover his face from the sight as he lets out a baffled cry. Each exposed bit of moonlight flesh, from foot to forehead, begins to sizzle and steam as if it were suddenly brought to a boil. The pain is devastating. So much so that the cleric can feel its phantom influence, through Julian, rip at his own skin.

The vampire darts behind the opaque glass pane in the center of the room as Celest stumbles to the floor, collapsing his hands over the tiny gem until the light retreats behind his cupped fingers. "Where did you find that?" asks the vampire in a savage growl.

"I-I'm sorry! It's—" stutters the elf.

"Where!" snarls Julian as his fist pounds on the glass that cracks like thick ice around the impact point.

Celest flinches at the violence and mutters, "It was at a shrine. In the woods." He clutches the stone, bringing it to his chest. The elf can feel his anxious heart pounding beneath its rib cage.

"That bastard had been *hiding* it this whole time?" shouts the vampire as Celest hears a brutal cracking of wood from the bed frame beyond the partition. "All this time! Is that the reason that fucking cunt refuses to stay dead?" Another blow, this time directed at the eastern wall, shakes the entire room.

The door to the hall swings open as the other vampires gather there, reacting to the noise. Iliya's concerned voice rings from the doorframe, "My lord? What is th—"

"Shut up!" he roars in reply.

Julian's phrasing settles in the cleric's mind, taking him aback. "What do you mean stay dead?" Celest squeaks through his throat. Salted tears well up and hang over his bottom lashes.

The vampire is silent. The question gives him pause. After a moment, he sighs. Returning to his normal composure, Julian says, "My little bird. Forgive me for my outburst." His black-nailed fingers round the partition's edge. When the skin fails to burn, they pull the rest of him within view. Julian's expression is soft again, but the noxious fury ablaze in his eyes isn't so easily hidden. "That gemstone belonged to my brother. I believed it to be lost to the ages. It simply startled me to find it in your possession. Now, be a good boy. Wrap that in a cloth and give it to me," he instructs.

"What do you mean *stay* dead?" repeats Celest. His grip is so tight that the stone digs into his palms. "The daeva. You..." chokes out the cleric. "You've tried to have them killed?" His knees begin to shake as the question is met with a lethal glare.

"No," responds Julian through his teeth. "Celest. Do not make me repeat myself. You will regret it." He steps forward to lord over the elf's crouched frame. Julian's inky waves of hair stretch down to drape over the elf's quivering shoulders. The strands feel like the throngs of a scourge whip, ready to chastise any further hint of disobedience.

Unable to voice his objection, Celest resorts to a silent, upward stare. And once his tears begin to fall, they don't stop. Two unbroken streams of salt-dense ribbons cut through his apple-round cheeks. His sobbing, too, is as quiet as a rogue. Only his pounding heart dares to fill the silence.

"I've frightened you," says the vampire. "I understand this, but you are mistaken. I have simply let out some frustration, and now you are convinced that I've plotted murder? Really, Celest, that is quite the stretch. Don't be dense." Julian's attempt to mask his irritation has vanished. The curve of his upper lip is marked with disdain, and his thick, black brows point downward over his eyes. The disparity between his current face and the one with which he used, just a moment ago, to attend to the cleric with luxurious affection gives Celest's tears all the more reason to continue flowing.

Though every impulse tells the elf to obey Julian's command, he can't scrub the vampire's remark from the forefront of his thoughts. There must have been a reason that Damion hid the sunstone from his brother, but regardless of that, the cleric's friends had entrusted it to him for safekeeping. What kind of ally would he be to anyone if he folded and gave the vampire his wish? He frantically searches his mind for a way to appease everyone. "I won't use it," Celest finally squeaks. "I have no intention to hurt you. I didn't even know that it would, I swear it. If I did, I would have left it at the tavern. Julian, please, just let me keep it. I can't betray the trust of my friends. You understand, don't you? Don't be upset, please."

"As I understand it, you have *been* betraying their trust. Did you not just admit that you're here in secret? Fool," spits the vampire. "I will ask you one last time. Take that towel at your waist, wrap it around that wretched gem, and place it at my feet. I will not tolerate this disobedience. If you fail to do that which I ask of you, my hand will be forced. Do *you* understand?" As Julian steps backward, his hair slides off the elf's shoulders, slashing his skin with the psychic sting of their whip-like tips.

Celest is faint. The struggle between fear and loyalty causes an aching thump in his skull. The elf's tear-soaked eyes roll to look down at the floor. His hands again grip tightly to the stone in an act that conveys a resolve to keep the little treasure despite the vampire's threats. His defiance is unnerved and unspoken, yet as legible as the print in a children's book. *"Celest!"* roars Julian with unnatural volume. The cleric pulls his gripped hands to his chest. "You... you ungrateful *peasant*! Do as I say!" he hisses with the poison of a viper tainting his voice.

The words only steel Celest's decision. "No," he shakily replies through gritted teeth, still looking away from the vampire's daggered stare. Behind the single word, though, a torrent of unvoiced objection storms through his mind.

"No?" echoes Julian in response to the cleric's insubordination. "No! That's what you choose to say to me?" His fist swings with incredible speed, and a twist of his waist, to impact the glass partition again. This time it shatters, falling like a sudden hailstorm onto the wooden floorboards.

Celest lets out a frightful gasp, pulling his knees to the hands clutched at his chest. His ears are downturned, shuddering like wind chimes during an earthquake.

"How dare you treat me this way? Do you wish for me to play the villain? After everything I have given you. After everything I've promised you," he growls violently. Then, collecting his rage into the fist balled at his side, he adds, "You have been so compliant up until now, sweet Celest. I had thought maybe you would need no taming. That was foolish of me. No pet is perfect from the start. It seems clear to me now that it is my responsibility to teach you a lesson. And next time you think it wise to disobey your new master, you'll have a reference for what punishment feels like."

The elf tenses his muscles to grip their bones. Somehow the even tone of his cruel, confusing words is more terrifying than the shouts. He sobs, expecting the vampire to strike him, but the beating doesn't come. Instead, he feels a gust of air hit his naked skin as Julian disappears from the room in a flash of movement.

Celest looks up just in time to see the curve of Julian's heel pass the doorframe. He is dutifully followed by Iliya, Seong, and Zoan. For a fraction of a moment, Zoan's eyes meet the elf's. They hold a look that's close to pity before disappearing down the hallway.

"W-wait! Where are you going? I... I'm sorry!" calls out Celest with all the volume he can summon. He stumbles to his feet and runs to the door, trying unsuccessfully to avoid stepping on the glass that covers the floor. When he reaches the hall, there is no one in sight. "Julian!" he wails. "Come back! I'm sorry! Please!" To his pleas, either unheard or ignored, no one replies. Only the sound of his own voice, echoing through a hallway that seems to expand like a telescope as he runs in panic, can be heard bouncing within its walls.

The elf is stopped cold as the towel under his arms falls to his feet, tripping him in the process. Leaving it in frustration, he hurries back into the room for his clothes. After failing again to avoid stepping on pieces of the shattered partition scattered across the ground, he quickly plucks small shards of glass from his feet and begins to dress. Before sliding his stinging soles into his boots, he tucks the sunstone securely into the side of his now blood-freckled sock.

For the second time, he runs after them. Unsure of where they would be, the cleric takes a chance at the dining room. The pair of iron doors, wide open to the patio, confirm his assumption. He rushes outside to the fountain's mirror and falls to his knees before the reflection. Trembling fingers touch the mirror's surface. The image inside is not that of the inn's round, orange windows. Instead, only his own devastated expression stares back at him.

"No... no, no, no, no, no," repeats the elf. "He couldn't have. He promised not to hurt them. He... no. No!" Celest's hands drop into the fountain's base with a splash. Their color appears white as salt, stripped by fear of their natural saturation. "I-I need to stop him," he stutters to himself, rising to his feet. "I need to warn them—oh goddess." Celest scans the balcony for an exit point while casting a glowing orb spell in his left hand. It illuminates the space around him in a warm, golden light. To his right, across the grand patio, a staircase leads downward and wraps around to the other side of the castle. He runs to it, slowing as he reaches the steps. Taking hold of the cold stone railing, the cleric descends. Reaching the landing, he nearly slips, but catches himself, takes the right turn, and continues downward.

A long, narrow patio stretches in front of him. The wall it clings to hosts a dozen plate-tracery windows, the glass of which is stained in vibrant lilac and blue. A single door stands between them. Its symmetrical, branching lines mimic the windows' decoration. Celest hurries over and tugs at its iron handle, but the door is locked. A drizzle of rain from the thickening clouds above begins to further dampen the elf's cheeks, still wet from his unrelenting tears. In a desperate frenzy, he checks the distance to the ground from the balustrade. About sixty feet below lies a garden. Two opulent, old gravestones in the center lay among the overgrown flower beds. Untamed red, pink, and white roses all but engulf them in their thorn-ridden bind. Directly below the patio, a line of willow trees hug the wall, lessening the distance by almost forty feet. The cleric clings to the railing, debating how effectively their branches would break a fall when an idea springs to mind. He darts back up the stairs and into the dining hall, where he finds the long, purple table runner and yanks it out onto the patio. He returns down the steps with frantic determination and ties one end to the balustrade's vertical spindle and the other tightly around his waist. The knots hold as he tugs and leans back with all his weight; then the cleric lets the golden orb of light drop to the garden below. He momentarily considers casting a spell to enhance his agility but begrudgingly decides the mana would be more efficiently spent healing from an injury than trying to prevent one.

"Please, oh goddess, keep me safe," he prays as he maneuvers himself over the railing. "For the sake of my friends, goddess, see me safely to the ground." With all his strength, he chokes the fabric and slowly descends with the aid of tiny footholds between slabs of black stone. Through some miracle, he manages to lower himself the length of the runner but stops a few inches short of reaching a willow branch. Holding his breath, he stretches out a gaping hand toward the foliage and grips its lance-shaped leaves in his shivering fingers. The knot attached to the spindle, however, begins to give until finally releasing. Celest sharply inhales as the thin branch he holds to bends and snaps instantly with his weight. He falls a distance as the leaf blades lash at any exposed bit of skin. His lower back makes a painful impact with a larger, lower branch that knocks away the air in his lungs before he falls prone on the tall grass at the tree's base.

He's alive, but when he collects the will needed to lift himself off the ground, a gritty, stabbing ache prevents him from standing. The elf's breath, too, is short. Each meager inhale is accompanied by a pain that makes him want to faint. Two ribs on his left side are broken. Realizing this, his focus turns to a spell. The act is difficult with his limited breath, but he handles it well enough to heal the internal wound with a glowing hand placed above the injury. Celest sighs as he stands, pressing his hands together in gratitude before picking up the light orb, and runs north through the wild garden to reach the castle's forecourt. It lies beyond a rusted metal gate with bars wide enough for the elf to slip through sideways. With little notice taken for his surroundings, he races down the wide pavement that leads away from the castle. He can see in the distance the main road that leads into the city, but the drizzle from above has turned to rain, and the pathway is steep. Clumsy as ever, Celest's foot catches a crack in the worn stone that sends him hurling forward. Unable to stop his momentum, the cleric rolls like a rag doll down the pavement. Its rough surface tears at the skin of his palms and stitches of his garb, ripping both apart with ease. A small boulder marks the end of his tumble. He hits it headfirst. A pounding ache wraps his skull as his vision blurs. The distorted, phantom faces of his friends are the last thing he imagines before slipping into a darkness that quiets him in the gnarled weeds beside the road.

Chapter Twenty-One

A thunderous crash, like a thousand mirrors all breaking at once, wakes Viktor from his restless sleep in the dead of night. "The fuck?" he spits, jumping from his mattress to the window. Pulling back the curtain, the warrior can just barely see aethereal shards of purple and gold laying on the ground where the magical barrier once stood. "Oh fuck!" he shouts, springing into action. He straps on his armor quicker than ever before, but as he slides into his boots, he hears a commotion of voices sound throughout the tavern, followed by the crumbling of brick and a hair-raising shriek that doubles his pace.

"No! Aah—leave her alone!" yells a raspy voice from down the hall. Viktor sprints to it with the speed of a stallion. Ahead of him, still only dressed in her frilly undergarment, Sable blasts open the door to room number eight with an arcane bolt. Cassianna is standing behind her, shaken to the bone. The witch runs inside, tailed by the half-orc. Upon entering, they are shocked to find Nyx crumpled on the floor, clutching a bleeding wound on their stomach. Blood seeps between their fingers and spurts as they try to scream again.

"Stop!" chokes Cassianna, pushing past the guildmates to hold them in her arms. "Sable, help her!"

Outside, four human forms are backlit by a shimmering lapis oval that leads to a place high up, overlooking the city. Three of the stunning silhouettes glide backward through the portal, while one, with long, black hair that billows forward from the wind behind it, stands and stares. It carries the kicking figure of Adinine securely with one arm, pinning her elbows to her waist. Its other hand is clasped tightly around her mouth, all but silencing her would-be screams.

In a split-second decision, Sable fires off three more bolts of energy aimed at the captor's head, but its eyes glow a deep gold in response. Her spell is countered with the vampire's own, and it fizzes out into nothing. The silhouette chuckles before backstepping through the portal.

Meanwhile, Viktor sprints toward the culprits, enraged. But by the time he reaches them, the portal disappears in his face. He runs into the wall of a building across from the inn with a knuckle-cracking thud.

"Uugh!" roars Viktor.

"Adinine," cries her sister. "Where did they take her?"

"W-what happened?" asks Nyx through a throat-closing pain. "Why? She... she opened the window for them." Glass and brick lie before the gaping hole where it was once inset.

"They used portal magic. There were four of them," Sable rambles between quick, heavy breaths. "Four. This changes everything. And that spellcraft? Sh-shit. The castle. They must have gone to the castle. We have no choice but to follow them now."

Viktor hoists himself upright and rushes back to inspect Nyx's injury. Hot blood spills through the claw-like gashes in their shirt. Grabbing a sheet from the bed and tearing it into strips, he dresses the wound. "Celest," he calls out at maximum volume while holding pressure on the fabric. "Where's Celest? Did they take him?"

Sable leaves the room in a rush and almost runs headfirst into the innkeeper, who is standing like a frightened dog in the hallway. "You," barks Sable. "What room is the elf in?"

"What's going on?" she whimpers. "Those screams. I heard brick breaking. What the fuck's happening in there?"

"We are under attack," explains the halfling with the speed of an auctioneer. "Vampires. There is no time. We need the elf. Where is he?"

"*Vuhm*-um. Room twelve. U-upstairs," she stutters in response.

Before she can ask any further questions, Sable dashes down the hall and up the steps. She finds the numbered placard and jiggles the locked door handle while calling out the cleric's name. Upon hearing no response, she again uses a spell to blast the door off its hinges. The room is empty. Judging by the chilling bite in the air, the window has been open for an unsettling amount of time. Not a single hint of the cleric's belongings are present. Even the bedsheets and pillows are perfectly arranged as if he hadn't even touched them.

"Celest," she calls, stumbling backward through the doorframe. The witch scrambles back down the stairs to the eighth room, again finding the barkeep standing in the hallway. Her mouth is covered in shock, taking note of the damages and her bleeding patron. "Miss," shouts Sable. "Are you positive about that room number? Did you see him leave the tavern at any point after I turned in for the night?"

She blinks without looking away, trying to absorb the content of the questions asked. "Room twelve," she repeats. "I'm sure, but no. I've been behind the bar all night. If the elf left, I would have seen him. Only my family and I have keys to the back doors."

"If anyone else is here, please tell them to stay put in their rooms until morning. That includes yourself," orders the witch. "The vampire can charm its victims. Lock the windows and draw the blinds. Go, tell anyone else."

Perturbed but compliant, the innkeeper runs off down the hallway while Sable reenters room eight.

"Where is Celest?" growls Viktor again. He and Cassianna are both huddled over Nyx. Their clammy cheeks are a pale gray as their eyelids flutter, holding weakly to consciousness, over unfocused, jade-green irises. Nyx mumbles something inaudible before slumping over onto Cassianna's lap.

"He's not here," confesses the halfling. "The window to his room is open. I... I have no idea. It appears that he's been gone. Maybe for over an hour. The room was freezing cold. His clothes are missing. He's missing."

Viktor lets out a lion's roar and strikes the ground with his fist before picking up the unconscious human off the ground.

Cassianna stands, taking her sibling from his arms. "Go, please," she chokes between sobs. "I'll take care of Nyx. Just go. Save Adinine. Sable, please. We can't afford to lose her. Please."

Sable nods, unwelcome tears welling along her waterline. "Viktor, we have no other choice," she whispers through the knot of anxiety on her tongue. "We head to the castle. Now. He could be there too."

He picks up his shield off the floorboards as Sable reaches to grab the lantern from the dresser. "I hope for his sake that he's not. Two versus four. We've had worse odds," says Viktor. "Cass, if—when Nyx wakes up, try to keep 'em awake. We'll be back with your sister and four fanged heads strapped to my belt. Good luck."

After leaving for a moment to dress, Sable returns.

He swings the witch up over his shoulders like a backpack and takes off, running out of the hole in the wall to the street. Usually opposed to being carried, the halfling swallows her pride for the sake of speed.

"Take this left to Main Street," she orders, clutching tightly with one arm to the strap over his shoulder. "From there, head north. Right. Adinine told me it's a straight shot from there, a few miles. Where the road ends, there is a pathway leading up to the castle."

They turn the corner and continue down the wet pavement. "Right on main. Hold tight," replies the warrior through a clenched jaw. He keeps his pace with athletic prowess, never once stopping to catch his breath, and within twenty minutes, they reach the outskirts of the city. The buildings here are by far the most neglected, appearing as if no one has stepped foot in this quarter for decades at least.

Some structures are no more than piles of rubble and dust. Bushy fern and scarlet basil, which were presumably once common yard plants, have overrun the man-made structures, reclaiming them for the natural world. If the halfling has time to spare, she might admire the haunting beauty of their surroundings.

Finally, Viktor halts. He kneels down to let the witch off his back, and they continue a brisk walk in lieu of rest. His massive shoulders rise and fall as he wipes the sweat and rain from his brow with his forearm. "Fuck," he huffs. "I'm worried about this. Do you think Celest went there on his own? He said last night that he wanted to try talking it out. I was acting like an asshole afterward and I think it pissed him off. What if I sent him over the edge?"

"I don't know," she admits, speaking as fast as the thoughts form in her mind. "He did mention a desire for... nonviolent resolution. But it's a stretch to think he would go out on his own to, what, reason with the enemy? It can't be. There's no way that's the answer here, but I can't think of a better explanation. Has he been charmed from the first meeting? I should have checked him. Fuck's sake—I don't know how they managed to break through the barrier. I'm deeply concerned with their level of magical ability. It's something I was not expecting. Did you see the way that vampire blocked my attack with just a look?"

Sable has to jog to keep up with the half-orc's quick stride.

"I've been too harsh on him. Maybe it was me," replies Viktor, whose heart rate is almost back to normal, "He's been acting... different lately. I've just been ignoring it. But yeah, I saw him block your spell. I really don't know how we're gonna pull this one off, especially without our healer. We might be marching to our deaths here. I'm gonna ask you one time. Do you think it's worth it? To put our lives on the line for these strangers? We could just find Celest, get out of here, go back to the guild, and get our next assignment."

"They're friends now, Viktor," mutters Sable with a determined gleam in her eye. "We promised to help, and it's not like this is our first deadly encounter. I know this isn't a guild mission, but we're adventurers. It's our job to be in danger. Let's not forget that Celest, too, might be there needing our help. We can't just run away."

The warrior nods decidedly. "Alright," he says. "But if I die in there and you don't, I'm gonna haunt your ass for the rest of your—" His words are cut short when his eyes catch a glimpse of something bright sprawled out on the side of the road that clearly doesn't belong there. "Is that... Sunshine?" he asks, calling out to the figure.

The pair race up to the elf's unconscious body, and Viktor is the first to arrive. A wound on his head turns a strand of his snow-white hair red as strawberries in the summertime, and a hundred smaller scrapes across his golden skin and robes make him appear as a sketched illustration. The warrior checks for breathing, placing his calloused hand under the elf's nose. "He's alive." Viktor sighs. "Hey. Wake up. Sunshine. Wake up." The warrior gently shakes his shoulder, and when that fails to work, he tickles the side of his ribs, but that also doesn't rouse him. Viktor notices, among the shallow cuts, deep purple kiss marks on the elf's neck that raise a whole host of new questions for the half-orc to consider. An unsettling ache in his gut gives him pause.

"Be careful with him. Hold his leg," commands the witch. "I read about this trick in a speculative medicine book once."

The warrior complies, and she rears back her leg and kicks the underside of the elf's foot with the hard tip of her shoe.

"Ah—ooh. Ow. Shit." The action leaves her big toe throbbing for a few moments, but Celest's eyelids quiver open.

Through blurred vision, he begins to see a brown face appear and beaded braids hovering over him. They swing to the side as the face says something indistinguishable as if he were hearing it through water. "C... st... ake up... Celest," it calls, increasingly clearer. It's Viktor, and Sable comes into sight over his shoulder.

"Where... where am I?" whispers the cleric, using his arm to sit himself up on his hip. His hand wanders to a pulsing pain on his skull and pulls away with its fingers warm and red. "Julian... He's—" begins the cleric.

"Celest, don't talk just yet. You need to heal yourself, quickly," interrupts Sable. "Where's the sunstone? That should help you." Before answering, her hands pat him until feeling a small lump in one of his socks. She reaches in, pulling the shining gem from the fabric, and curls his bloody hand around it. "Focus," she insists. "A full heal. You've got this."

Celest does as he's told, and the moment a whisper of holy magic collects in his fist, radiant warmth spirals around him. Bright beams of sunlight escape through his clenched fingers. And as his blood pulls back under his skin, his eyes burst open, glowing yolk-yellow as the sun at high noon. His mouth gapes to exhale, and it too, spills sunlight past his lips. In a quarter of the time it would normally take, Celest is feeling like himself again, perfectly healed. He immediately lunges forward, catching the two of them in a tight hug as tears dribble from his eyes.

"Oh, thank the goddess," he blurts out. "You're safe. You're safe." His cheeks press into their own, which yields a soft smile from the witch and a pained grimace from the warrior who pulls away first.

"Where the hell have you been? What happened?" asks Viktor in agitated desperation. He stands, pulling up the elf with him.

Sable takes a handful of the cleric's robe in her hand and leads him forward toward the castle. "There's no time for that," she informs. "They've captured Adinine. We need to stop them. Hurry."

The warrior's hands return to the cleric's shoulders. Staring him in the eyes, he repeats sternly, "Celest, what happened? What have they done to you?"

Guilt and shame weigh visibly heavy on the elf, who squirms under Viktor's gaze. "I wanted to make peace. At first, he agreed, but I was a fool. They hurt me. They threatened you. I'm so sorry."

His grip loosens until it falls. "Let's go kill these fuckers," says Viktor before taking off up the pathway.

"I'm so sorry, Sable," Celest says as they run after him. The rain is full now. It falls like darts from the woolen hands of the night-black clouds, adding challenge to the already difficult ascent.

She lets out an aching sigh and repeats, "I said there's no time for that. You're safe now. Focus on your footing. We'll talk later."

Led by the warrior, they run like hell toward the monstrous structure before them. Its black stone face almost disappears in the darkness of the hour, but dim light from inside illuminates its windows as if it were expecting its guests. As they approach, an unnerving melody reaches their ears. The music possesses a grandeur, vibrant and clean, with an eerie thickness that resonates deeply into the listeners' skulls. Its pitch range is incredible, and its musician is masterful.

They stop at the foot of the stairs leading up to the entrance's grand double doors. They stand at least ten feet tall, bearing ornate metalwork that resembles the head of a raven toward the top and gilded feathers below it. Two long, stained glass windows flank each side like wings. Without a second thought, the half-orc charges up the steps and bashes through the right window with his shield. After a quick look from left to right, he beckons his teammates to follow.

Helping them both over the ledge, they find themselves in the castle's entrance hall. Gray marble floors are centered with plum-colored qua-trefoil rugs, and decorative suits of armor are set into semicircular dips in the walls. Hanging on the high ceiling, elegant quartz chandeliers light the main hallway that leads deeper into the castle's roaring belly. The music vents down the hall from that direction. Viktor gives himself a motivating shake and prepares to rush the noise but is paused by a hand on his arm.

"Wait. My blessings," says the cleric. He traces the symbols for bear's strength in elvish with a glittering finger in the air before pressing it through Viktor's chest. The half-orc's muscles swell slightly in response as he lets out a feral breath through his nose. Next comes hawk's eye, which he bestows on Sable, whose pupils dilate with newfound keenness. Lastly, for himself, he casts cat's grace to counteract his own clumsiness. "I'll remind you that these will last thirty minutes to an hour," explains the elf. "I hope... we won't need to use them."

Heated within from the enchantment, the words' implication causes the warrior to finally snap. He roughly grabs the cleric by the robes over his chest and lifts him onto his tiptoes. "Celest," he snarls. "I swear on your goddess, if you think this won't end in death, you're mad. Let's make sure it's not ours."

The elf nods meekly, is unhanded, and the warrior leads the party once more. Chaotic emotion rots the cleric's chest with each step forward. The plans of action slip away from him one by one as the feeling grows, and it makes even blinking a labor of will.

The others, although anxious, show no signs of trepidation. Their conviction to rescue Adinine from the vampires' wretched grasp propels them on. Whatever happens now, it ends tonight.

Ahead, the hall opens up into a grand ballroom, aglow by hundreds of candles in sconces and an enormous chandelier that hangs from the center of the ceiling. It's ringed with painted frescoes that depict humans naked and bound in all manners by blooming rose bushes. The expressions displayed are diverse, ranging from exalted euphoria to sheer agony.

Each is pierced with thorns. Each bleeds into the others around them. The style is not at all like the portraits admired by Celest upstairs or the pieces in the shrine. The strokes are deeper, darker, and hyperreal. At the furthest end of the ballroom, four marble steps lead to a platform that secures the largest instrument the three have ever seen. Its pipes stretch toward the ceiling in sets like soldiers standing in rank on the battlefield. With unseen breath, they sing each rich note through slotted mouths close to their base. And, below them, three sets of keyboards, akin to that of a piano, are layered like stair steps on top of one another.

Fingering the keys in expert time is Julian Markov.

His back is turned to them, and the raven hair on his head falls past the seat he's taken. Another layer of key-like foot pedals are being pressed by his shoes. Laying in front of the seat is an unconscious Adinine. Copper-colored hair covers her face, and a thin stream of blood from her wrist trails down the white marble. At the trail's end is Seong, dipping her finger in the little puddle there and bringing the crimson liquor to her lips. To her right sit Zoan and Iliya. Leaning on each other, their eyes are closed as if to fully immerse themselves in the serenade. The music slows to a stop once the three adventurers reach the ballroom's threshold, and Celest nearly collapses at the sight.

"Viktor. Sable. Sweet Celest," says Julian, turning on the seat to face them. "Welcome to my home."

Chapter Twenty-Two

Three adventurers, standing at one end of the palace ballroom, collectively clench their fists. For two, the reason is simple fury. The sight of Adinine, limp and bleeding at the foot of the massive instrument's seat, is more than enough to spark a blazing rage in their chests.

For the third and most sensitive among them, a vacuum pit of betrayal threatens to consume him from the inside out. It chokes the air from his lungs. The feeling only grows as his eyes dash from his newly acquainted suitors to the unconscious human at their whim. Finally, they land in a fixed stare upon the monstrous man that, even still, despite his wickedness, holds sway over his tender heart. Celest breaks into a fevered sweat and freezes at the sound of Julian's voice.

Viktor's roar fills the chamber as fully as the organ pipes once had. "Step away from that girl," he shouts with the force of an explosion. In one swift movement, he takes the silver dagger from his belt and brandishes it.

Sable, too, readies into an offensive casting position. The air around her crackles with arcane energy, prepared for release at a moment's notice. The cleric, however, remains trapped in his own mental anguish, still as prey in hiding.

Seong sits up on the steps and lets out an arrogant laugh. Her lips are tinted red with Adinine's blood. "My nails are longer than that blade, big man," she scoffs. "Do you think that's a weapon? I'd pick my teeth with that little thing."

"Now, now," mumbles Zoan. "Let's not emasculate our guest. It's unbecoming."

"Surely," adds Iliya. "Where are your manners?" She slides over to Seong and lays her head down onto her lap, petting the chin-length, black hair that frames her face.

"Step away," roars Viktor again. "Now. Or else I'll show you how deep I can get this little dagger into your necks."

This time Seong's laughter is shushed with Iliya's finger pressed onto her lips.

Julian smiles, reclining on his arm and casually crossing his legs. "Pardon my dear pets," he says. "I will, however, have to decline. You see, Viktor, this girl belongs to me. She always has. But worry not. She is still breathing, although I may have been overzealous when feeding from her. It appears that she has fainted, and I'll need her awake for this next part."

Through stuttering teeth, Celest pushes out the words, "J-Julian. Please. St-stop. You don't have to do this." He leans forward a few inches as he attempts, and fails, to approach the vampires. The cleric catches Seong rolling her eyes at his plea while the rest wait, unafflicted with emotion, for him to say anything further.

When he doesn't, Julian replies, "Oh, but I do, my sweet. The responsibility has fallen upon me to teach someone a lesson. I've been slighted and simply will not allow that to go unpunished." The vampire looks down at the body at his feet and, with the toe of his shoe, flips Adinine face up. The pastel blue nightgown she wears begins to soil with blood from her wrist, and hair falls away from her face, yet she remains still as a corpse.

Another rage-filled roar erupts from the warrior, and he stampedes like a bull toward Julian. Simultaneously, Sable conjures bolts of energy from her palm and shoots them forth with the speed of arrows.

Barely moving his wrist, Julian shoos away the advances, dispelling the witch's attack and knocking Viktor backward with a barrier spell. It advances across the room and hits Celest and Sable like a strong wind, causing them both to flinch.

"Let us not act hastily now," hums Julian. "You've only just arrived. And I know you're eager to save this weakling, but I am afraid it's out of the question. Her soul belongs to me, and it has for hundreds of years. All those who enter my domain become unable to leave. In a way, you all are mine already."

"I'd die before I'd let that happen," growls Viktor, squaring up to charge him again and clenching the muscles in his jaw.

Each vampire laughs at the sentiment before Julian responds, "I do like your passion. But, unfortunately for you, death would not be a release. Like all others, the moment you entered, your soul became trapped in this place. Death would be a momentary reprieve from my company. But you would soon be reborn. Your features might change slightly with each new birth, but your soul will remain the very same. You might like that, seeing as your bloodline is tainted. It's likely, though, that you'll come out with tusks and be cast into the river. Or perhaps, your family will lock you in a basement, ashamed of their deformity of a child. I bet you'll be killed and reborn hundreds of times until you're finally made correctly."

The half-orc grunts through his nose at the insult and again sprints forward.

"Viktor, wait!" shouts the witch, but he doesn't listen.

He gets in closer than last time, but before he can reach the steps, Julian whispers Zoan's name. The vampire, almost equally matched with the warrior in stature, appears between him and his target in an instant. A stone-dense kick to his chest again sends Viktor flying backward and sliding across the marble floor on his knees.

Julian yawns theatrically, and says, "Ah, so brutish, Viktor. It must be that orcish heritage of yours. Little Sable, though, seems relatively keen. Not many here possess magic, and even fewer realize that they do. I'm glad to have you. The blood of a mage is a vibrant flavor. It's the favored treat of one of my pets, in fact." His tongue glides tauntingly over his teeth, and he winks in her direction, causing her skin to prickle at the insinuated violation. He makes no attempt at subtlety. "I wonder how yours tastes," he adds.

Celest can feel the halfling's agitation radiate from her body like static in the air on a dry winter's day as Julian continues, again looking down at his victim. "This one, though, might prove difficult to train. She already holds such resentment toward me. Not to mention, her loved ones are still living. Probably. Iliya left quite the mark on that little blind one. And the other has a habit of taking, uh, *her* own life. This latest incarnation of that particular soul is the oldest it's ever been. Usually, around age fourteen, it kills itself. It's fascinating, really, to witness these human cycles repeating over and over again like an opera. But I digress. Maybe I should let this version of Katya die and save myself the effort of polishing out her disdain for me, especially considering the fact that I have a few new toys occupying my interest." He pauses, still sitting, to scan his eyes across the length of her body. "Three centuries ago I was forced to end her after she was sired. It robbed me of the pleasure of tasting her last breath. I know hers would be the sweetest... In any case, I've not decided just yet."

Celest's eyes are cracked wide with worry. After absorbing the information, he finally chokes, "What-what do you mean we're trapped here? And you... you said the curse would break if your love was reunited.

You... lied to me." The elf's heart threatens to break through his chest and shrivel on the ballroom floor.

Sable moves to his side, confusion marking wrinkled lines on her face, but her body language remains grounded. "Don't listen to a word that snake hisses, Celest. It's all just a ploy to frighten you. Keep focused. Ready your spells," she whispers.

"What was that, little mouse?" he asks in a sinister purr, flamboyantly tucking his hair behind his ear. "Did you call me a snake? Do you so wish for my venom?" As he turns to face her, one side of his robe falls from his shoulder. Only dark trousers, that tighten as he spreads apart his knees, are underneath. "I could give you just that if you're begging for it," he promises.

A rotting sensation in the elf's gut gives way to nausea. The feeling, though seldom explored, is evident. It's a bubbling, viscous anger. It tears at his throat as he shouts across the room, "Did all your words mean nothing? Are your promises as fragile as dried daisies, ready to crumble upon the slightest touch?" His shoulders shudder as tears fall from his lashes onto the marble floor.

Attempting to read into her teammate's outburst, Sable's gaze follows Celest's to Julian, who looks down his nose at the cleric as the corner of his lip curves into a sadistic grin. Taking advantage of her temporarily enhanced perception, she picks up something else to his countenance. The yearning of a lover is glazed over his eyes, but there's no time to calculate the possible implications that arise within the witch's mind because of it.

Entirely unaware of his guildmate's new concerns, Viktor's boot stomps the floor, and its echo bounces across the ceiling. "Enough pageantry, freak show," taunts the warrior. "Which one of you ugly corpses wants to fight me? Come here, and we'll see how long you can last."

Seong's ruby eyes light up in excitement as she wiggles away from Iliya to stand at the foot of the steps. "I'll take you on, dog. You do look like the most fun of the three," she chirps. "I can't wait to rip each fiber of muscle away one by one from those big bones of yours."

Her left leg wraps behind her, and just before dashing forward, Sable picks up on her intent. "Celest, now," she commands. "Aim at Viktor."

Without thinking, the elf complies with her direction and casts a holy blast while the halfling uses an arcane bolt once more. The cleric's golden ray, flanked by a swirling helix of the witch's thin purple bolts, flies toward the warrior in perfect sync at the same time that Seong begins charging for him.

Her speed is incredible, reaching his location in just a few seconds to slash her clawed nails into his chest piece as she pirouettes on the ball of her left foot. The blow isn't nearly as brutal as Zoan's, but its force again pushes the half-orc back across the marble.

In that same instant, the spells impact, blasting into the smallest vampire with their combined strength. Her pained scream is piercing, she stumbles to the right, and Viktor takes his opportunity to strike back. The edge of the silver blade kisses her cheek, only slightly splitting it but singeing the skin upon contact before she retreats backward by forty feet.

"You rats!" she exclaims at the party, then looks back to Julian. "Why didn't you shield me?"

"You dare speak to me in that tone? That's yet another mark against you tonight," he replies coldly. "You wanted to fight without awaiting my command, did you not? Why would I waste any energy to help you? You absolutely deserve the pain you've been dealt, maybe more."

She huffs an aggravated exhale through her nose and fights to keep her mouth shut.

"But, I am in a good mood," he continues. "Additionally, I require time to decide what I am to do with poor Katya. So, if it's a fight you all are craving—" Julian closes his eyes for a moment in contemplation as he speaks, and Sable again takes the opportunity to strike with her bolts. She attempts to shoot them silently, with as little fanfare as possible, but without even looking, Julian casually falls back onto the seat and dodges the attack. His smiling gaze meets hers, dripping with hubris, and he finishes his thought, "A fight you shall enjoy. Iliya. Zoan. Seong. Entertain our guests. Do with them what you will but return Celest to me as unscathed as possible. That is an order. As for the other two... I'll leave them to your discretion. Surprise me. Go."

The two vampires seated on the steps rise and flank their smaller ally. "I want the big one. I'm gonna tear him apart like tender pork," hisses Seong through her fanged teeth. Her scarlet eyes twinkle with feral excitement.

"I'll take the cute little lady," hums Iliya. "I've never tasted halfling before, and she looks like a perfect bite-sized morsel, no? A light snack?" Although she blows a sensual kiss in Sable's direction, the witch is anything but amused, and unfazed by her voluminous beauty. Instead, she hones in on the dip of her neck like an archer to their target.

Zoan throws his hands behind his head nonchalantly, remarking, "That leaves me to capture our lord's prize. Hello again, Celest. Why don't you be a good boy and just come to me now? You could save us both a lot of trouble. You'd absolutely be in our lord's good graces if you'd come back begging on your hands and knees for forgiveness. He's fond of you. I would advise you to take advantage of that."

The cleric swallows a knot of emotion as Viktor sidesteps closer to his allies.

"You won't touch either of them, freaks," growls the warrior. He actively tries not to imagine what they've already done to Celest, but a fear of the unknown quickly gives way to a boiling rage within him. With no intention of abandoning each other, the guildmates poise themselves to fight back against the villainous trio that taunts them. "Well?" grunts Viktor. "Bring it the fuck on, then."

Chapter Twenty-Three

The battle begins in an instant with the forward shift of Seong's right foot. The three attackers advance at terrifying speeds, the smallest being the quickest among them but not faster than Sable's reaction time. Accompanied by an outcry from her chest, the witch casts a thunderous wave of electricity that catches the vampires in its area of effect, slowing them by a considerable amount. Aside from that and slight flinches in their facial expressions, they seem relatively unfazed.

Before retreating to the backline, Celest reaches his arms outward toward his allies, his eyes flash with light, and blesses them both simultaneously with a shield of faith. The spell encases them in an aura of glittering gold that follows their movements like a second skin.

"Ah, I know that spell," comments Julian, spectating from the comfort of his seat. "It is impressive that you can cover two targets at once. Be sure to keep your focus, though, my sweet. You wouldn't want them succumbing to some terrible—"

In a protective fury, the warrior barks back, cutting him off, "Enough of the fucking pet names."

Julian continues as if uninterrupted, "As protected as they might be now if you lose concentration you'll be leaving your friends vulnerable to my pets' attacks." The cleric ignores him but does exactly that, clearing his mind of anything other than the safety of his guildmates.

Zoan is the first to escape the electric cage, strafing out to the side instead of a forward advance. Giving Viktor a wide berth, he passes behind him. His dilated pupils are fixed like a leopard to Celest's gazelle-thin frame.

The warrior attempts to cut him off but is confronted head-on by the second opponent to leave the purple lightning of Sable's spell.

Seong swings into a kick aimed at the half-orc's face but is blocked by his leather bracers and additionally by the cleric's shield-like aura. "Eyes on me, big man," she warns, going in for a slash to his abdomen that is all but unfelt due to the holy spell's protection. "If you can keep up with my speed, that is."

Viktor slams both fists down in retaliation, followed by a flurry of punches that fail to make contact with her quick, liquid form.

She dodges each with ease, chuckling. "I hope that's not your best, beast."

While distracted with Seong, Zoan takes the opportunity to dash past the half-orc, toward the elf, as Iliya finally escapes the electric web of the witch's evocation. Sable wastes no time, casting a holding enchantment on the advancing blonde by reaching into her pocket, pulling out a coin inscribed with the spell's sigil, and throwing the object at her feet. It succeeds, paralyzing her limbs in place with a ghostly rope that bursts from the enchanted object and wraps securely around the pink-tinted skin at her ankles and wrists. Translucent fibers then pull the skirt of her pine-green evening dress close to her body, further accentuating the plentiful curves underneath.

"If you wanted to tie me up you could have just said so, little witch." starts Iliya, gently biting down on her lower lip. "I would have eagerly complied." She purposefully gapes her mouth as the spell crawls up her neck then between her teeth, silencing her.

Ignoring the flirtation, Sable readjusts her gaze to track Zoan.

The vampire is nearly to Celest, who is hastily backing up to one side of the massive staircase. It leads to a balcony on the second floor that overlooks the ballroom beneath.

"Celest," shouts the witch. "Two sets of stairs on either side leading to the second floor. Get distance. Avoid him." Taking full advantage of his own blessing, the cleric uses his temporary grace to hop onto the wide, curved railing and runs up it as fast as possible to follow her strategy and create distance between Zoan and himself.

Compared to Seong, at least, this vampire moves more slowly, allowing for the cleric's escape. He follows but slows further to a deliberately casual stride as he ascends the steps.

The witch then turns to aid the warrior.

Engaged in a dance of sorts, he swings his fists with wild abandon and slashes with the dagger gripped in his right hand.

The dexterous vampire, less than five feet tall, easily avoids the attacks with twirls and skips as if it were as easy as a children's game. When the half-orc takes a moment to catch his breath, she gloats, "Aww, tired already?" She parts her lips to continue the insult, but Sable has already cast three arcane bolts in her direction. They strike the vampire in the center of her chest, knocking the breath from her lungs that she was going to use to further taunt him. Despite her bolstered ego, the surprise stuns her.

Viktor roars as his left fist makes contact with the underside of her button-round chin. The force lifts her off her feet, and he stabs the dagger into her hip, turning its blade while shoving it deeper inside. She shrieks as it burns her flesh, and she kicks off his chest to land as far back from the warrior as she can. Landing hard on her knees, she shakes on the marble floor as she looks up at him with a rage that cracks blue veins into her forehead. "Aww, had enough?" spits Viktor. "Two hits, and you're ready to give up? You don't have to let pride get you killed, corpse bitch."

Despite his provocation, his breath is noticeably heavy. Beads of sweat drip from his rounded nose and plop onto the breastplate of his armor.

Before her holding enchantment breaks, Sable casts one more bolt evocation, but Seong is ready for it this time and rolls out of the way.

Julian chuckles and reaches his hand behind him to play a disparaging riff on the organ keys. "So close, little Sable," he hums. "But you should be paying attention to your own opponent."

She looks back over her shoulder to see her spell fading and Iliya biting clean through the ghostly rope that binds her tongue.

"Ugh," she scoffs. "So rude to shut me up with something other than your tender skin." She rips through the rest of the cords as the spell dissipates and stomps on the coin, flattening the sigil engraved into it. "There, enough of that" Iliya sighs. "Now, where were we?"

Meanwhile, Zoan reaches the top of the steps, locking eyes with the cleric who is poised at the railing of the opposite set of stairs. "Alright, Celest," says the approaching vampire. "I'll give you one more chance to come quietly to me. Let's go watch this play out by our master's side, shall we? He'll surely be pleased with your change of heart. Your little party would be spared. Come now. Don't make this difficult. You'll most definitely regret it."

The elf ignores the vampire's threats and invitations, solely concentrating on shielding his friends from harm. Zoan stops for a moment, ten feet or so away from his target. "No?" he asks. "Is that really your final decision? Well... Don't say later that I didn't warn you." He springs forward toward the elf but just barely fails to grab hold.

Celest evades by sliding down the railing on his feet as if he were a sportsman boarding down a snow-covered hill.

"You're going to make me go all the way back down there?" bemoans Zoan as Julian politely applauds the impressive maneuver. The cleric then runs back to the base of the opposite staircase he ascended in a continued effort to ignore and evade his pursuer.

With the warrior busy trying to catch Seong as she strikes at him with the vigor of a woodpecker, the witch faces Iliya alone. Adrenaline surges through her system as she casts a mirror image, creating three identical copies of herself.

"Mmm," hums the vampire facing her. "Three on one? Well, now it might be a fair fight."

One of the three versions of Sable takes off running toward Adinine's direction, shooting a lesser bolt of fire at Iliya, who hones in on her movement without skipping a beat. It misses. A second and third flame, however, cast from the two who stayed back, spit through the air and both hit their target. They strike the vampire's exposed shoulder and cheek but sizzle out quickly, not even leaving a mark.

To catch the witch by her ankle, Iliya swoops forward as she nears the steps where Adinine lies unconscious. But, as soon as pressure is applied by her grip, the witch turns to vapor, revealing itself to be one of the copies.

"Seong," calls out Zoan, who is leaning at the center of the second-floor railing and watching the battles beneath him. She looks up at him briefly, but it costs her a shallow slash to the thigh by Viktor's dagger. He lazily continues, "Be a good little sister and help me shepherd this disobedient lamb." She grits her teeth together in frustration, rushes forward toward the warrior, then slides under his legs before he can retaliate. By the time he turns around, she is already chasing the cleric up the staircase.

Both versions of Sable follow Seong's movement and try to call out to Celest in warning but are stopped by Iliya's beet-red heels that screw through the air like projectile weapons and strike each in the stomach. The copy evaporates instantly, but the original curls forward in pain.

"Found the real one," she sings. "What's my prize for winning?" In an attempt to further separate the three, Iliya positions herself between the witch and her guildmates while she recovers from the blow.

Stumbling up the steps and shouting profanities, the warrior gives it his all, trying to catch up with Seong's deathly speed, but he isn't fast enough. At the top, Zoan cuts off Celest's exit and forces him down a hallway deeper into the castle. "Good work, love," praises Zoan. "I'll let you pick the next book we read together." His pursuit begins again, striding down the hall behind the cleric. "Provided you can defeat the beast at your heels, that is."

Dark blades of chin-length hair swipe across her cheeks as she turns with quickness to face Viktor again. Tiptoeing backward up the remaining steps, she avoids the edge of his blade and the grip of his calloused fingers by mere threads of space.

Once solidly situated on the second floor, she looks about. To the left, she could run across the second-story overlook, down the other staircase, and back into the ballroom, or into the western hallway, a mirror of the one behind her. To her right, on the other hand, is a tinted-glass window with a midnight view of the courtyard. An idea pops into mind, grafting a sickening smile into place. "Come on, half-blood," she taunts. "Come 'n get me."

And, like a bull to a red cape, the warrior charges. Lashing at her and gnashing his tusked teeth, he runs full force in her direction, but she uses his approach against him. Running up the side of the wall, just out of reach, she now stands behind his back. As he is mid-turn and at his least balanced, she leaps up, swings from a bronze candle sconce fastened to the wall and kicks him in the shoulder blade with both her tiny feet. This, along with his already forward momentum, leaves him tumbling toward the window. In a frantic, last-resort maneuver, Viktor unhooks the shield from his back and holds it close to his face. The center metal disc makes first contact with the glass, breaking it all at once into a spiderweb of pieces. Down falls the warrior through the splintered window and crashes to the ground below.

Chapter Twenty-Four

"Viktor!" Sable screams. "Celest!" Their names echo on the walls, but neither reply. She can feel the spiritual shield held in place by the cleric's concentration gradually thinning, and desperation now seeps into her expression. Backed into the top right corner of the room, her dread is palpable and thickening.

Making things worse, to her right, a vampire plays a chilling composition that quickens in intensity with each breath she takes. And, just ahead, another enemy licks her lips in anticipation while gently inching closer.

The set of double doors behind her is the witch's only possible saving grace. She withdraws to them, placing her gloved palms to the seam where they meet in the middle. The polished, antler-bone handles are set perfectly above her head as if they were her own, but instead of reaching for them, she recites aloud, *"Veranthya mahn heckta. Sevos."* The solid wood liquifies in place as her eyes flash an arcane purple. The witch slips through its temporary form like oil through water to make it onto the other side and finishes her spell. *"Relehvii,"* she demands, and the doors obey, sealing themselves together and reinforcing into the walls to become one solid obstacle for her attacker.

On what just a moment ago had been the set of doors, a terrible strength pounds twice. Muffled, Sable hears Iliya chuckle, "What a neat trick, you little magician. Are we playing hide-and-seek? Better hurry, or it won't be any fun." Already halfway down the hall, the witch snaps an illumination spell onto her thumb. The gentle, twinkling light reveals an ornate archway flanked by unlit sconces, the details of which are effortlessly captured by her enhanced vision. Its etchings are that of spiders, fish hooks, open eyes, and grapes, all hanging tenderly on green copper vines. Another pound is accompanied by the sound of wood beginning to crack. It shocks her forward and under the arch, placing her in the entrance of the castle Markovia's eastern library.

The walls stretch three stories high into a cone-shaped glass ceiling that invites a clear view of the cosmos choked by a layer of rain clouds. The architecture's effect means to instill in its viewer a sense of the inexhaustible pursuit of that which can be known and all that has yet to be discovered. Books of every kind are stacked along the walls to the ceiling, most accessible only by way of wheeled metal ladders. Filling in the center space, a long desk with many chairs holds what looks like hundreds of old tomes, flipped through and scattered across the tabletop. Religious lore, mathematical textbooks, poetry, maps, and many more lie on and over each other like lovely courtesans waiting to be plucked through at leisure. On any other occasion, being here would be a dream, but yet another pound and crack remind her that it's nothing if not a nightmare.

Bordering the center table, sets of bookshelves stand in obedient, mirrored rows. Sable scurries to the right, hides behind a stepping stool in the second aisle, and tries to solidify her next plan of action.

Back out in the hallway, Iliya smashes through the melded doors. Splintered bits of wood clatter to the ground followed by a high-pitched creak and snap as the vampire widens a space to crawl through. "Oh, little morsel," she sings. "Ready or not, *here I come.*" There's a texture to her voice, one that wasn't there just a moment ago. *"Where aaaaaare youuuu?"* she asks in a pitch that bends like a broken spine.

Sable dispels her light, and primal horror forces the halfling's hair to stand on end as she covers her nose and mouth to muffle the quickened breath and urge to scream. The fear isn't creeping. It smacks into her at full speed. The halfling's eyes begin to water as she idles, as helpless as the child who watched her village burn all those years ago. As a torrent of tears threaten to swell past her eyelids, she hears something enter the room. No longer do Iliya's steps sound like that of a prim and proper debutant. Something heavier takes their place, something elongated, something with claws.

Another sound, that of a book falling to the floor, disturbs the silence. It comes from the opposite side of the library. *"Silly snack,"* gurgles the vampire. *"You give yourself away."* The creature slides its weight across the floor toward the unexplained noise. Flesh squeaks over the stone floor tiles as it moves. In horrible disbelief, the witch questions her sanity. What, in fact, is she hiding from? Sable can't imagine the feminine beauty that was Iliya to be in any way comparable with the creature that searches for her now, lurching across the floor like a rat dragging a slug. The unknowing chills her to the bone. Has she gone mad with fright? Cold sweat beads on her cheeks, and dizziness weakens her legs until she grabs herself by the torso and holds herself in a tight hug. Sable's eyes pinch shut, and, in silence, the witch steals back her agency.

When her midnight eyes reopen, she notices scraps of ivory parchment at her feet. They look to be phrases ripped from books. Each piece is slightly off-color from the next and different in size and font. Together, they read:

"Not a sound

brave soldier for

Unholy death

focus on

the heart."

Again, the hardback spine of a fallen text on the other end of the room distracts the beast away from the witch. A slimy chortle echoes behind it.

Reaching a shivering hand down to the strange message at her feet, a sudden vision takes hold in the eye within her mind.

She finds herself in the castle courtyard.

Flashes of lightning bolt down from an angry sky as the image of Julian Markov shoves a fist through the torso of a younger man. They look related, sharing a similarly raven-toned hair color, but the latter is much shorter than his attacker. The man clings to the vampire's shoulders with a desperate weakness until the grasp goes limp, and he crumples to the ground. His skull hits the pavement with a crack, and his eyes slide lifelessly back in the witch's direction. As if breaking from the scene, a force puppets his mouth, warning, "Brave Sable. Her heart. Aim for her heart."

Spoken through death, the sound of her own name fills her with sickness. But, before she can purge it, the vision skips ahead in time.

Now she is placed within the room she had just escaped, the ballroom. Most of its features remain unchanged, but the fresco painted on the ceiling depicts a very different scene. Angels, cherubs, and birds dance together among a blooming of purple flowers. It would have been a true masterpiece had the eyes of every creature not been carved out by a malice-driven vandal. Below, again stands the vampire.

Two women are on their knees before him, one of which being the lovely Iliya. Her hand is on the other's back. She appears to be comforting the familiar woman, whose fists are clenched in rage by her sides. It takes a moment for the witch to realize this woman is Adinine. Her hair is a slightly darker hue and thicker texture, but the real difference is an unmistakable, inhuman beauty.

"Back away from her," seethes Julian. "Katya had her second chance, and she's wasted it."

"My name is Sofia," growls the woman in response. "You cannot make me your—" He slaps her heavy-handed across the cheek.

"*You* will not tell me what *I* cannot do," his sharp tongue spits as Iliya obediently flees to a safe stop on the northern wall. "You, a mere peasant that latched on to this family like a leech!" He strikes her again with a force that knocks her to the side. "Even then, when I loved you more than Damion ever could, you *denied* me!"

His boot kicks her in the gut, and she wails.

"You cannot continue to deny me!" he roars, pouncing on her with violent speed, and the vision blurs as if to shield the halfling from its vile reality. Once the distorted screams and brutality quiet, the scene is clear once more.

Iliya cries to herself silently, hands over her mouth, and slips into the hallway unnoticed. Standing over the woman, Julian pants with rage. Her body is twisted, her clothing torn, and one leg is broken beyond repair. The fasten of his pants is undone. "Look at what you've made me do," he says. "Look at yourself. Disgusting. You've ruined it. Again." He lurches across the ballroom floor to the staircase and rips a baluster away from the handrail. The splintered edge drags across the marbled floor as he returns to her. "And now it falls to me. To end it. Again." Julian stamps his boot to pin her shoulder, and a final shriek escapes her teeth before she's stabbed through the heart and dissolves into ash.

Dripping liquid from the ceiling pulls the witch's attention upward. Black tears fall from the defaced eye sockets of an angel above them. It goes unnoticed by all but Sable as the scene breaks again. The fresco speaks, "Through the heart to kill the beast that hunts you. She'll smell you soon enough. Steel yourself, brave Sable. Vanquish this monster, then the next." With those words to guide her, the vision ends. Her senses are back in the library to face a present as awful as the memories she bore witness to.

Across the room, the beast of Iliya grumbles, *"Are you playing silly tricks, magician?"* A long, wet sniff is followed by the words, *"You can't hide from me for long, sweet treat."* The halfling quietly clenches her jaw, preparing to be found, and readies two spells in either tight fist. Slugging over the floor, the monster approaches the other side of the tall bookshelf that hides her. Mouth parting like a spoiled sludge swamp, Iliya speaks, *"I can taste your—Ah!"*

She is cut off by Sable, who loosens her left hand that holds a barrier spell. The witch casts it at the bookshelf, pushing forward and crashing the structure down onto the vampire's head. It writhes under the books and wood as one fleshy, clawed arm pierces through the wreckage. It's quickly followed by another, then a foot that's just the same. A tangle of hair begins to surface, but before she can emerge, Sable casts with her right hand a powerful ball of purple fire that blasts from the center of her palm with a loud boom. It easily catches the papers and splintered wood around the monster in a bright, engulfing blaze that leaves the creature panicked and screaming. The witch reflexively backs away as its form becomes visible, then she is halted as her spine hits another shelf behind her.

Loose from the wreckage, Iliya squirms across the room as she frantically shakes off the burning flame. Her limbs are elongated and knotted at the joints. Inhuman fingers stretch like the claws of a lizard into sharp, serrated points. On all fours, its stomach drags to the floor and feeds into a tube of a rib cage that balloons out asymmetrically at the chest. The creature oozes saliva from the loose, needle-toothed jaw that hangs from its face as the last bit of charred skin is snuffed, screeching all the while. It then quiets, turning its hollowed gaze to meet Sable's.

Between them, the wreckage fire continues to burn and reflects off their two sets of widened eyes. Instinct fueling action, the witch gathers a torrent of arcane force behind her, but not soon enough. The monster thuds forward, piercing straight through the halfling's shoulders, pinning her to the bookshelf. Excruciating pain shocks the air from her lungs and is replaced by the vile stench of old blood and rot from Iliya's disfigured maw. She shrieks like murder inches away from the halfling's face.

"Fuck!" the witch screams. "You!" Following her words like an order, the tomes behind her shape into sharpened cones and rocket from their shelves at the creature. The impact sends it hurtling backward, but as its embedded fingers shred their way out of the halfling's shoulders, the sawtooth serrations hack new damage into the flesh. Whatever pain she had felt before came nothing close to this, but her focus only wavers a fraction of a moment. "Eat," she cries again, tearing at her vocal cords. "Shit!" More books from other shelves join the attack. Her hands outstretch to guide them to the beast and pin her like an insect, high on the western wall.

It rebuttals between primordial screams almost unintelligibly, *"I'll slice you into little bits and eat you like hors d'oeuvres."* Spoiled ichor flows from its wounds, soaking the wall as it drags downward, but disgust is set aside as the witch calculates the next piercing blow through its chest. Before contact is made, a wet gasp is followed by an internal gurgling as something inside the creature moves to the right and dodges the attack. *"No,"* Iliya pleads. *"No, stop!"*

Sable follows its movement, sending another weaponized tome through the beast. Again the organ escapes, this time down past her rib cage.

"Please, I'll spare you, little witch!" Iliya's facial features soften, folding back into the beauty she once portrayed. "Please, don't! I can help you and your friends escape this place! I can distract my lord—please!"

A battle cry erupts from the halfling's lungs as dozens of books bend to her will, all at once striking the vampire through every bit of exposed flesh, succumbing her to dry, flaking ash.

Out of breath, without a care, and nearly out of mana, Sable stumbles away from the burning library and heads for the ballroom.

Chapter Twenty-Five

Outside, pouring sheets of rain-blackened clouds smother the moon's light. Viktor lays prone on top of his shield, burrowed in a bed of stained glass and roses. The bush at least has broken his fall, but the blunt force of it has left him bashed and bruised. A pained moan bumbles past his teeth as he begins to shake his daze and push himself upright. The courtyard is ahead of him, its slick stone appearing as a dark, still ocean.

Above the warrior, a voice laughs, "I see that tumble didn't do you in. Good. I'm not done fucking with you yet." Seong sits on the windowsill, kicking her legs back and forth, framed by the shards of glass that still hang to their encasing.

The half-orc rolls off of the rose bush with a grunt and realizes that Celest's holy protection has all but faded. "Still up for it?" asks the vampire. "I could turn around and finish off the little bitch if you don't want to keep playing." After a pause, she adds, "I'll let you guess which one of those weakling friends of yours I'm referring to."

Viktor stands to his feet, spits some blood from his mouth, and roars, "Come at me, cunt. Let's play your game. Watch me win." He shakes himself fully awake and picks up the dagger that had clattered to the stone as he fell. Shield at the ready, he braces into a defensive stance and awaits her next move.

The vampire giggles. "Perfect." Seong slides off her perch and descends the side of the castle, catching every tiny foothold with the ease of a spider until her bare feet land with a splash on the courtyard stone. She circles him slowly. In the dark, robed in a loose, black dress that reaches just above her knees, she is almost invisible to the half-orc's eyes. The candle-lit castle windows barely illuminate the exposed skin of her arms, face, and lower legs. "Can you even see me?" she muses. "Can you hear my steps?" She deliberately silences them, moving closer with extra care.

"Fuck around and find out," growls the warrior in response.

Smiling wide, she juts forward. Wind whistles past her as she moves while her tiny feet splash through a puddle, kicking up rainwater behind her.

Viktor uses the sound to anticipate her direction, and as she jumps into the air, fist raised backward to swing, he bashes her in the side with the front of his shield, still fueled with unnatural strength bestowed on him by the cleric. It knocks her to the ground, and he follows through with a slash from his silver blade that she rolls to avoid. The warrior retreats back into defense, unable to get a clear view of his opponent.

Seong stands upright. The dress, now soaked through, clings tightly to her slight frame. Agitated, she wonders aloud, "So can you see me? Or, can you hear me?" Hair falls over her face as she tilts her chin downward and slinks back near the bushes, out of reach from the castle's dim light.

The warrior steadies his breathing, taking the opportunity to assess his surroundings for an advantage. Trimming the castle are the wide rose bushes onto which he had fallen and where the vampire currently hides. The courtyard itself is a large, open space, aside from a single tree that has long grown through what was once a small crack. Its roots have overpowered the stone slabs at its base, reducing them to rubble. They hold the broken pieces like treasures. More trees like it skirt the courtyard's edges.

Viktor grips tightly to the brace of his shield and harkens back to his training, but oddly, an older memory of his sister comes to mind.

They stand together in the highland desert of his homeland, spears in hand. Brown shrubs freckle the landscape alongside the occasional gourd tree, its fat, gray trunk a source of clean drinking water in even the most brutal drought. "Prey will hide on instinct if it can smell a hunter nearby," she says in the orcish tongue. "Even when you don't know where it is, anything that moves leaves a trace." He walks behind her to a nearby tree. Its base has been gnawed at, and a bit of liquid still streams from the wound.

"Still fresh, Roushul," a prepubescent Viktor replies. "That means it's close. But how do we find it?"

She kneels down, pointing to a few broken twigs on the ground, and follows a path of disturbed dirt with her finger to a thick bramble. "Take aim, brother," she instructs.

He does as he is told and throws his spear. From the bush, a squealing boar emerges and is quickly felled by his sister's weapon that whistles in the air and pierces through its hide. Viktor extends a fist in celebration and Roushul bumps it with her own.

"Always use your environment to your advantage, Vikthorus," says Roushul as she pulls him under her arm in encouragement. "Not every problem can be solved by running into it head-on."

In the present, the warrior takes her old lesson to heart. He sprints toward the lone tree and slams into the side with his shield, causing an avalanche of crispy, orange leaves to fall all around him.

Seong's voice taunts from the shadows. "Feeling okay there, big man? Has the stress gone to your head? That fall must have really messed you up." Her laughter splits through the rain as she continues to mock him. "Confuse me for a tree? How sad. I didn't know I was fighting a dimwit. I guess a mercy killing is in order."

The warrior stands as a silent sentinel among the fallen leaves as they settle to the ground. "Trouble speaking? Growing bored?" Her voice sounds closer. "Me too."

From behind, he hears crunching as she approaches with swiftness. Without a moment to spare, he slashes with his dagger. It slices her across the clavicle, again sizzling the skin upon contact. She cries out in pain but is gone again in an instant. Holding his breath, he tries to hear where she escaped to. It's quiet. Viktor turns slowly, monitoring the area for any glimpse of the vampire lying in wait. After a moment of absolute stillness, however, he is attacked from above.

As Seong drops down from a tree branch, Viktor looks up just in time to be headbutted between the dead center of his brows. It knocks him on his back away from the tree, causing the back of his skull to thud against the stone floor.

For a few seconds, he loses consciousness.

Seeing this, the vampire kicks away the hilt of the dagger from his palm. She sucks in air through her teeth as it burns the bottom of her heel, but he begins to rouse. Another kick to his temple sends bloody spit flying from his mouth and buys her a few more moments. She uses the sharp points of her fangs to split the leather braces of his shield, removes it from his arm, and throws it with all her strength. It speeds through the air, slices deep into the tree trunk, and stays there, jutting out halfway. Amber sap oozes slightly around the edges, and raindrops ping off the metal. "There," she growls, stamping a foot onto his chest. "Now I can finally have some real fun."

As Viktor reawakens, he dizzily reaches his arms up to grab her by the ankles, but she flips off his chest to evade him. The warrior roars, stumbling to his feet before she comes at him again. Now, caught in her dance, he brings his fists and forearms close to his body, ready to block.

All too fast, the vampire approaches. She spins to the left, slashing his arm between the shoulder pad and bracers with her pointed nails. Then she goes low from behind, cutting through his pants to the skin of his calf. "One thousand cuts." She giggles maniacally, striking the same leg twice. "That's how I'll do it. 'Till you're unrecognizable, flayed meat."

He tries to catch her with a right hook when she comes in again, but she moves to the side, uses his arm as a bar to hoist off of, and scratches her claws across his cheek.

It is no use. Without a way to anticipate her movement, it's like sparring with a phantom. The rain pours down even heavier than before, masking the sound of her splashing footsteps. He has to get back to the leaves. It is only a short distance away, but if he runs, he'll open himself to more critical attacks.

Before her next invasion, the two are startled by a loud boom emanating from the eastern end of the castle. Distracted by the sound, Seong turns to face it and is punished with a ferocious blow to the rib cage. She staggers a distance away.

"Sounds like my Sable is working her magic," he spits. "I bet she blew her pasty-ass head clean off." He begins backing slowly to the fallen leaves, not wanting to give his plan away. Just then, he notices something worrying. He can feel the effects of Celest's blessing waver. The strength he wields will soon be only his own.

"That's impossible," Seong replies. "My sister has probably scared her so completely that she'd rather torch herself than fight."

"Don't look like sisters," he scoffs, keeping her distracted.

"You dumb fuck," says Seong, taking the bait. "My sister. My kin. My wife. My family. Ugh, it doesn't matter."

"Sisterwife? Gross. You lot are sicker than you look," he continues, nearing the perimeter. "So you all just skulk about in that castle fucking and sucking each other? Preying on poor girls when one of you can't get off?"

"Enough," erupts the vampire. She sprints forward again, cloaked in rain and darkness.

He doesn't see the hand as it comes in close, held sharp and straight like a blade. It stabs through the armor, fastens at his side, and pierces the length of her fingers in the flesh above his hip. Viktor wails, bringing his elbow down in retaliation.

She evades, continuing her onslaught. Wild slashes, scratches, and stabs harass every bit of him that isn't covered by thick leather. She is merciless, and the barrage leaves him dizzy as he is turned around in circles trying to protect himself.

A crunching of leaves underfoot, however, marks her next movement, and the warrior lunges forward, locking her into a desperate grapple. His heavy arms clench around her waist, trapping her wrists at her side. The vampire squirms to break free, and it takes all of his extra strength and then some to keep her. Head down, he roars, shallow veins bulging from an adrenaline rush.

Barreling forward, Viktor imagines ramming her into the ground but is stopped in his tracks as the two bodies hit a tree trunk that cracks and groans upon impact. He holds her there, yelling, as the last of Celest's spell fades from his spirit. The warrior is racking his mind for his next attack when he feels something wet seep into his braids. Viscous crimson dribbles down his forehead, dripping onto the roots below, and to his confusion, the body he holds tight to is limp. "What the... fuck?" he asks, head tilting cautiously upward. The shield in the tree is now painted dark red, and in his arms is a body without a head. Its severed neck squirts and bubbles. "Wh-haa—fuck!" he exclaims, loosening his grip as a shiver scrapes down his spine.

Viktor backs away, releasing Seong's body and slapping her blood from his face. It crumples onto the ground and lies there motionlessly. Atop the shield, displayed like a pheasant on a dinner platter, sits her head. The eyes are open, rolled upward to the night sky, and her mouth is agape. Viktor turns away almost immediately, huffing quick breaths through his pursed lips. "Okay," he whispers. "Yeah, okay. One down."

Firelight from the eastern side of the castle leads him back to its front steps, but before reentering to face his next foe, a silver glint catches his eye. The dagger that was cast away lies in a puddle under a thin layer of rainwater. "It must be my lucky night," says the half-orc. He kneels down to retrieve it, but the damage of his battle has taken a hefty toll. He grunts, righting himself. Everywhere, the pain throbs. "Alright, Viktor," he groans to himself. "Let's keep this ball rolling."

Chapter Twenty-Six

R unning down the second-story hallway, Celest berates himself for splitting from his friends, both now and in the nights leading up to this one. As he attempts to round a corner that leads to another hallway with stairs at its end, his stride is stopped by Zoan's arm slamming into the wall in front of him with a thud. He all but fills the way ahead with his massive frame. "That's far enough," he says calmly. "No more running from the inevitable."

The vampire's boot makes heavy contact with the center of the cleric's chest, causing ribs to crack like twigs in the hands of children. The force sends Celest into the bedroom behind him as the door breaks off its hinges and falls to the floor.

The cleric gasps for air, trying to sit up, but Zoan kicks again. This time the impact lands at the base of the door causing it to slide with Celest across the floorboards until they both crash into the back wall. The elf holds a shaking hand over his chest to repair the broken bones underneath his skin.

"Yes," praises Zoan. "Heal yourself. Heal so I can break you again. How convenient that is. I wholly understand why our lord would want to keep you mortal. Endless entertainment. A soft body to break, and break, and break."

He approaches slowly and then smacks the elf across the face with the back of his hand so swiftly that Celest is unable to react before the hit lands. It splits his bottom lip. Blood wets his chin and drips onto his robes, further soiling the white fabric with fresh dots of red. The shock gives the cleric pause. His eyes glaze over as his awareness attempts to disassociate from the pain.

"Heal yourself," Zoan demands again. "This might be the only time I'll get to play with you on my own. Heal. Now." His iron grip takes hold of the elf by the hair as if to puppet his compliance. "Now," he repeats.

The elf considers his position and fears the worst. In a pathetic attempt to appeal to his assailant, the cleric looks up at the vampire and desperately whimpers, "Julian... would be upset with you." Celest continues breathlessly. "He would want me unharmed. Please. Don't do this. You disobey him... explicitly."

He stops short of a full heal, attempting to conserve the mana for his friends who he hopes are faring better than himself in their own battles. The bones fix back into place, but the more superficial wounds remain. The abuse has begun bruising his skin, and the damaged nerves send frenzied signals to his brain that feel like bolts of fire as the inflammation sets in. "Please," he repeats.

Zoan's expression is as neutral as ever, emotionally unswayed by Celest's desperation. He leans closer to the elf and unexpectedly steals a kiss. The vampire's tongue licks at the blood seeping from his lip, and it stings deep inside his chest. The elf wriggles to avoid it and beats on his assaulter's chest but fails to pull away. Curled, black fingers hold his skull in place by the hair as his lips are forced to shape. Stray tears become sobbing, and when the kiss stops, the cleric is firmly slapped again. He winces after the fact, bringing his arms up to cover his face.

"Submit. Don't. It doesn't matter. It won't change my actions. Unlike our lord, who prefers prostration and obedience, I think I'd actually rather you struggle. I'll remind you, too, that our lord isn't here. He can't punish me if he doesn't know what I'm doing, and I'm usually so well-behaved. I doubt there will be much consequence as long as I keep you alive," growls the vampire. The threat, taken to heart, spurs the elf to instinctively reach for the holy object tucked into his sock, but Zoan's boot falls on his wrist before he can retrieve it. The pressure exerted on the ribbons of muscle in his forearm curls the cleric's fingers into a fist and nearly cracks the bones within.

Celest's eyes glow white as he casts a command spell in panic. *"Flee,"* he orders with divine persuasion, but the vampire is unaffected.

He stays squatted over him, firmly planted and newly armed with arrogant amusement. Only then does the elf remember that this spell, in particular, has no sway over the undead.

"Was that supposed to do something," asks Zoan sarcastically, "or were the theatrics intended to frighten me? I'd hate to deflate your confidence any further, but a street cat is more intimidating. A kitten could give me more of a start than that pathetic display." His boot presses down slowly with each word he speaks until the bone underneath it breaks.

Celest cries out in agony as both of his hands erupt with golden-white flames. Self-preservation guides his free left hand as it hurls an aethereal blaze at the vampire's chest. The other blackens and burns the leather of his boot.

Zoan releases his grip and stumbles backward, swatting away the otherworldly flames.

The cleric uses the opportunity to scramble to his feet and begins posturing for a spell of banishment. Carving symbols into the air with his fingers concentrates the energy required to cast it, but the intricate movements are difficult to achieve with a broken wrist. The elf disregards the pain but still isn't quick enough to act before Zoan is at him again.

"Quite the trick, kitten," growls the vampire as he lifts the elf by the collar of his robes. "My turn." With what seems like all his incredible strength, Zoan throws the elf into a bedpost. He crashes through the wood and onto the mattress. The frame underneath it snaps like a dry biscuit.

Celest lays still among the splintered post and white linens, failing to find his breath. His hair blends with the sheets and streams over his face, making it appear as if he were sinking beneath the fibers. A wish to sink further, below the soil, be forever forgotten, and never again bothered by the suffering of the world above lingers in the forefront of his thoughts—to give up and give in. But, again, he begins to breathe.

"Oh, kitten," purrs the vampire. "Where did that fight of yours go?" Zoan takes the foot end of the sheet and tugs the elf closer to him. One of the sharp pieces of the broken bedpost stays put underneath him, however, and slices a gash up the elf's back. He lets out a yelp and jolts to the right out of shock. His hand holds the wound for a moment, then pulls away with wet fingers. Blood oozes into the sheets like cherry syrup on soft bread.

Celest can barely feel it, though, desensitized by the repeated injuries, but the sight of his palm dripping with precious, liquid rubies saps the rest of his strength. He mouths the only word he can think to say as Zoan's hands travel from the elf's ankles to his thighs. "No, no, no, no, no—"

The vampire's eyes are glossy and fixed on the growing red stain on the sheets. "How unfortunate," he whispers slowly. "So much of your sweet nectar, wasted."

Celest screams as he is flipped onto his stomach, nearly stabbed again by the jagged piece of wood underneath him. Crawling onto the bed, Zoan hovers over the wound and then runs his index finger across its length. Another pained noise, now muffled by the white sheets, escapes the cleric. "You really shouldn't tempt me like this," warns the vampire. "We ate before you arrived, but dessert is sounding better by the moment."

Somewhere in the castle, a loud boom shakes the walls. But the two, preoccupied with their own situation, barely register the sound. A cold, wet tongue begins to lap at the gash and is followed by the rumbling moans of pleasure that Zoan breathes into the cleric's low back. After a moment of this, the wound begins to numb, and after another, a surprising tingle of satisfaction accompanies the sensation.

For the first time all night, Celest's heart rate evens, but the elf is barely aware of this change. A protective detachment keeps his focus in an elsewhere that doesn't exist.

Zoan, however, is acutely aware.

"Aww, pretty kitten." He sighs. "Are you feeling a touch better?" His stone hand grips Celest's thigh, just above the back of his knee. Continuing, he explains, "There's a component of our saliva that nullifies the pain of a feeding. Some have mistaken me, before I've swallowed them whole, as their savior. It's as if a pleasant death was the pinnacle of their pathetic lives. A younger me would give final pleasures to the dying exclusively, but time passes, and curiosities arise. When I'm feeling ruthless..."

Two sharp nails dig through the skin and into the thick ligament that runs on the side of the elf's thigh. He cries out in agony as the tips of Zoan's cold fingers are stained red.

"I don't have to use my tongue," mutters the vampire. He dislodges himself, sucks the blood off his fingers, and moans with a muted delight.

Celest's cheek rolls to the side to turn his head away from the blood-drunk blankets. The smell of iron sickens the air as he watches Zoan's pupils contract into sharpened blades while he indulges himself. Eyes fluttering with exhaustion, the cleric reaches his able hand beneath him and shifts the broken post into his palm. The vampire is silent now, save the revelrous growls of a satisfied predator. He seems almost distracted as he cups at the oozing, crimson streams, then drips what has gathered onto the length of his wanting tongue. The vampire's eyes close in ecstasy as he licks at the heel of his palm, and the cleric sees a silver thread of opportunity that he acts on without a second thought to dissuade him. Celest pulls the makeshift weapon from under him and sets it ablaze in a roaring, holy fire. All his will concentrates on the single burning tip of wood as he sinks it into the side of Zoan's neck. The wound is superficial, but the flesh hisses and bubbles from the heat. As the vampire rears back in shock, the broken post falls to the floor, and the cleric again reaches for the warm stone in his sock. He grabs it just at the moment Zoan recovers enough to spring back toward him with teeth bared.

Sunstone exposed, misting the room in a soft, orange light, Zoan is halted in place for a brief moment, then staggers to the back corner of the room. His eyes bulge slightly from their sockets, either in fear or pain, but not a sound escapes him as his skin begins to sizzle.

Celest is frozen too. Left arm shaking and hyperextended, he holds the stone between his fingers with desperate resolve.

Zoan struggles out the words, "You wouldn't. I'll ki—" His threat is overtaken by globs of golden fire that the cleric channels through the stone. Wrapped with flame, the vampire wails and churns his body in agony but doesn't fall.

Celest expects a quick demise, but a searing hatred within the vampire's expression burns as brightly as the flames that engulf his body and pin his feet like they are pierced by steel rivets. Even steel melts with time, but the ticking moments feel like ages. Every scream pricks the elf like a rusted knife, and every convulsion drives him further into an impatient frenzy until he picks up the broken post once more and charges forward with the intent to bring Zoan's suffering to a final end. The wood stabs into the boiling skin just above his clavicle and lets out a gush of blackened blood as it pulls back out from the wound.

Still, Zoan screams but doesn't concede. His arm muscles through the impossibly thick fire to grip the elf by the throat. He's weak, but a weakened Zoan is a strong man, and Celest is choked nearly to the point of asphyxiation. He doesn't relent, however, and sticks him again with the weapon, this time in the shoulder, then again in the neck, and lastly, the heart.

As if it were imagined from the start, the clutch across the cleric's throat doesn't loosen but instead dissipates all at once. The holy flame, unburning to the cleric's touch, briefly retreats back to its caster and evaporates around him. What's left is crumbling, black ash in the shape of a man that then dissolves weightlessly to the floor in a pile. After slipping through Celest's blue fingers, the broken post clatters beside it and is followed by the elf himself, who collapses to his knees, weeping in equal parts despair and relief. The vampire is dead.

Quicker than ever before, the elf finds his composure and picks himself off the floor. Staggering backward, he hits a wall and leans there as the broken bones of his arm are set into place with a sunstone-enhanced incantation. To stitch together his gashed back and the slashes left from Zoan's fingers, the cleric uses another healing spell while trying to preserve as much of his depleted mana as possible. It's just enough to stop the bleeding and does nothing for the pain, but that is the least of his worries.

"Viktor... Sable..." Celest wrings the names from his swollen throat. "Just wait for me. I'm nearly there." He takes off out of the room in the wrong direction, running straight ahead into the hall that had previously been blocked by Zoan. Balance wavering as his grace spell begins to fade, he slows, looking around in confusion. Upon realizing his mistake, the cleric turns around but is stopped in his tracks by a familiar metallic scent emanating from a room to his right.

The door is already cracked ajar, but an itching curiosity causes the elf to push it fully open with a haunting creak. Celest gasps, clasping his hands to his mouth at the sight. Blood. Everywhere. It's splattered on the walls, puddled on the floor, and even dotted like cruel stars on the ceiling. On the bed lies the body of a girl, tortured, disfigured, and buried under a pile of her own insides. Ripped away pieces tangle into matted locks of curly black hair and set into its skull, two bloodshot blue eyes bulge out lifelessly as if to escape the carnage. A mangled hand on the floor, severed from its wrist, seems to reach for the cleric in desperation. "T-this... This is Briar," sobs Celest. A volcanic pit in his stomach gurgles as he wretches in disgust. The elf purges himself dry of the meal he had shared with the monsters capable of this unbearable violence.

Unable to stand the sight any longer, Celest staggers down the hallway from the direction he had come. The thought of his friends falling to a similar fate carries him forward, back to the ballroom, to face his gruesome lover.

Chapter Twenty-Seven

M usic fills the ballroom. Its tone captures a violent yearning, starved, yet patient as death. Julian commands the notes with his fingers to the keys. Powerless to object, the instrument wails his song from the heart of his castle. The sound bleeds through the halls and pours out from the broken windows. Still playing, the vampire's gaze slides upwards to the ceiling's fresco. As his irises shimmer a momentary gold, the painting writhes in rhythm with his song. Its victims dance in place as far as their thorned bindings allow. They move in agony, lust, or confusion toward a freedom they will never be allowed.

Julian tilts back, smiling at his hypnotic creation, and the grin stretches further as he hears two little feet clicking closer with each step from the eastern hallway. He pretends not to notice as a book, shaped to a point and buzzing with arcane light, speeds through the smashed double doors. It aims to hit his heart. Waiting until the last possible moment before impact, he flicks his fingers, and the projectile bursts into a fine black dust. Julian falls forward, feigning death, his arms slamming against the keys, causing an uproar of dissonant noise from the instrument's pipes. "Oh no," he hums dramatically. "The hero witch has felled me. What a travesty. What an awful fate this is."

From the shadows of the hallway, Sable yells, "Release the girl, and I'll consider sparing you."

Julian laughs loudly as he pushes his dark hair behind one ear. "My Katya?" he asks. "She might be already dead. You'll have to come closer and check for yourself. But if that is the case, you could always try saving her in the next life." Sable peeks out slowly from behind the cracked wood. Adinine appears to have not moved an inch since before, but the assistance of the cleric's spell has already faded, and it's hard to be sure of from this distance. One-handed, Julian continues to play but turns on the seat to face her direction. His leg is propped up on the other, looking all too comfortable. "I'm impressed that you've bested my dear Iliya," he praises. "This is the second time she's been killed, poor thing. It took quite some time to scrub away the new person she had become. I only hope that she'll retain her beauty in the third life and those cute pointed ears. You'll keep me entertained enough in her stead, though, won't you? You are quite special."

His words do nothing to pull her. The vampire's glamor is all but repulsive, knowing his character, but the halfling decides to play into his ego. At the least, it might buy her friends some time to regroup. "You aren't upset with me?" she asks in the meekest voice she can muster, sliding out of hiding into the wreckage of the doorway. The blatant prostration physically pains her, but she bites her tongue and continues the act. A lifetime of being underestimated has culminated in the ability to use that perception to her advantage.

"No, little mouse," he replies with a dazzling smile as the melody of his song becomes gentle and light. "I'm enticed. As I have told Celest, I mean you no harm. All that I require is obedience. Is it not the right of a ruler to expect his subjects to obey?" His own question marks irritation on his expression. "Though," Julian's ruby gaze pierces through her, and he says, "I've found that strong-willed women tend to try my patience."

Sable successfully repels the bubbling anger at the remark from her face.

"Come, little witch," he continues, relaxing again. "Subjugate, and we may move past this."

"You will allow me to check if Adinine is alive?" she asks, taking a step onto the ballroom floor.

"Of course, I will. You only have to trust me." He finishes his song and stands to lord over the body at his feet.

Sable hesitates. This is obviously a trap, but her objective is clear. Adinine needs protecting, and it's impossible to do that from the outskirts of the room. The witch swallows her trepidation and begins her approach.

"There," purrs the vampire. "I knew you had some common sense." Before reaching Adinine, however, Julian steps over her body and meets the halfling on the ballroom floor. Sable freezes, trying to anticipate his next move. Crouching down to face her, he attempts to bring a hand to her cheek, but she flinches.

"Will you move aside?" Sable asks firmly.

"Yes," he assures, but continues the motion and gently touches her face. A black-nailed thumb explores the plush skin over her cheekbone as he comments, "So very small. I've never met a halfling in the flesh. It's fascinating." His hand moves to pet the tight coils of hair cut close to her scalp. "How tall are you, little mouse?" he asks, breathing honey-sweet myrrh across her face as he speaks.

"I'm three feet and an inch," Sable responds with a muted expression. Behind the facade, her skin crawls. Rage simmers the blood in her veins, but she maintains her composure. "Now, please, let me attend to her."

The hand moves again, this time to her chin, and he tilts it upward. The vampire's eyes bore into her own as he asks, "Your heart rate is climbing. Could it be fear? Anger? Or, perhaps it's excitement."

She keeps a tight lip, afraid that the next words out of her mouth will curse him.

He stares for a moment, then continues speaking. "Please, what, little Sable? Please, *who*?"

She swallows her pride again, replying, "Please... *sir*. Allow me to go to her."

A satisfied smile etches into his expression, and he stands, moving out of the way. Rushing up the few steps to the body, Sable checks the pulse at her neck immediately. It's weak, but she's still living. The witch takes a cloth from her dress pocket, ties it around Adinine's wrist, and applies pressure to the wound. "Adinine," calls the halfling. "Can you hear me? You need to wake up now." The human's eyelids flutter a bit, but ultimately she stays unconscious.

The witch begins casting a spell to detect the use of magic but is interrupted by Julian remarking, "I didn't charm her to sleep if that's what you're wondering. She is simply faint from blood loss, but enough with her. Where were you and I?"

Just then, storming through the center hall, Viktor yells out, "Back off, bitch!" He steams toward them, but with a casual wave of the vampire's hand, the railing posts that flank the warrior are bewitched and animated. They twist into snakelike creatures that wrap around his ankles and force him to the cold ground. Returning to its solid, wooden form, the railing pins Viktor in place.

"Even you survived? Hm. I don't think I will," scoffs Julian. He turns his attention back to the two women and reaches out to grab the witch, but she holds tight to Adinine and projects a shimmering barrier around them. He chuckles as his palm hits the purple boundary. "Really?" He sighs. "I thought we were getting along."

From across the room, the half-orc roars, cracking his binding with brute strength.

"Do you think this pitiful excuse of a spell will keep you safe?" asks the vampire, tapping his nails on the surface like a fishbowl. Molding his hand into a fist, he hammers down onto the barrier, shattering it like glass.

Sable raises her palms and yells, again casting a ball of flame, but only a splattering of embers fire off. They cool and dissipate before catching anything of his alight.

"Miserable," spits Julian as he grabs her by the wrist. "Out of mana already?" Irises melting gold, he commands, "No more fighting me. Be calm."

For a moment, she tries to defy the enchantment from taking hold of her mind but ultimately has no choice. It bores like a parasite into her skull and nests itself in place, causing a wave of ease that makes her go limp. The vampire kneels again, pulling her close, and plops her down on his thigh to sit.

After snapping through the wood that held him, Viktor is finally free. "I said back—*the fuck*—off," he growls, again running full speed ahead.

Julian gently raises an open palm, then abruptly clenches his fist. The air around the warrior seems to thicken, and suddenly, gravity pulls him to the floor. The force is almost painful, slowing him to a useless crawl.

Viewed under the vampire's influence, she can't bring herself to feel any sense of worry, but some core piece of herself still cries out in opposition. Unable to properly express her discomfort, the halfling giggles.

Julian wears a slippery grin, asking, "Isn't that funny, little mouse?"

"No," she says plainly, through a slight smile.

A twitch of surprise at her response can only last a moment before he is distracted again by the warrior who pushes forward under his spell's weight and groans.

"Fight me... like a man."

"And what will you do once you get to me, Viktor?" Julian hums as he takes Sable's face between his fingers. "Punch me?" Taunting him further, the vampire laughs to himself, then plants a soft kiss on her cheek. Like a doll, she simply sits and watches.

The warrior forces himself to his feet. "Don't touch her!" he roars. Each step closer takes his maximum effort.

"You'd like me to touch her? Like this?" he moans, sliding his tongue up the length of her neck.

The violation is repulsive. A furious disgust crackles underneath her skin and snaps the witch out of his enchantment. She slams her elbow into his nose before attempting to flee, but he wraps her across the waist with his arm.

"Stupid cunt. Sleep," he growls another charmed command into her ear, and she quickly slips into involuntary unconsciousness. Julian's grip tightens, forcing shallow breaths from her lungs. "Fine," yells the vampire. "If you want her, catch."

As gravity's pull releases the warrior, Julian flings the halfling across the room at a terrifying speed. Darting to the side, Viktor uses his body as her shield, but both are sent crashing into the staircase that clings to the western wall. The half-orc gasps for air, caught in a nest of splintered wood, but the feeling of Sable, still breathing on his shoulder, brings him more comfort than anything else at that moment could. Trying to right himself, however, causes nauseous waves of pain. After the abuse taken tonight, his body is finally at its limit. All he can do now is hold onto his friend and keep breathing too.

"This is becoming more trouble than it is worth," Julian dryly comments. "Killing you both sounds like a better idea by the second." Collecting in the ball of his hand, a massive glob of gold and red arcane light begins to form. It swirls together like malice, deadly and barely contained.

"Julian, stop!" screams Celest, sprinting from the second-story hallway to the landing between the set of stairs.

"Oh hello, Celest," says the vampire evenly. "You're just in time to say your goodbyes."

"No, please," he cries, rushing down the stairs to protect them, but his foot misses a step halfway down. The elf tumbles a few feet before catching himself and scurrying over to his team.

Viktor is barely conscious. Eyelids begin to droop as he focuses on the cleric's tear-stricken face.

"You're hurt, but," bumbles the cleric as he brings forth the shining sunstone from his pocket, "my mana is—"

"Celest!" roars the vampire, loud enough to fully fill the empty space between them. "That thing is the very *reason* for this punishment!"

The cleric ignores him, leaning over the two and casting the last of his holy magic to heal only their deepest wounds. Golden-flecked white light bathes them for just a moment as Viktor's spine audibly cracks back into formation. Without the aid of the sunstone, the cleric's available magic would have barely mended a scratch.

Enraged, the vampire fires off his malice to hit the floor in front of them. Its impact is ferocious, shattering chunks of stone flooring that scatter like roaches into the air and then down again.

During the commotion, Viktor weakly slips something from his waist belt into the breast of the elf's clothing. He pats the object onto his chest and delivers a look that conveys to the cleric that their fates now depend on him alone.

It petrifies him, thoroughly. Celest can't help but stutter.

Dust still hanging in the air, Viktor wipes a streaming tear from his friend's cheek and encourages, "You've got this, Sunshine." After a gentle smack to the side of his face, the warrior's arm falls to cover Sable, and his eyes slide shut in exhaustion.

"Do you think I enjoy this spectacle, Celest?" growls the vampire as the last bits of rubble settle to the floor. "Have I not proven to you firsthand how reasonable and accommodating I can be when I'm afforded that luxury?"

The elf stands, spins around to face him, and pleads, "Julian, I'm so sorry. Please, just listen to me." He grips the sunstone tightly in his palm to hide away its warm light.

"Sorry. A simple apology isn't enough for what you've done," spits the vampire. He stands like a shadow in the evening, stretched and haunting. "My dear pets lie dead in my own home because of your disobedience. You think you can wash that away with a sorry, still gripping that vile memory in your hand no less?" Julian's long, obsidian hair practically stands on end, coursing with a wrath that spews out from within.

Celest steps forward, falling to his knees before the rubble, and sets the sunstone on the ground. It glitters across the broken floor, blooming bits of light around itself like a tiny star. Julian shields his eyes with an arm, seething at the sight before the elf grabs a chunk of stone flooring, lifts it over his head, and smashes down with all his might. It bursts with a crackle. And, like a lantern extinguished, the light fades into a gray smoke, then dissipates forever. "There." The cleric sighs, looking up at Julian through watery eyes. "I should have done this hours ago."

Caught off guard, the vampire falls silent. Disarmed from the act, the tension in his shoulders releases as he exhales. "You want absolution?" he asks, then commands, "Come here." Celest complies. He makes his way across the ballroom, arms hugged to his chest and a knot clogging his airways until he finally reaches Julain. The two stare at each other wordless for a moment before the vampire takes the elf's face in his hands. "Why should I forgive you," he whispers, "after what has transpired here tonight?"

Celest, again, begins to cry, replying softly, "Julian... I love you."

The declaration, like water to a flame, extinguishes his wrath for the time being. He sighs, wiping away his paramour's tears, and rests the elf's head on his chest. "Sweetest Celest," consoles the vampire. "I would set aside any other pleasure to accept the love you have to give." Sincerity rings true in his tone. Julian is taken wholly and solemnly with the idea that Celest, in his seemingly infinite capacity for compassion, is the remedy he has sought out for centuries.

The cleric raises his head and tilts his neck, exposing the pale, golden skin ripe with blood beneath its surface. "Take it," he whispers tenderly. "Bond to me. Make me your own." Julian hesitates, searching into the elf's gaze, but is met only with a desperate yearning, a look of pain and promise. All else around them disappears.

"As you wish," he answers, brushing back the white, silken strands that still cling to the elf's neck. Julian starts with a kiss. His lips steal away the warmth underneath them. His eyes close to savor the feeling of his tongue wetting the skin. And then, he bites. Fangs pierce the flesh with delicate precision, then pull out just as gently, leaving two punctures that well up with fresh crimson. It stings for a moment but is quickly numbed as the vampire begins to feed. He sucks Celest's life through his teeth and guides it with his tongue. Numbness becomes a bliss like snowflakes that melt into glittering dew.

The vampire's pleasure is contagious, seeping through the cleric and coloring his thoughts. His is the pleasure of conquest, a full moon, old wine. Julian's fingers play through the elf's hair, absentmindedly for comfort, gripping and releasing as he indulges in the taste. Keeping him there, bound to him, Celest gingerly cups the back of his neck, and Julian seems to melt, enraptured by belonging, fully embraced.

A feathery moan floats past the vampire's throat but is cut short as a stinging pain pierces through his chest. Julian gasps, pulling back to see the silver hilt of a dagger held by his dearest Celest, stuck straight through his heart. Solid streams of tears begin to slice both of their faces into fractions as the vampire falls to his knees.

"No," he whimpers as the metal sizzles inside him and looks up at the cleric with eyes blighted by betrayal.

"You don't deserve it," cries Celest, "my love."

The vampire rests his hands weakly over the elf's as if to tear him away, but Celest holds tightly to the dagger and twists, and Julian turns to ash in his arms. He falls forward into the pile of dust, sobbing with the full force of his lungs. Pain rips through his heart like a saw blade, and as it does, a viscous, black smoke rises from the ash. It lashes and twists, like a net full of eels, then forces its way into the elf's open mouth as he screams in despair. He coughs as it chokes him until it finally slithers down his throat. Panicking, Celest beats down on the ash, fueled by wild rage the likes of which he had never known himself capable of. But during his outburst, the world around him changes. Seemingly out of nowhere, his next blow is received by frost-laced, brown river stones. The startled elf recoils and then darts his head around in exhausted confusion.

A lazy river drifts by ahead, and in the distance, the cliffs of the Elvyn Wilds peek over the treetops. Winter has cast away the colorful autumn, and through the wispy clouds, the morning sun brightly shines. It kisses his cheeks like a mother welcoming her child home. A weary groan from behind the elf turns him around in an instant.

"What... where..." mumbles Sable. Propped up at the base of a tree trunk, held in each other's arms, she and Viktor begin to wake.

Celest stumbles over and wraps them both in a desperate hug.

"You did it, Sunshine?" groans Viktor as he rights himself.

"We're back where we started," says the witch, "but the others—Adinine. Cassianna—How did you..." She stops herself and hugs him back as he cries softly into her shoulder. "You're safe now, Celest. We're all safe now." A worry in her chest aches for her new lover, but she sets it aside to care for the elf.

Celest pulls them in tighter, afraid of ever letting go. "I'm sorry," he sobs. "I'm so sorry." The two console him, huddled together on the riverbank.

"Hey, Sunshine," Viktor sighs, dejected but relieved. "I don't need you to tell us everything, but next time you get the craving to chase after a charming villain, please just keep us in the know. Maybe you didn't learn this growing up, but we... Friends are there to watch your back. Ah—How do I say this? Sable? Birds? Bees? Making sure your friend isn't fiending over a psychopath?"

Celest nods as he wipes his eyes.

"I think he gets the point. We have much to discuss, and even more to worry about. But for now, we have each other, and that's important." The brisk air nips their noses, but the heat of their voices fights back the chill.

After a moment, the three fall silent, letting the questions of their experience take a back seat to the collective relief they share. But left in the silence, a familiar voice from the back of the cleric's mind, so quiet it seems almost imagined, whispers to him.

"Do you think you've escaped me... my sweetest Celest?"

To be continued...

About the Author

When not caught up in his own personal fantasies about courageous heroes, flamboyant villains, or ancient magics, Cyril spends his time inches from a monitor playing video games, trying to make his friends laugh with silly voices during D&D sessions, and flirting with his boyfriend to the point of obsession.

As a trans-masculine nonbinary person, Cyril is passionate about the continued fight for bodily autonomy in all forms, intersectional justice for minorities, and opulent gothic fashion.

The quickest way to get his attention is by mentioning vampires, but if you don't have a few free hours to discuss the ins and outs of vampiric mythology, it's best not to bring it up at all.

Curious how Celest met his unlikely companions?
Unlock the prelude to *An Empty Embrace* by subscribing to Cyril's newsletter.
Exclusive content and insights await. Don't miss out!

<u>Join Cyril's Devoted</u>